Praise for Joseph Flynn and his novels

Digger

"A mystery cloaked as cleverly as (and perhaps better than) any John Grisham work."
— *Denver Post*

"Engrossing ... non-stop action and original plot ... rapid-fire suspense."
— Phillip Margolin
New York Times Bestselling Author of *Wild Justice*

"A deftly mapped thriller. Page-turner of the week."
— *People Magazine*

"A straightforward, pulse-pounding novel ... a forceful hard-boned book."
— Carsten Stroud
New York Times Bestselling Author of *Deadly Force*

"Mix Dashiell Hammet's *Red Harvest* and T*he X-Files* and you'll get some idea of how original this concept is. Recommended book."
— Thriller Editor, *amazon.com*

"An exciting, gritty, emotional page-turner."
— Robert K. Tanenbaum
New York Times Bestselling Author of *True Justice*

"Surefooted, suspenseful, and in its breathless final moments, unexpectedly heartbreaking."
— *Booklist*

The Next President

"Flynn [is] a master of high-octane plotting."
— *Chicago Tribune*

"Flynn keeps the pages turning in this well-done thriller."
— *Houston Chronicle*

"An original, suspenseful thriller that will keep you turning the pages."
— *amazon.com*

"A thriller that's fast enough to keep reading straight through (in) one sitting."
— *Rocky Mountain News* (Denver)

"(A) tough, stylish tale ... (Flynn) propels his plot with potent but flexible force, using just the right mix of pressure and release to maintain suspense deep into the story."
— *Publishers Weekly*

"Readers raved about this book ... cat and mouse suspense ... full of twists ... a well-written, timely thriller. Highest marks."
— *Barnes & Noble Guide to New Fiction*

"Flynn is an excellent storyteller with a well-tuned ear for dialogue and a gift for creating memorable characters placed in believable settings ... *The Next President* bears favorable comparison to such classics as *The Best Man, Advise and Consent,* and *The Manchurian Candidate.*"
— *Booklist*

Look for . . .

The President's Henchman

It's inevitable, and probably not too far off, that the United States will elect its first female president. Which will make her husband ... what?

Well, if he's the ex-cop who solved the murder of the president's first husband and brought the killers to justice ... and if he's not the kind to stand on formality ... and if he doesn't want to be appointed head of the FBI ... and if he takes out a private license and becomes the first private eye to live in the White House ...

That would make him *The President's Henchman.*

Coming soon from Joseph Flynn

By Joseph Flynn

The Concrete Inquisition
Digger
The Next President
Hot Type
Pointy Teeth (short stories)
Farewell Performance

GASOLINE, TEXAS

Joseph Flynn

SPRINGFIELD, IL
2007
Stray Dog Press, Inc.

Published by Stray Dog Press, Inc.
Springfield, IL 62704, U.S.A.

First Stray Dog Press, Inc. Printing, July, 2007

Visit the author's web site: www.josephflynn.com

Flynn, Joseph
     Gasoline, Texas / Joseph Flynn.
     256 p.
     ISBN 978-0-9764170-6-4

Printed in the United States of America

PUBLISHER'S NOTE
This is a work of fiction. Names, characters, places, and incidents either are the product of the author's imagination or are used fictitiously; any resemblance to actual persons, living or dead, events, or locales is entirely coincidental.

Book design by Aha! Designs
Typeface: Adobe Caslon

For

Catherine,
My own Texas rose.

Acknowledgments

Everyone in my family, all my friends, and all the people who've bought my books over the years, especially the ones who've taken the time to write and ask, "What's next?" You've kept me going.

GASOLINE, TEXAS

CHAPTER ONE

There hadn't been any gunfire by eight p.m. on Election Day, but that was about to change if Buckminster Musgrove had his way.

Buck was the campaign manager for Laddy Johnson, and he had blood in his eye as he asked to hear one more time the report his son, Ben, had just brought in.

Ben was perfectly willing to repeat himself in the exact same tone of outrage he'd used to announce his news moments earlier. "The goddamn 11th precinct polling place is still open and letting people vote, an hour after the law said it had to close. When I went over to say, 'What the hell do y'all think you're doing?' two of Win-Win's boys pointed scatterguns at me. Shit, if I hadn't been alone ..."

Ladbrook "Laddy" Johnson and Edwin "Win-Win" Winslow were competing for the office of mayor in the town of Gasoline, Texas, a gathering of 20,000 souls at the southernmost point of a ragged triangle with Houston to the northeast and Austin to the northwest.

Win-Win was the incumbent; Laddy the challenger.

1

Even by Texas standards the race had been spirited.

Meaning it was a surprise blood hadn't been spilled already.

"You did the right thing, Ben, not getting shot," Laddy said, sitting behind his desk, his feet up, not looking the least perturbed at hearing the election might be stolen right under his nose. "No sense in anyone getting killed."

A point with which Ben's father begged to differ.

"Fuck that shit, Laddy," he said. "Bastards think they can steal this election and threaten my boy's life, I'll waste every last one a them. Tie Win-Win to a tree and skin him alive."

Hardly the usual strategy for a Democrat. On the other hand, Buckminster Musgrove was a former Marine and handy with both a gun and a knife.

"Buck," Laddy said calmly, "as much as we like to romanticize the Wild West hereabouts, none of us would actually care to live in the 19th century. What we'll do is send Ben back to the 11th precinct. Have him take Mary Sue Parker from the *Beacon* with him."

Mary Sue was the reporter covering the Johnson campaign for the town paper. She'd compromised her journalistic objectivity by sleeping with Ben Musgrove on the second night of her assignment. She'd also promised Laddy good press if he got her résumé to the executive producer of *Entertainment Tonight*, whom Laddy had met exactly one time for three minutes.

The candidate continued, "Let's get Ben up on the roof of ... what's that building across the street from the 11th precinct polling place? Is it still a jewelry store?"

"Fein's," Buck nodded, restraining himself until he saw where Laddy was heading.

Contrary to his candidate's assertion, Buck would have

been perfectly happy giving up his modern creature comforts if he could more often settle matters with his own two hands. Only thing he couldn't do without was Friday night football. No real Texan could live without that.

"Ben," Laddy said, "you get up on top of Fein's with a videocam. One that has a date and time stamp in the frame. Shoot any illegal voting going on. Shoot Mary Sue asking the boys with the shotguns if maybe they're allowing only Win-Win's voters in; keeping everybody else out at gunpoint. Make sure Mary Sue's discreetly miked so she can record whatever they have to say."

Buck shook his head.

"Win-Win's the biggest advertiser on KYHA." YEEHA-TV, channel 85, was the Fox affiliate in town. The only station with a local newsroom. "They ain't gonna air anything we bring in, no matter how damning it is."

"We'll get the Houston and Austin stations," Laddy said. "They'll go with it. CNN'll pick it up. People in Gasoline will get the news."

"Unless Win-Win's bastards jam their TV signals."

The notion sounded like Castro jamming TV Marti to Laddy. Cold War paranoia. He was tempted to laugh. But he'd been back in Texas only a little over a year, returning from 15 years of living in L.A. Maybe interfering with federally regulated broadcast signals wasn't as outlandish as he thought.

He shrugged. "Be that as it may. This campaign will not initiate any gunfire."

For just a moment, Buck Musgrove's look said he'd backed the wrong horse.

But he turned to his son and said, "Go on, boy. Get Mary Sue and do like you were told."

For his part, Ben looked relieved. Eager, even, to be pulling a scam with Mary Sue instead of charging into battle with his father and a posse from Johnson headquarters.

Buck closed the door to Laddy's office, just the two of them in the small space now.

"You're gonna hate yourself if you lose 'cause a this," Buck said.

"Not nearly as much as if you or Ben or someone else got killed."

"Don't you *want* to win?" Buck asked.

"I promised my mother I'd do my best," Laddy told him.

Laddy's mother, Arcelia Dominguez, was said by some to have been the teenage mistress of the late President Lyndon Baines Johnson. She never made any such claim herself ... but she never denied the rumors either. Those with a conspiratorial turn of mind loved to point out certain "facts" which they said lent credence to the stories of illicit goings-on.

Young Ms. Dominguez had grown up in Austin where her family operated a small but successful Mexican restaurant and catering business. Austin was but a 34-mile drive to the LBJ ranch outside Johnson City. At the speed with which Texans customarily drove that was a spin around the block. Then there was the photograph: a picture in which the former president was standing directly behind the 18-year-old Ms. Dominguez at a gathering of Texas oil and political barons held at a dude ranch midway between Austin and Johnson City. Normally, the catering staff was not photographed with the swells, but this time LBJ had insisted on a "one big happy family" shot.

There were those who said it looked like Lyndon had his hand on Arcelia's ass when the shutter clicked. Of course, the young woman's body blocked the viewer from seeing any direct contact, but LBJ, Arcelia, and John Connally, who was standing next to Lyndon and checking things out from the corner of his eye, all wore the same mischievous smiles.

Then there was the timing of Johnson's death and Laddy's birth. The 36th president of the United States died of a heart attack in San Antonio on January 22, 1973. Ladbrook Johnson was born in Gasoline, Texas September 22, 1973. The conspiracy theorists had it that the news from Arcelia that she was pregnant with Lyndon's child was what killed the former president.

No record was ever found that Ms. Dominguez had been in San Antonio that day, but the conspiracy buffs said she could have delivered the news by phone. There was no document to bear out this contention, but then who had access to a former president's phone records? The NSA maybe, but they weren't talking.

All the speculation would have been cleared up if the child had closely resembled LBJ, but young Ladbrook looked like his mother with black hair, dark brown eyes, strong and generously sized features, and a copper complexion. But topping out at six feet three inches tall, he was eight inches taller than any of his Dominguez kin and pert near right on a level with Lyndon.

And, of course, there was Ladbrook's surname. Arcelia explained that she'd always intended to give any child she'd had an American name, and after the president had tipped Dominguez Catering $1,000 on top of their fee for lunch at the dude ranch, Johnson it was. She never did say where she got the Ladbrook.

Shortly after LBJ had succumbed, a "relative" of Arcelia's left her a house and a business in Gasoline, a trust fund for the child she was carrying, and a guarantee that should the child turn out to be even an average student, he would be guaranteed admission at UT Austin.

Those who investigated the name of the mysterious relative who'd left this generous bequest to Arcelia were always told the records were sealed, contrary to the way probate matters were routinely handled, i.e. being public records. Those who persisted in snooping received a phone call from the managing partner of a 500-lawyer firm in Dallas and were informed that if they kept prying they'd have their own lives gone over with a fine-tooth comb. How would they like that?

Nobody much did, and the question of who Ladbrook Johnson's daddy was passed into Texas folklore. Lots of fun to gossip about. Downright dangerous to examine too closely.

Arcelia, meanwhile, raised her boy while running Gasoline's only public bathhouse.

"Sonofabitch," Ben Musgrove muttered from his perch atop Fein's Fine Jewelry. Just his forehead and his eyes showed above the parapet of the building, but he could see things had changed at the 11th precinct polling place. For one thing, the damn doors were locked. Nobody was doing any after-hours voting now. For another, the two goat-ropers with the shotguns were gone from out front. Replaced by Walker Winslow, Win-Win's boy.

Whose chest Mary Sue, goddamnit, just put her hand on. Like she was about to unbutton his shirt or something.

Laughing at whatever that prick Walker had just said to her. Bastard. Bitch. Ben wanted to throw his camera at them, but he had a job to do so he kept on shooting. Grinding his teeth so he wouldn't jump up and shout out anything stupid.

Ben had to duck down right fast when Mary Sue turned and looked his way. Walker was lifting his head in Ben's direction, too. Ben thought he'd been quick enough to avoid detection but as he sat with his back against the parapet he heard Walker's laugh. Mary Sue, too. Then they talked some more, but he couldn't catch their words.

Didn't stop his imagination from filling in the dialogue.

Mary Sue saying, "Yeah, that dumb Ben Musgrove is up on Fein's roof with a camera, all right. Hoping to get some dirt on your daddy's campaign."

Walker answering, "Fat chance. Likely as not, Ben's got at least two fingers in front of the lens and a thumb up his ass."

Both of them ragging him. All three of them had been at Gasoline High together.

Back then, Ben had never even dared to fantasize having sex with Mary Sue. But when the opportunity came along, her asking him how about it, his heart skipped a beat but his hands sure didn't. He might even have scared her a little how fast he had her clothes off. But she got right into the spirit of things. Ben fell half in love with her right there that first time.

Only thing was, when she should've been moaning and screaming and clawing the hide off him, she was yapping at him instead. Every time they did it, it was the same thing. Asking him this and that about the campaign. Or how many movies Laddy Johnson had been in. Had he always been a stuntman or did he ever have any speaking roles? Was it really true a big star like Joanna Wells had been Laddy's college girlfriend, had lived with him, and kept leaving all of her husbands to get back with him? Was all that true? Did he know any secrets he could tell her?

Being a healthy young man, Ben could be interviewed and still complete his mission every time he had sex with Mary Sue. Twenty-three times now, but who was counting? He even brought her along most times and got her to shut up a minute or two while she caught her breath. But sitting up there on Fein's roof reflecting on matters, he had to conclude that Mary Sue's main interest was finding out what Ben knew about Laddy Johnson.

It was enough to make a person develop a healthy mistrust of the media.

Ben even had the queasy thought that Mary Sue had been planted on the Johnson campaign by Win-Win in the first place. Just listen to the two of them cackling down there.

Her and Walker.

Mary Sue's old high school boyfriend.

That fucking five-foot-four Chuck Norris wannabe.

Buck Musgrove was formulating how Laddy Johnson could demand an investigation of voting irregularities at the 11th precinct polling place in the event the election went Win-Win's way when Eveleen Nellis, the campaign's treasurer, poked her head into the office without knocking. Eveleen had an unlit cigarette in her mouth. She hadn't smoked in years, but she enjoyed sucking on unfiltered Camels, asserting you could savor the taste of the tobacco that way and get yourself a nice little buzz when the leaves mixed in with your saliva.

She refused to simply chew tobacco, saying that was unladylike.

"Her majesty's on the line, Laddy," Eveleen said. "Want me to tell her you had a stroke?"

"No," the candidate replied. "Just say I'm constipated real bad, and you don't know when I'll be out of the bathroom. But if I don't have a heart attack before I have my bowel movement, I'll get right back to her."

"You are a pisser," Eveleen told him with a grin.

"And you two are just awful," Buck told them, not sounding like an ex-Marine at all. "I'll go talk to Joanna. I always find it a pleasure."

"Miz Musgrove know that?" Eveleen asked.

Buck stomped out of the candidate's office as Laddy and Eveleen snickered.

Laddy Johnson and Joanna Wells, nee Wallersteen, had, in fact, been college sweethearts at UT. She'd graduated with her bachelor's degree in theater arts. He'd dropped out after his sophomore year to accompany Joanna to L.A. She'd said he should have stayed in school and gotten his degree in secondary education. Laddy's goal had been to teach high school history, hoping to find a school that would allow him to go beyond the textbook and fill young minds with the real dirt done by men and women of power and influence.

Might've had something to do with the fact that all his life he'd heard the rumors about who his father had been but wasn't able to get Mom to cop to the fact.

To alleviate Joanna's guilt, he told her he'd transfer all his credits to UCLA. Get his degree out there in La-La Land.

"Can you do that?" she asked.

"Sure. UT's a big name school and I'm a dean's list student."

"But I thought, you know, a place like UCLA would make you take at least three years of their credits to get a degree with their name on it."

Laddy's first impulse was to say he'd talk to his mom. He was sure the people she knew in Texas, whose names she'd never reveal to him, must know people in California, and they'd fix things for him. But he decided on the spot not to go that way.

He said, "That's okay. If I have to go an extra year, it'll be worth it to be with you."

Joanna threw her arms around Laddy and told him, "Oh, I love you so much."

"I love you, too," he said, liking the way she felt all rubbed up against him.

Until she held on so long his arms went numb.

Besides Joanna's love, which Laddy didn't doubt for a minute, he knew she also felt a sense of gratitude for the support he showed her. She needed it because of her own sense of desperation.

Joanna had yet to give her first professional performance, had yet to set foot in L.A., and was only 22 years old, but she felt she was already getting old fast. She didn't have much time left if she was going to become a major movie star.

Joanna's parents gave her a $5,000 grubstake as a graduation present. But Darren Wallersteen told his daughter, "That's all she wrote as far as this acting stuff goes. You can't make it on that, come back home and I'll pay your way through dental school."

Birdie Wallersteen rolled her eyes and let Joanna know she had money of her own she could send her, so never mind her father's bluster. Who then blustered some more.

"I'm serious, Birdie," Darren told his wife. "If Joanna was confident she could make it out there in L.A., she wouldn't've changed her name. Lookit Meryl Streep. You think Streep looks any better on a marquee than Wallersteen? A girl can act, she don't need to change her name."

Joanna's father said, "Ow, shit!" when his wife pinched his cheek. With Darren properly chastened, both of the Wallersteens kissed and hugged their daughter goodbye.

Laddy was already waiting for Joanna behind the wheel of the '67 Ford Mustang he'd bought in high school, restored, and kept running like a top ever since. Darren stepped away from his daughter and wife and came over to have a private word with young Mr. Johnson.

He extended his hand to Laddy and held on while they talked.

"I know you're a fine young man, Laddy," Darren said. "I've met your momma and she's a wonderful lady."

"Thank you, sir."

"I know you make Joanna happy, too."

"I try my best."

"I'm smart enough to know that you make her happy by doin' more than just carrying her books to class."

Laddy decided it was time to keep quiet.

Darren said, "I'm all right with that. Might surprise you but I remember how it feels to be your age."

Laddy only nodded.

"I just want you to take care of my little girl is all. And when you bed her down, do it like a Texan should."

Laddy wasn't sure if Mr. Wallersteen meant he should

leave his boots on. But all he said was, "That's the only way I know how, sir."

Darren gave Laddy's hand a final affirmative squeeze and said, "Good, that's all I wanted to hear."

Ten minutes later, after Laddy and Joanna had driven off from the Wallersteen home, Joanna said, "Daddy told you to take care of me, didn't he?"

"Yeah," Laddy answered.

"What else?"

Laddy told her and Joanna laughed.

"What'd he mean?" Laddy asked. "Like a Texan should."

"Well, Daddy's afraid that ..." Joanna blushed.

Laddy looked over at her and said, "What?"

"I overheard him and Momma talking last night. It was really kind of nasty. Weird, too, the stuff parents can worry about. Guess it's a fearful thing to let a daughter go."

Laddy stopped at a red light and gave Joanna a look.

"Oh, all right," she said. "Daddy's got this notion that all the men in California, even the straight ones, are half gay."

"What?"

"It's his idea, not mine. Anyway, he wants to be sure that I'm with a man who knows he should put his thing where God intended it to go. Not where some gay guy might like to put it."

"Huh," Laddy said as the light turned green and he pulled away. "Don't think I'll have any trouble keeping him happy on that one."

Wasn't a movie studio in Hollywood holding its breath waiting for Joanna Wells to hit town. But that's the way it was for any young fool who wasn't related by blood, business or blackmail to some movie hotshot. Laddy got a job bussing tables at a Mexican restaurant, even though his trust fund was providing him $2,500 a month. His working environment was familiar, friendly, and he got a chance to keep current on his Spanish cuss words.

He also got into UCLA and, as Joanna had thought, had to take three years of classes before he could get his degree. Which was okay because Joanna had post-grad studying to do in the dramatic arts. Mainly eliminating any trace of her Texas accent. Possibly cultivating posh British tones. The two of them went to school during the day and made love according to the divine plan after Laddy got home from his shift at El Gallito Rojo. The Little Red Rooster.

After a couple of months in town, Joanna met Beeb Bidwell, who was working in the mail room at William Morris. Beeb invited Joanna and Laddy to a party at his home in the Hollywood Hills. The two Texans didn't exactly have trail dust on their chaps, but their jaws dropped when they saw Beeb's house and its view of the city: a million twinkling lights against a black velvet sky.

"Mail room work must pay pretty well," Laddy told their host when he greeted them at his front door. "I might have to drop out of college again. See if I can't operate a Pitney-Bowes for someone."

Beeb laughed. "It helps to get into the *right* mail room."

"Yeah? How do you do that?"

"It helps if your dad is somebody *big*."

"My dad was president of the United States," Laddy said.

Beeb laughed again, looked at Laddy as if maybe he should be the one trying to get into the movies, told Joanna her boyfriend was a hoot. Yeah, she said, and gave Laddy a shot to the ribs the minute Beeb turned his head. Actresses didn't like their boyfriends stealing the spotlight.

Back at campaign headquarters, Laddy and Buck listened to Ben's tale of perfidy, with its subtext of heartbreak.

"Mary Sue just went off with Walker Winslow. Got in his SUV and drove away."

"She left you up there on Fein's roof holdin' your wienie?" Buck asked, highly agitated once more at the way the world was treating his boy.

"No. Before she left she called out, 'Ben, you can come down now.' Then she and Walker laughed at me, and then they drove off."

Ben hung his head in shame. Buck wanted to kick some ass. Couldn't do that to Mary Sue, though. Laying a beating on a woman just wasn't in the cut of his cloth. Now, Walker Winslow was another matter. Little runt thought he was some kind of kung-fu master, but Buck was sure the boy wouldn't last ten seconds with anyone who'd ever had any USMC hand-to-hand training.

Problem was, Ben had never been in the Marines, and this matter really was his fight. It was proving to be a highly frustrating night for Buckminster Musgrove.

Laddy stepped into the breach. "Ben, you did us two real big favors tonight."

Both Musgroves looked at the candidate.

Ben asked, "How's that?"

Laddy said, "One, you exposed Win-Win's trap."

Buck asked Laddy. "What the hell trap was that?"

"Yeah," Ben added.

"The one certain people around here wanted to rush into. You know, go charging off to the 11th precinct polling place, loaded for bear, looking to right wrongs, shoot down the opposition, skin Win-Win alive. Of course, our men would've arrived after the polling place was closed, there were no longer any armed men outside, and everything was peaceful. Which isn't to say there weren't a dozen or so well-armed cops, all of them friends of Win-Win's, inside the polling place just watching out for trouble. Cops and maybe a TV crew from KYHA."

Buck looked as sheepish as a 6-foot-4, 240-pound, ex-Marine with a fist for a face can look. "Jesus, that was close. Why the hell do you let me run anything around here?"

Laddy said, "You're good with organization; you're great with team spirit; and you have an effervescent personality."

Buck snorted and Spit into Laddy's waste basket.

Laddy turned back to Ben. "Two, you exposed a spy in our midst, Ben. And don't lose a minute's sleep over Mary Sue. I've seen a hundred like her. She seems real sweet now, but inside of five years she'll be sour enough to pickle your pepper, if you're fool enough to have another go at her."

The candidate thought that coming home and listening to country music again was having a definite effect on how he turned a phrase. Probably a political advantage.

Just then, Eveleen poked her head in with a word from the state's most exalted country singer. "Laddy, Governor Freyman's on the phone. Said to tell you Win-Win's on the Austin TV channel calling you a bastard again.

Beeb Bidwell was planning to become the biggest agent in L.A. and he was laying the groundwork by scouting for young talent he could groom and bring with him on what he said would be his meteoric rise. He already had his house in the hills, a Shelby Cobra, and reserved tables at all the best restaurants in town. Of course, all of that was thanks to his father, who'd put a Cinderella witching-hour on his largesse. Beeb had to make a splash within 18 months or everything turned back into a pumpkin and mice for him.

He explained all this to Laddy at his house party.

"That was a pretty good joke," Beeb told Laddy, "saying your dad was president of the United States."

They were drinking long-neck bottles of Lone Star beer, which Beeb had sent out for. Joanna was standing at Laddy's side, looking for a way to turn the conversation toward her. After all, damnit, she was the one who'd gotten the invitation to Beeb's party in the first place.

"No joke," Laddy said. "My dad was Lyndon Baines Johnson."

Beeb looked Laddy up and down. Grinned and said, "Yeah, bullshit."

"No bullshit," Laddy said. "I'm LBJ's love child."

Beeb choked on his beer. Some came up out of his nose.

"He is a bastard," Joanna said. "I'll vouch for that."

Beeb doubled over laughing.

Laddy said in his best Texas twang, "Mah fella Amurricans ..."

"Stop, you're killing me," Beeb pleaded.

"See," Laddy said, "I sound just like him, don't I?"

Which, thinking about it, came as a revelation to Laddy. He'd never done an impression before in his life, but his LBJ was dead on. The way Johnson sounded on old black-and-white videotapes, anyway. *Shit.* He was the man's son.

Beeb departed, pleading the need to pee before beer came out his ears. Joanna turned her back on Laddy, highly miffed. And Laddy wondered how his mother would react if he ever phoned her using Lyndon Johnson's voice.

* * *

Lucan Thorn came through Beeb's front door like Don Pardo had just introduced him on a game show. Smiling ear to ear and ready to be adored by everyone. Beeb was off irrigating porcelain and Joanna still had her back turned on Laddy. Thorn was a pretty boy with wavy dark hair, a complexion almost as bronzed as Laddy's, and gym-cut muscles. Laddy made him for an actor the minute he saw him, though Thorn was a little taller than most, maybe five-ten.

One look told you no one else could ever love him as much as he loved himself. And the way he cocked his head suggested he might be from New York. That was how Laddy read things, anyway.

There was no room for misinterpretation about what happened next. Thorn made a beeline for Joanna, didn't give Laddy a glance though he was standing right next to her. The first words out of his mouth were, "Those are the finest tits I've seen in my life."

In fairness, Laddy agreed, and Joanna's cocktail dress did offer quite a view.

Thorn's voice confirmed his New York origins.

He wasn't satisfied simply offering a verbal appraisal of Joanna's charms. While she looked at him like he was some kind of bug she'd never seen before, Thorn cupped her breasts in his hands.

"Perfectly balanced, too," he judged.

Laddy didn't bother to tell Thorn to step outside. Didn't give him a bit of warning. Some things a fella should just know are going to stir people up. Laddy hit Thorn a hard left to the nose. His follow-up right lifted the New Yorker off his feet and dropped him on his ass. Thorn looked up as if to see what had hit him, but his eyes crossed and he fell backward to the floor unconscious.

Still a bit worked up, Laddy thought a few bootprints might improve Thorn's appearance, but before he could act on the notion two big old boys who made him seem dainty grabbed his arms and rushed him out the door, as applause sounded behind him.

Laddy thought it was his turn to catch a thumping, but the gents who evicted told him to just mosey along. *Mosey.* In a Texas accent. He'd gotten lucky.

"But my girlfriend —" Laddy started.

"Is old enough to find her own way home," one of the giants said.

"And if she has one too many, one of us will drive her," said the other.

Laddy nodded. Waved goodbye. Knowing when not to push his luck.

He didn't know just *how* lucky he'd been. Beeb Bidwell had taken a real shine to him. Wasn't at all put out Laddy had busted up another of his party guests. Only regretted he hadn't seen the action. He called Laddy and told him he wanted to make Laddy a star.

"You're still delivering mail?" Laddy asked.

"Won't be for much longer," Beeb said. "Then you'll have to listen."

"Unh-huh," Laddy said.

In fact, it was only three weeks later that Arneson Bidwell, Beeb's dad, passed on. Arneson's fourth wife, a limber Brazilian, had shown him a capoeira kick which he tried to duplicate. The result was a hernia so grievously strangulated that the pain produced a fatal heart attack. The widow Bidwell was pre-nupped from A to Z and every day of the year. Including February 29th. That left Beeb with most of his old man's gelt.

Including daddy's client list. Arneson Bidwell had been the biggest agent in town. A mantle that had now passed to his son, Hollywood being a bastion of primogeniture.

Beeb was now too big to represent any of the nobodies he'd recently been cultivating.

But hardly too big to handle LBJ's love child.

Problem was, Laddy had never wanted to be an actor. Had tried acting only once. Under unique circumstances. He was sure he would stink, if he tried to be in the movies. He was better suited to working at the Little Red Rooster.

Beeb was dumbfounded. Who had ever heard of such a thing in L.A.? If he told his friends what Laddy had said, they'd never believe him. At the same time, he couldn't let his friends hear a word of it. If it got around that anyone said no to him, much less a busboy, he'd be finished. He had to change Laddy's life in some magical way. Some way Beeb could eventual brag about.

"Look," Beeb told Laddy, "you remember the two guys who threw you out of my party?"

"Sure. It was nice of them not to bust me up."

"Well, they kinda liked your accent and the way you used your fists. You know what their day jobs are?"

"No," Laddy said, not sure he wanted to know.

"They're stunt men. How'd you like to work with them?"

Beeb figured he would put Laddy in the movies without him having to act.

The idea had a certain appeal for Laddy. He'd always liked a good action scene.

"Pay any good?" he asked.

"You could buy a house with a pool. In the Valley."

"Maybe you could take Joanna on as a client?"

Beeb fell silent. Then he said, "I can't. But I have a kid in my mail room. Smart. He's going to be big. Maybe as big as me someday. I'll have him take Joanna on as his first client. How's that?"

"Deal," Laddy said.

So, as fate would have it, Laddy wound up in the movies before Joanna. Her new agent, Freddie Smith, was hustling for her, had gotten her a couple of shampoo commercials, but no movies, not even any TV shows. She had to work harder on losing her Texas accent, Freddie said. He sent her to Farrah Fawcett's old voice coach. Which Laddy gladly paid for even though he thought Freddie was full of shit.

"Be who you are, baby," he told Joanna. "Your voice is part of your charm, your identity, your American heritage, for Christ's sake."

Joanna only rebuked him through her tears, "Easy for you to say, goddamnit. That fucker Beeb's already got a movie lined up for you."

Which was true. Laddy got to be the body-double for an assassin who got thrown under a train by Tom Cruise. The job paid some damn fine money, you didn't mind your character getting sliced into three separate sections. Tom getting to say, "He went to pieces."

Joanna sucked it up and they went to the premier in Westwood. She was easily the most dazzling woman between the San Gabriel Mountains and the Mexican border, if you asked Laddy. But his sentiment didn't matter because after Tom and his leading lady entered the theater none of the media gave a rat's poop about anyone else. Nobody took a single picture of Joanna.

Another sore point that evening was the fact that along with his sports coat, silk T-shirt and jeans, Laddy insisted on wearing a Stetson and his cowboy boots. Joanna was working hard to distance herself from her past and Laddy was reveling in it. When the train cut off Laddy's head, Joanna cheered loudly enough for Tom Cruise to turn around and give her a smile and a thumbs-up.

For a little while, things improved when Laddy and Joanna went house-hunting in the Valley. There's a natural excitement in any young couple's life looking for their first house, and they found a beauty, for a price that would have bought 500 acres back in Texas, but which they could afford because Laddy had work lined up for the next three years.

What with getting the house furnished and decorated and swimming enough laps in the pool out back that Laddy thought Joanna might be able to swim to Hawaii if she tried, there was a month or two of relative calm between them.

Then three things happened.

Joanna got a call from her mom saying how absolutely thrilled she and her father were at the way things were working out for Joanna and Laddy. Meaning Laddy was working, Joanna was keeping house, and as far as they knew he wasn't sticking his thing up her butt.

Next, Joanna started reading the *L.A. Times* aloud as a voice exercise. One of the stories she read told how the San Fernando Valley, where she and Laddy now lived, was the porn video capital of the United States. Great, she thought, sinking into depression, things kept up the way they were she'd wind up being either Betty Crocker or Jenna Jameson.

Lastly, Joanna's voice coach, in a measure of desperation to separate his pupil from the intonations of her youth, suggested she watch every movie Katharine Hepburn had ever made. Then she was to do her best to imitate Ms. Hepburn's voice, the hope being that such a radical change would jolt Joanna out of her normal speech patterns.

The experiment had an unhappy ending when Joanna happened to watch *The Philadelphia Story* on the same day Laddy came home early after being kicked by a horse. The kick, luckily for him, had been a glancing one that caught him above his right knee instead of on it. In the macho way of stunt men in particular and Texans in general, Laddy had declined medical attention and said he could drive himself home. A little rest and he'd be fine in the morning.

Maybe all he needed was a soak in the hot tub with —

Tracy Lord, Hepburn's imperious heiress in the movie Joanna had just watched. She was the one who greeted Laddy at the door as if he were C.K. Dexter Haven, Cary Grant's role as Hepburn's wandering ex, and someone to be dismissed with contempt.

The assault of an East Coast nasal honk coming out of his Texas rose was more than the wounded Laddy could comprehend. He looked for other signs of demonic possession. Joanna's lunatic rant continued, telling him that George Kittredge, the role of Tracy's fiancé played by John Howard, was twice the man he was. Laddy had no idea what she was talking about, but her verbal assault made his leg hurt worse than the horse's kick. All he could do was clamp his hands over his ears and yell, "Stop!"

Joanna took this injunction as criticism of what she'd thought had been a spot-on performance. Her face collapsed from Hepburnesque hauteur to the dismay of a crushed little girl. She started to bawl and ran for their bedroom. Laddy took one step in pursuit and collapsed. This time, he felt like a train actually had cut off his leg.

He yelled to Joanna for help. Yelled twice more. Got not a peep of response. Somehow, like a teenager in a horror movie, he managed to drag himself to the closest phone and call for help. He gave the emergency operator his name, his location, and his condition.

"I think I'm dying," he said.

Then he dropped the phone and crawled back toward the open front doorway, his thought being he'd better get to where the ambulance crew could see him. Joanna obviously had been taken over by the pod people. She could close the door on him and with a smile on her face tell the paramedics that his call had all been a big mistake.

He was four feet from the door when he blacked out.

Governor Freyman told Laddy, "Win-Win called you a bastard straight out tonight. Said he was just telling it like it is."

"He's the one finally came up with the documentation, huh?" Laddy asked.

Buck had left Laddy to speak to the governor alone. He wasn't a fan. Thought *Flake-o from Waco* was an apt description of the state's chief executive. Especially thought the lyric about him "hosin' heifers" was on the money.

Laddy tried to tell Buck the song was written by someone else and was just a parody of Merle Haggard's *Okee from Muskogee*. But Buck wouldn't hear any of that; he loved Merle.

"Joanna says she's sick of hearing Win-Win call you

names," the governor said.

"She's called me a bastard more than once herself."

"You sleep with a woman, that's bound to happen. She says you ain't taking her calls because you're too full of shit. Once I heard that, I sent you a bushel of my special Texas-strength psyllium husks. Those suckers'll clean you out bet-ter'n Roto Rooter."

"You're too good to me, governor."

"Yeah, well, us show biz folks have to stick together. So why don't you pick up the damn phone the next time a movie star calls? Do somethin' about Win-Win, too. I'd hate to see him back in office. Kick his ass on TV, why don't you?"

"You'll give me a full pardon for any grievous bodily injury I might cause?"

"A pardon and kiss on the lips, you want one. But only if you talk to Joanna."

"You're a regular Jewish mother."

"Some people'd tack on a couple more syllables," the gov-ernor said.

Laddy laughed and said goodbye.

He thought maybe it was time to talk to Joanna again.

Kick Win-Win's ass on TV, too.

Something like that might help in case of a recount.

"Jesus, why didn't you tell me you were hurt?"

Joanna's face was the first thing Laddy saw when he came to. Then the hospital room came into focus: the bed with the safety railings; the hospital gown he was wearing and the sterile wrap around his right leg; the monitor going *beep-beep* with reassuring regularity; and the IV-line coming out of his arm.

"My piercing pleas for help weren't a clue?" he asked.

She looked at him blankly. "I never heard that. I just came out of the bedroom and saw you on the floor. I ran to get the phone and call 911, but the ambulance guys were already at the door. I made them take me with you."

She didn't say that she'd emerged from the bedroom with the intent of telling Laddy she was leaving him, if he could maybe lend her ten grand. And she didn't mention that before she ran to get the phone she'd given him a little kick to see if he was faking things to get her sympathy.

"The doctors say you won't lose your leg," she told him.

Laddy's eyes got big just hearing of the possibility.

"But then I guess you didn't know that," Joanna said.

He shook his head mutely.

"I called your shoot and found out what happened, that horse kicking you. What the kick did was tear your quadriceps muscle. You shouldn't have been walking around on that leg at all. A vascular surgeon told me if the angle of the kick had been a little different it might've hit your femoral artery. If the flow of blood to your lower leg had become insufficient, gangrene would have set in. Then they'd have had to amputate."

Laddy was glad he was in a bed with bumpers, as he suddenly felt woozy.

"Of course, if the kick had severed the artery," Joanna said, "that would have killed you. You'd have bled out before you ever got home."

Laddy closed his eyes and dealt with thoughts of mortality for a moment. Without looking, he extended his hand to Joanna. Felt a world better when she took it. Started to get excited when she stroked his arm with her free hand.

She laughed and he opened his eyes.

"I know what happens when you get goose bumps, buddy," she said. "Something else pops right up, too."

Laddy scanned the room. No one else was there. The door was closed.

"Forget it," Joanna said, seeing him look around. "It ain't gonna happen here." Then her voice softened. "But I sure would've missed you if you'd died on me."

He loved the way she sounded like herself again.

"I'll take you home when you're ready," Joanna told him. "Take real good care of you."

He smiled. She smiled back and brushed a tear from her eye.

"Even get myself a nurse's uniform, if you like that kind of thing."

Joanna kept her promise and waited hand and foot on Laddy, bringing him back to health. He went back to work: falling off buildings, driving off cliffs, flying airplanes into mountains — but he drew the line at horses. He was one Texan who wasn't going to climb back into the saddle. He'd had it with *Equus caballus*. His right quad had knitted back together, but the big muscle ached in rainy weather and he'd lost a step in his 40-yard dash. Fucking nag.

Freddie Smith acquiesced to Joanna's decision that he would have to find work for her with the voice she had, not Katharine Hepburn's, Oprah Winfrey's or Bugs Bunny's. Freddie said he'd do his best, but would she, in return, do one little favor for him? Learn to speak French.

This, of course, was yet another ploy to modify her inflections. You learned French, you had to at least attempt to speak with a French accent. Ordinarily, this suggestion would have been unacceptable. But during Laddy's convalescence Joanna had indeed played the randy nurse for him, and they'd both felt a tremendous surge in the health of their relationship. So much so that they'd gone on to explore other role-playing games: one being the French maid.

But even Joanna thought her faux-French accent was *tres de fromage*. Really cheesy. If she wanted to perfect her maid's role or someday even play Marie Antoinette for Laddy she really ought to know the language and speak it properly. She accepted Freddie's proposal.

In turn, Freddie got Joanna work in places where her native Texas tongue was an asset: the *Blue Collar TV* show, and interviewing country singers on CMT. Which was a definite step up from shampoo commercials, but far from the feature film stardom the *cum laude* graduate of the University of Texas' theater department longed for. Still, she gamely stuck it out for two years, hoping better things would come. Which as it turned out they did.

With a Hollywood ending. The *real* kind of Hollywood ending.

Laddy came home one day, after being eaten by a giant squid, and found Joanna in tears on the living room sofa. She was so forlorn he could reach only one conclusion.

"Jesus," he said, putting an arm around her, "was it your momma or your daddy?"

Who died, he meant. But Joanna only looked confused.

"What?" she asked. Then she understood and told him that both her parents were fine.

"Well, what is it then?" he asked.

"Freddie is leaving me."

For a dizzying moment, Laddy thought Joanna was confessing an affair with her agent, but then he caught on.

"Freddie's leaving Beeb's agency?" he asked.

"No," Joanna sobbed, "he's moving *up*. They want a girl from the mail room to handle my career. I'm the nobody who always gets passed on to the new trainee."

"Well, shit," Laddy said. He'd never liked Freddie much anyway. And maybe working with a woman would be better for Joanna. Maybe the new girl was a real winner. But he knew better than to offer any of these rationalizations.

So he said, "I'll give Beeb a call. See what I can do."

Joanna kissed him hard enough to chip a tooth. She had the phone handy, too.

He said he'd make the call from the den, and don't listen in, the conversation might turn nasty. Joanna promised she wouldn't, but Laddy made the call from his cell phone just in case. He returned to the living room five minutes later.

It killed him to see how anxious Joanna looked. He thought he should tell Joanna they should just get married and have a child. They had enough money to go home, buy a house, start a family and a business of some kind.

But that wasn't Joanna's dream.

"That was fast," she said warily. "Did he take your call?"

"Beeb always takes my calls."

"He does?"

"Yeah, 'cause I told him the day he stops, I'll be by to kick his ass."

Despite herself, Joanna grinned. But just for a moment. "What'd he say?" she asked.

He said if you really want to stay with Freddie, okay, he'll fix it. But he thinks you'd be happier with Melanie because not only is she smarter than Freddie, she's faster off the line. She's already got a movie audition for you. But if you want Freddie, Melanie will send another actress over."

On first hearing Beeb's spiel on the phone, Laddy realized what a masterpiece of manipulation it was. But at the time he didn't know the half of it.

"I'd be a fool to go back to Freddie," Joanna said.

"Yes, you would."

"This isn't a cable movie, is it? she asked."

"Feature. Hundred-million-dollar budget."

Took the breath right out of Joanna. When she got it back, she was even more nervous.

"I don't have to do anything extreme, do I? No full-frontal nudity."

"Only for me," Laddy assured her. "Beeb told me Freddie did do you one favor."

"What?" Joanna asked suspiciously.

"The role requires a beautiful woman, sort of a young American Catherine Deneuve, who can speak perfect French because that's what she's pretending to be, French."

"That's me, that's me!" Joanna bounced up and down on the sofa twice, then launched herself into Laddy's arms.

"I've worked hard, Laddy. My tutor says my French accent is *plus que parfait.*"

"Don't I know it?" He kissed her, happy for her, but suddenly anxious for himself. Still, he mustered the grace to say, "Knock 'em dead, sweetheart."

"I will. I will. I ..." She pulled her head back and looked him in the eye. "Laddy, if I don't get this part, I'm done. I'll go back to Texas and beg you to come with me."

At that moment, Laddy dared to hope they'd live happily ever after.

Which was a damn fool thing to do.

Joanna got the star-making role. The whole thing had been wired from the git-go. The leading man, whose participation got the project financed, had demanded that Joanna be cast. Her part had been rewritten specifically for her.

When Joanna came back from the two-month shoot in Europe she was engaged to marry her leading man. Lucan Thorn.

The same grabby New York prick Laddy had sucker-punched more than two years ago.

Payback had been a long time coming, but it was indeed a motherfucker.

Edwin "Win-Win" Winslow had made his fortune with a car dealership like no other. Win-Win didn't limit his store to any one manufacturer. Rather, it hewed to a theme revered by Texans from Brownsville to Amarillo: *Bigger is better.* Win-Win sold Cadillac Escalades, Lincoln Navigators, Hummers, and for those on a budget, GMC Suburbans. He called his dealership Texas Rolling Stock. TRS, for short.

Even when gasoline sold for $3 per gallon he had no shortage of customers. But then half of his clientele came from Persian Gulf countries where price was never an object, and the sheiks were the buggers who set the damn price of gas in the first place.

Well, for most people they did. The town of Gasoline, Texas had its own municipal oil field and refinery. Residents paid 25¢ per gallon of gas, plus a few pennies tax. Made it a lot easier for the locals to own and operate the biggest, fanciest SUVs on the market.

Win-Win was of a scale to appreciate a bronto-sized ride. He was six-four and 260. Played two years at nose tack for A&M. Every time he'd run for mayor, prior to this one, he'd made a point of standing next to his opponent as often as he could. People couldn't help but see how stunted and shriveled the sumbitch cowering in his shadow was, and being Texans they always made the right decision: *Bigger is better.*

He'd tried that trusty old approach only once with Laddy Johnson.

At six-three, Laddy wasn't but an inch shorter, and with him having a full head of hair and Win-Win's thinning out into a comb-over it looked like a draw in the height department. Just as bad, Laddy weren't no string bean neither. Had to go 220, which made Win-Win look like the one with 40 pounds of suet on him.

On top of all that, the bastard was good looking and had worked in the movies for years and years. Not being some pansy actor or commie director, either, but as a tough as nails stuntman. Laddy's first campaign commercial made use of that, was the best political ad anyone had ever seen, from Texas to Timbuktu.

Started out with clips of Laddy's movies when he was a young man, Tom Cruise tossing him under that train, then Laddy getting shot, stabbed and blown up. But he always kept coming back. Damn commercial even got the staff at TRS whooping and hollering when it came on in the customer waiting lounge. But the clips were only the setup.

When they finished, there was Laddy looking like he did now, a grown man come home to Texas. Before he can even say a word, wham! A great big fist comes out of nowhere, sets Laddy down on his ass. But is he knocked out? No, sir. He gets up with a smile, a little dab of blood at one corner of his mouth, and dusts himself off. He looks right at the camera and says, "You vote for me, Laddy Johnson, for mayor, and we'll see who wins the tough fights around here."

He starts toward the camera with his fists up. The screen goes to a card saying *Vote Laddy Johnson for Mayor.* But behind it you heard three hard punches landing, and you just know Laddy Johnson is kicking ass.

Win-Win's ass.

"They didn't fall for it, Daddy," Walker Winslow said as he and Mary Sue Parker strolled into Win-Win's office at his campaign headquarters, a/k/a Texas Rolling Stock.

"Didn't really expect they would," Win-Win said.

"Buck Musgrove would've," Mary Sue informed the mayor, taking a seat.

Walker remained standing. At five-four, without the lifts in his boots, he was a foot shorter than his father. At a little over 130 pounds, he was a Big Mac more than half his daddy's weight. So he took every opportunity to stand when Win-Win was sitting.

There was no denying they were father and son, though. The eyes, nose, and mouth, they were all the same. One was just XXXL; the other was handy travel size. Some folks speculated that when Win-Win sired Walker he must've used only one nut. *One Nut* was one of Walker's two most despised nicknames. The other was *Booster Seat.* That one got started when daddy fired a grease monkey from TRS and the sumbitch put out word that Walker's Hummer had a custom upholstered driver's seat so he could see over the steering wheel.

Walker had laid a serious beating on the weasel for that one. Serious enough that no one in town made fun of him to his face. But from then on he had his Hummer serviced in Houston.

"So Buck would've bought it, huh?" Win-Win asked.

"He got real upset hearing your boys pointed their guns at Ben."

"Laddy reined him in?"

Mary Sue nodded.

"Good to know how things work over there," Win-Win mused. "This election's bound to go to a recount. Maybe, while the ball's still up in the air, we can get ol' Buck to shoot his wiener off yet."

"Or Laddy's," Walker suggested.

Win-Win laughed without humor. "That sumbitch, you shot his dick off, he'd prob'ly grow himself a new one."

Mary Sue changed the subject. "Mr. Mayor, I believe my usefulness as a spy in the Johnson campaign is over. So if you don't mind ..."

Mary Sue didn't have her hand out but she wanted her money. Win-Win gave her a fat envelope which she tucked discreetly into her purse. "Thank you, sir."

"Don't you go runnin' off to Hollywood just yet, Mary Sue. I'm sure I'll have another chore or two for you."

"Yes, sir."

"What about me, Daddy?" Walker asked. "Am I done for the night?"

Walker wanted to take Mary Sue home. He hadn't slept with her while she was sacrificing her virtue to Ben Musgrove. Her reasoning had been: "How's it gonna look, I'm in the thick of things with Ben and I call out your name?" Which made sense to Walker. But now that her play-acting was over he wanted to remind her what a real man was like.

Before Win-Win could answer, his campaign manager, Norman Oklahoma, who was also the sales manager at TRS, knocked and entered Win-Win's office.

Norman got his family name from his great-granddaddy, who had come to America through Ellis Island. The immigration man had tried to read whatever the hell the great-granddaddy's name had been back in Transylvania or someplace like that and failed miserably. According to Norman, the original family name had started with an O and a K, all right, but after that it was a twelve-car pileup of consonants no regular American could ever pronounce. So the immigration man just changed it to Oklahoma. Norman's momma then gave her son his first name as her own little joke. Norman's daddy had been old country and didn't know his wife was playing a trick on their baby boy.

Norman's momma had been tipsy on the night she'd given him life and his name. Tipsy being her usual condition. Perhaps as a result of fetal alcohol exposure, Norman himself rarely thought anything was funny.

Except for Walker Winslow's nicknames. He thought they were hilarious. But he kept quiet about it.

"Hey, Norm," Win-Win said, "got any good news?"

"Don't know if it's good, Mayor, but the TV just said Laddy Johnson's 'bout to make an announcement."

Win-Win picked up his remote control and clicked on the office flat-screen.

Everyone turned to watch.

Laddy sent a card to the happy couple to congratulate them on their wedding. He addressed it to Joanna and Luke Anne Thorn. He reminded Joanna of her daddy's concerns that most men in California didn't know where to put their things. She sent him back a Polaroid showing Lucan knew where to put his just fine. The snapshot didn't show any faces, of course; Joanna wasn't about to give Laddy a picture he could sell to the tabloids for a million dollars.

But she didn't have to show Laddy her face. He knew Joanna's terrain by heart.

The ironic thing was that Laddy was probably as responsible as anyone for Lucan Thorn becoming a big star. Before Laddy has busted Thorn's nose for him, giving him some character and what one reviewer gushed was "a dangerous look," Thorn was just another pretty face going nowhere fast. But right after the swelling and discoloration from Laddy's beating had faded, the guy started getting work and just kept on going till he was a big enough star to steal Joanna from Laddy.

Big enough to be represented by Beeb Bidwell, who then cut Laddy loose. After the agent had lined up enough work for Laddy that he wouldn't get his nose busted, too.

Things settled in for a number of years after that. For Laddy, anyway. He worked, he paid off his house, he invested conservatively, dated with even greater caution, and found the time to get his BA in History from UCLA. He became certified to teach but he never entered a classroom because the L.A. Unified School District seemed a more hazardous place to earn a living than the deck of a ship on fire in the middle of a hurricane: one of his favorite stunt settings.

Joanna, on the other hand, divorced Lucan Thorn after two years of wedlock when she found out that he'd set up another household in Manhattan with Melanie, the agent who'd sent Joanna to the audition that had been her big break. By then, though, Joanna no longer needed Thorn as a co-star. She was bankable all on her own.

She called Laddy soon after the split-up with Thorn. But they couldn't go out in public for fear of the paparazzi, and Joanna wouldn't go back to the house she'd shared with Laddy. A big star like her didn't schlep out to the Valley. And Laddy would be damned if he'd go to the estate in Bel-Air that Joanna had shared with Thorn. They stopped talking after half-a-dozen phone calls.

Joanna married three more times, including once more to Thorn. She called Laddy after each divorce. The calls became briefer, more perfunctory, each time. But after her Thorn redux nuptials ended she said to Laddy, "Maybe it's finally time I married you. We could have a kid or two before it's too late."

Her words hit him like a sledgehammer to the heart.

Joanna had never had a child by any of her husbands.

All he said, though, was, "You've got two or three more good years of box-office left. Give me a call then and we'll hope you're still fertile."

Seemed harsh, but she didn't tell him to get fucked. She went out and made another hit movie and got engaged to another leading man. But that wedding never happened because her fiancé decided he could take the risk of coming out of the closet. Shortly thereafter, Laddy's phone rang again, but this time it was his mother calling him.

"You tired of California yet?" Arcelia asked. "How'd you feel about coming home and running for mayor?"

Gasoline's original name was Puttberry, Texas, given to it by the first Anglo settler to reach the area in honor of himself. An outpost of no great distinction or populace, it came to be known derisively as Buttberry. As in the ass end of nowhere. That was in 1839.

By 1901, everything changed when a well-digger hired by the town during a particularly hot and dry summer hit oil instead of water. The discovery of petroleum set off three days of anarchy as various parties tried to assert their claims to the land on which the oil was found. In a span of 72 hours, three mayors had seized power and been shot to death; the first two gunned down by their successors. The entire six-man town council also died violently. The citizenry divided into three armed camps, each of them trying to decide who to shoot first and how to make their ammo last.

That was when word came that the governor was about to send in the Texas Rangers to restore the peace. That and, no doubt, grab the oil for himself. Confronted with a common enemy, the three rival leaders came to a responsible solution. The land on which the oil had been found would be owned by the town in perpetuity. Each head of a household would have an equal share in access to whatever oil was produced and could use it for his own purposes or sell it, as he saw fit. No individual could own more than one share of the oil rights even if he bought more than one house in town. No extended family could own more than three shares of the oil rights. No combinations of families, friends, or businesses would be allowed to pool their votes or resources. The town boundaries and lot sizes of homesteads were fixed so the original inhabitants wouldn't be overrun by late arriving profiteers.

And, finally, the town name would be changed to Gasoline.

Everybody'd had a crawful of Buttberry.

* * *

After the Municipal Field was brought in, a town refinery was built. Gasoline sold its gasoline on the open market. But it wasn't long before the major oil companies undercut the prices of all their small scale competitors. Fucking majors had to sell at a loss to do that, but they were willing to bear the pain long enough to rid themselves of small-fry pests like the town of Gasoline. Some of the big oil companies even added insult to injury by referring to Gasoline by its old nickname of Buttberry.

Then the bastards from the majors had the brass balls to try to buy Gasoline's oil field and refinery for pennies on the dollar. That proved one insult too many for Mayor John Tyler Tunbridge. On July 2, 1906, he threw a lawyer for a big oil company based in New York out of his office by his shirt collar and the seat of his pants.

The lawyer rose to his feet on the sidewalk outside of City Hall with a sneer on his face. He gathered the papers for the proposed sale into his satchel and warned Mayor Tunbridge: "We'll get your oil. We always get what we want."

"Maybe so," the mayor replied, "but you'll never see it."

With that, the mayor drew his pistol and shot the lawyer dead.

He went back into his office and opened a bottle of whisky. He'd finished all but the last inch by the time the Texas Rangers came for him. He was tried and hanged before the month was out. By the following April, the town had erected a statue of Mayor Tunbridge. It defiantly faced toward Austin and the governor who'd sent the Rangers to arrest the mayor, and had later refused to pardon him for what everyone in town had come to judge a justifiable homicide. Texans knew when somebody needed killing.

At the statue's dedication, the people of Gasoline vowed that no one would ever have use of its oil but them. Now and for as long as there was a God and a Texas.

A little more than a century later, Mayor Edwin "Win-Win" Winslow decided he wanted to change all that. He had a hundred million reasons why. He had Mayor Tunbridge's statue removed from its place of honor. For refurbishment, he said.

That was when Arcelia Dominguez decided it was time to give her son, Laddy, out there in California, a phone call.

"They're trying to buy us out, Laddy," Arcelia told her son that day.

"Who is, Momma?"

"It's a consortium of the majors." She gave him the names involved.

"How much are they offering?"

"Half-a-million for each household."

"Huh," Laddy said. In California, 500K would barely get you a one-bedroom condo in Playa Del Rey. But in rural Texas it was a fortune. Far more than most people would ever see at one time.

"You add up all the households in town," Arcelia said, "the tab is better than three billion dollars."

Which was serious money anywhere west of the Pentagon.

"That how much the reserves in the Municipal Field are worth?" Laddy asked.

His mother told him, "I had some friends up at UT check it out for me. At even four dollars per gallon of gas, they're offering a billion dollar premium. Based on an estimate of what we should have left in the ground."

"That doesn't seem right," Laddy said. Oil men weren't known for philanthropy unless it was also good public relations, and Laddy didn't see how any oil company could spin this purchase to its advantage. "So what's the rat we smell here, Momma? You and your friends figure it out?"

"We're not positive. Well, hell, I am. What it is, the way the price of gas is going, folks look at us and see us paying two bits a gallon here in Gasoline, what are they going to think?"

Laddy knew. "That maybe they could fill up for a whole lot less, too, if they had their own oil wells. Like maybe the majors should be shoved out the door and the industry nationalized. But how would folks square that with their free-market beliefs?"

"Son, people'd vote for Vladimir Putin if he delivered cheap gas."

"And didn't mess with Friday night football."

"Well, of course," Arcelia said.

"Who's the mayor I'd be running against?" Laddy asked. He hadn't kept a real close eye on Gasoline, Texas politics. "He has to be in with the oil companies on this."

Arcelia said, "Win-Win Winslow's our mayor."

"Hayley's daddy?"

"Mmm-hmm," his mother agreed without elaboration.

Which reminded Laddy that for some reason he'd never learned his mother didn't like Hayley Winslow.

"How deep is Win-Win in the consortium's pocket?" Laddy asked.

"We figure 50 minimum, 100 tops," Arcelia told him. She didn't have to specify multiplying each figure by a million.

Laddy thought about that a minute.

"Momma, if these people are willing to spend that kind of money, any seriously contested election is going to be a real shitstorm."

Arcelia didn't argue the point, didn't say a word.

Finally, Laddy told her, "You know what, Momma, I am getting a little tired of Hollywood."

Laddy stepped out the front door of his election headquarters with Buck, Ben and Eveleen following him. Laddy had told them what he was going to say. There were three TV crews waiting for him: one from KYHA and one each from Houston and Austin.

"Give me a minute to speak my piece and then I'll answer any questions y'all might have," Laddy told the reporters. Squaring himself to look directly at the KYHA camera, he said, "I've heard that Win-Win Winslow has gone on TV tonight and called me a bastard. Which is nothing new. Up till now, I've ignored it. Took it as just one man cussin' out another in a heated situation. Nothing really to get upset about. But tonight Win-Win said it one time too many. My mother called me. She said even if I wasn't taking it personal, she was. It hurt her heart to hear Win-Win speak ill of me and, by implication, her, too.

"So right here and now, I challenge Mayor Edwin Winslow to come on by within the next 60 minutes and call me that name again to my face, knowing that if he does, he'll have to fight it out with me until one of us is no longer standing. I further challenge him to accept that the winner of that fight will be the next mayor of Gasoline, Texas because the loser will agree to drop out of the race. Now, I know I'm younger than Win-Win, but he's bigger than me.

And I've heard that in the past he always liked to stand next to his opponents and overshadow them. Well, let's see if he's got the Texas gumption to stand in front of me right now. Win-Win, I'm calling you out. Bring your boy, Walker, too, if you want. I'll whip his ass when I'm done whipping yours."

"What about Mrs. Winslow?" the KYHA reporter called out.

White-haired Margaret Winslow might have been the toughest member of the family. One night when Win-Win and Walker were out of town, an eco-terrorist group had tried to burn down Texas Rolling Stock. But Margaret, a bookkeeper by training, was in a back room doing a snap audit of the books to make sure no one was stealing from her family. Just as the terrorists were about to hurl their Molotov cocktails, Margaret burst out the front door, whipped off her trademark strand of pearls and all but garroted the terrorist leader. The others promptly ran away.

Not that Laddy was truly afraid of Win-Win's wife, but no way was he going to fight her. He wasn't sure even Governor Freyman would pardon him for beating up an old lady. But if Mrs. Winslow started snapping her string of pearls around, she could take an eye right out of his head. Turned out, though, Laddy neither had to fight her nor answer the reporter's question.

Eveleen stepped forward, lit the cigarette dangling from her mouth, and said, "I'll do the honors on that one."

"Y'all have 59 minutes left, Win-Win," Laddy added.

"Let me have him, Daddy." Walker Winslow pleaded. "I'll bust him up into a million pieces."

Win-Win loved his boy's spunk. Willing to fight so far

out of his weight class. But that was the problem. Walker was small. Looked like Win-Win could carry him around in his vest pocket. So what would the voting public think of Win-Win sending in someone that tiny to do his fighting for him? They'd think he was yellow. He'd never get another vote in his life. Not in Texas, he wouldn't.

Mary Sue summed up the situation neatly, "Laddy's got you by the short and curlies, Mayor, and the clock's ticking."

"Fucker did that on purpose, setting that time limit," Win-Win grumped.

"Sure. It's a Hollywood chestnut, but it does builds tension," Mary Sue said.

Norman Oklahoma looked around from the picture on the flat screen.

"Mayor," he said, "Houston and Austin TV are sending helicopters to get aerial pictures of the fight, and they report heavy volumes of vehicular traffic heading this way."

"Sumbitch," Win-Win said.

"I can do it, Daddy, I can," Walker keened. "You want me to do it fast, I can put him down in the blink of an eye." Walker whirled around backward, doing a vicious spin-kick. Looked just like Chuck Norris. Except Chuck kicked guys in the head. Walker's kick might've caught Laddy an inch or two above the knee.

"C'mere, boy," Win-Win told his son. Reluctantly, Walker stepped forward. He knew what was coming. Daddy was going to put his arm around Walker's shoulders. Their size difference would make Walker look like he was maybe in middle school. Win-Win told Walker, "I do want you to jump in fast, son. No warning at all. Take the bastard right out, like you said. If you can."

"I can, Daddy. I swear I can," Walker said, smiling ear to

ear, hardly believing his father was giving him this great opportunity.

"But, Walker," Win-Win told him, "I gotta be the first one to give the bastard a go. I was the one he called out. Someone called you out, you wouldn't want me to step in for you."

Much as he yearned to, Walker couldn't counter his father's argument. It was just like when Mary Sue explained why she couldn't have sex with him while she was screwing Ben Musgrove. Everywhere Walker turned he was confronted by unassailable logic.

It was enough to piss him off. He didn't want Laddy Johnson to whip his father's ass, but if it even looked like he might, Walker'd be on him like a buzzsaw.

"You could just call your chief of police," Mary Sue said, throwing ice water on the macho moment. "Tell him Laddy's threatening you with physical violence."

Win-Win directed a cold smile at her. She knew as well as he did that calling in the cops would look even more cowardly than letting Walker fight for him. Mary Sue was just pulling his pud. Having herself a little fun.

The mayor hadn't laid so much as a finger on the young thing. But they'd had their private little chats. Nothing was said directly that might be covertly recorded and be damning if replayed in court, but there was a lot of innuendo between the two of them. Phone sex without phones or the "Oh, baby, do it to me now!"

Mary Sue went on, "Or you could say you'd like to fight, but your doctor forbids it. You know, on account of an old football injury."

Mary Sue smiled innocently.

Laughing like hell at him on the inside, Win-Win knew.

"Daddy, you got an old football injury?" Walker asked.

Win-Win gave his son an affectionate squeeze, careful not to hurt the boy.

"I'm just fine, son."

Actually, Mary Sue had done Win-Win a favor. Reminding him of his football days at A&M. Reminding him how he'd enjoyed knocking the snot out of a bus load of old boys a lot bigger and meaner than Laddy Johnson. It'd been a while since he'd done that, but he reckoned if there was any ass-whippin' to be done tonight he'd be the one to do it.

"Walker, go saddle up that new Hummer Gargantua we just got in. Let's you 'n' me arrive in true Winslow style."

That'd mean Walker'd have to sit on a phone book to drive, but he was too excited to care.

"Right away, Daddy!" Walker left at a trot.

Norman Oklahoma said, "Mayor, TV says there could be 10,000 people in Tunbridge Square by the time of the fight. We're gonna need crowd control."

"Might be 20,000, Laddy's nice enough to wait for the out-of-town fans," Win-Win said. He was getting his game-face on now. He remembered how the crowds would cheer for his big hits on the football field. It'd felt good enough to make his pecker hard on more than one occasion. He told Norman, "The police are to keep order, but not interfere with the fight in any way."

"But what if —" Norman bit his tongue as the mayor looked at him. He hurried from the room.

Mary Sue finished Norman's question for him. "He meant what if Laddy is seriously whipping your ass and Walker's, too? Just like he said he would."

Win-Win only smiled at her for a long moment. Mary

Sue didn't look away.

"You're a very naughty girl," he said at last.

"Makes you tingle all over, don't it?" she asked.

It did, but Win-Win didn't say so. It would be just like Mary Sue to have a recorder going right now. He gave her a little wave and left.

Mary Sue got up and grabbed Win-Win's desk phone. She called the *Beacon* and told the city editor to send a photographer over to Tunbridge Square right away. She'd be covering a big story there ... in just about 45 minutes.

CHAPTER TWO

If Laddy hadn't stirred things up enough by challenging Win-Win to a fight, Joanna got into the act. She'd seen Laddy on TV, watching from the governor's mansion up in Austin, having just flown in from the Coast. As Laddy wasn't taking her calls, she called KYHA-TV and got put through to Reva McClatchy, the reporter on the scene at Laddy's headquarters, by promising to give the station an exclusive interview for its next sweeps period.

Reva called out to Laddy just as he was about to step back inside his headquarters, "Mr. Johnson, Laddy, I have a phone call for you."

Laddy turned to look at Reva, wondering how much peroxide human hair could absorb before it disintegrated. She was holding her cell phone out to him.

Win-Win responding to his challenge already, he wondered.

"Who is it?" Laddy asked.

Reva smiled giddily. Even waggled her penciled-in eyebrows. "Academy Award nominee, Ms. Joanna Wells."

True enough. Joanna's most recent movie, *Desperate Hours*, had been her best work and earned her an Oscar nomination. She'd played Marilyn Kendricks, the mother of Alan Kendricks, a man wrongly convicted of murder who was on Death Row, one day away from his execution. A crusading reporter, Talia Donati, had exposed all sorts of holes in the prosecution's case against Alan, but the governor, Ellery Horton, was running for reelection and couldn't afford to look soft on crime. He refused to pardon Alan or even stay his execution. So Marilyn kidnapped the governor's mother, Claresta, and passed the word to Talia that if her son died so did the governor's mother.

"One innocent life for another," Marilyn said.

Thing was, Governor Horton didn't like his mother a whole lot. As Joanna's character, Marilyn, was to discover, Claresta was far more loathsome than her condemned son was made out to be. Indeed, Alan had come to terms with his awful fate, had made his peace with God, and asked that those who were about to take his life be forgiven when it was found out how terribly wrong they were.

Governor Horton, ironically, was now as much of a hostage as his mother. He could either look soft on crime by delaying Alan's execution or he could look like a heartless monster who would sacrifice his own mother to advance his political ambitions. Either way he was sure to lose votes. He was mad enough to shit, spit, and throw a fit.

Meanwhile, Marilyn tried to explain her actions to Claresta, who remained coldly indifferent. Marilyn's son was about to be mistakenly executed? Too bad, Claresta said. These things happened. Over and over again, the infernal woman made Marilyn want to kill her. But only for a moment or two. Then Marilyn would feel forced to tell

Claresta another story about Alan, herself, or her late husband, Ted. Each and every time, though, Marilyn's attempt to humanize the situation was callously rebuffed. Claresta would gleefully tell Marilyn of the terrible consequences she was going to face for kidnapping the governor's mother. Marilyn's fate would be the same as her son's.

Finally, Governor Horton worked out a way to escape his predicament. He went to Alan's cell on Death Row and asked him to plead with his mother to spare the governor's mother. The governor said he was *not* going to stay Alan's execution in any case. So why not minimize the consequences for Marilyn? Wasn't that the least he could do for her? After hours of prayerful soul-searching, the condemned man agreed. Not to save Claresta, but because he didn't want his own mother to destroy her soul.

From his cell, Alan made the televised plea.

That was followed immediately by Governor Horton's announcement that Alan's execution would proceed as scheduled. Both Marilyn and Claresta were hit hard by their sons' words.

Marilyn could do no more than hang her head and cry. She told Claresta, "You win, you and your son. But I can't live another day in a country that kills innocent people. I'll call the police in a couple of days when I'm somewhere else. Somewhere better. You'll have to hold out until then."

Marilyn walked out, leaving the hateful Claresta tied to a column in the condemned building where she'd been holding her. Marilyn barely got out of the building, though, before the police caught her.

Meanwhile, Claresta was watching her son being interviewed on the television that had been left on. Horton was saying he loved his mother dearly ...

"Liar!" Claresta screamed. She pulled hard against her restraints.

The governor continued, "I'm sure Alan Hendricks' plea for mercy will spare my mother's life ..."

"You little bastard, you have no way of knowing that!" Claresta pulled harder, shaking the unsound column to which she was tied.

"But as governor, my paramount responsibility is to the people of this state."

"You just want to be president, you little —" Claresta pulled hard enough to actually dislodge the column that had held her hostage. But she was far from free.

Outside the building, the two cops who'd arrested Marilyn left her cuffed in their patrol unit. They ran toward the building where Claresta was being held but soon came to a dead stop. In fact, they turned and ran back the way they came — because the building they'd been about to enter was now imploding.

Claresta died in the rubble. Alan was executed. Marilyn was jailed and charged with capital murder. And Governor Horton was reelected, riding a huge wave of public sympathy for losing his mother.

From a legalistic point of view, justice was served in every regard.

Joanna's heart-rending portrayal of the tortured Marilyn Kendricks, her courage in gaining 30 pounds and having her hair dyed gray and her faced seamed with wrinkles, earned her a nomination for an Academy Award for best leading actress.

In any other year, she'd have been a shoo-in to take the Oscar. But that year Meryl Streep played a Uruguayan Indian woman who had started a land reform movement in

South America and she took home the prize.

Upon hearing that decision, Joanna had smiled graciously at the Oscar telecast, giving what Laddy considered the very best acting performance of her life. Joanna's portrayal of a good loser was made all the more difficult by the fact that the producer, the director, the lead actor, the supporting actor and supporting actress, and even the stinking screenwriter of *Desperate Hours* — *her* movie, damnit — had all won all their Academy Awards. She'd been the only one who got skunked.

It was such a depressing turn of events, Joanna hadn't even considered marrying her leading man.

All in all, Laddy had to wonder if the actor's life wasn't beginning to pall for Joanna.

"You ready to come home?" he asked her, speaking into Reva McClatchy's phone.

All three news cameras were pointed straight at him recording his every word and every expression on his face. The three TV reporters were even pretending they knew how to take notes like real journalists. But Laddy could see Reva McClatchy was making out her shopping list.

"I am home," Joanna told him. "I'm an Austin girl, remember?"

The camera operators crept closer, trying to pick up Joanna's end of the conversation.

Laddy turned his back on them. They tried to maneuver around this evasive tactic, but Buck and Eveleen cut them off.

"You staying with your momma and daddy or is Governor Freyman letting you bunk down at the mansion?"

"I'm at the mansion. I'm going to stop in and say hi to momma and daddy, but I've got my own place, a little spread just outside of town."

Laddy hadn't heard about that. It kind of hurt him that Joanna had started to reestablish her Texas roots without telling him. Maybe his fertility crack had pissed her off.

She said, "Governor Freyman and I are thinking about flying in for the fight. But he wants to know if you think that big tub of shit, Win-Win, will actually show up."

Laddy looked at his watch. "He's got thirty-five minutes left. My gut instinct is he'll milk things and arrive at the last minute. You want to watch in person, you better get the governor's chopper in the air."

"Laddy?"

"Yeah?"

"Is your leg okay? You're up to this fight? You're going to win?"

His leg. He hadn't even thought of that. Leave it to Joanna to remind him, and now that she had, the damn thing did seem a bit tight. But he said, "I'll be fine. Win-Win shows up, he won't. Be fine, that is."

"So, I should get a bet down on you?" Joanna asked.

Laddy had to laugh.

Joanna went on, "Win-Win probably fudged his drawers when he heard you call him out. That's what's holding him back, right?"

Laddy smiled, loving Joanna at that particular moment.

"Hey, let me talk to the media a minute," she said. "Give the phone back to that reporter."

Laddy did, but only because he was curious what Joanna would say.

After a personal hello from the movie star to the TV reporter, Reva McClatchy held her phone out to the three cameras in front of her, smiling with teeth as unnaturally white as her hair was unnaturally blonde, and Joanna Wells spoke to the people of her natal state.

"Hello, y'all. This is Joanna Wells ..."

The media being as incestuously conglomerated as it was, Joanna's voice was also on radio and being listened to by Win-Win and Walker Winslow as they motored in their Hummer Gargantua toward Tunbridge Square.

"Hey, Daddy," Walker said. "Joanna Wells. I wonder if she's gonna come to the fight. She sees me in action, I bet I could get some kind of try-out for the movies. 'Specially after you 'n' me whip Laddy Johnson's ass."

Win-Win cut his son a sideways look. "The word is audition not try-out. And Joanna Wells is Laddy Johnson's sweetheart."

Walker frowned. "Maybe once upon a long fuckin' time ago. But she's been married to Lucan Thorn and half the actors in Hollywood. Maybe *all* the straight ones."

Win-Win just shook his head. The things his son didn't know. You put 'em all together, they'd be thicker than a New York phone book.

As if to prove Win-Win's point, Joanna said through the Hummer's 24 speakers, "I'd just like y'all to know that if I lived in Gasoline, I'd've been proud to vote for Laddy Johnson for mayor. I'm sure he'll win and do y'all proud, too."

"Why, that little bitch," Walker said, mashing his foot down on the gas pedal. Fortunately, his leg didn't extend very far in the Gargantua and he only got the monster truck up to 45 miles per hour. "What's that damn Laddy Johnson got that Lucan Thorn don't?"

"Apparently, his brand on that little gal's heart," Win-Win answered.

The mayor's philosophical poise disappeared as soon as he heard what Joanna had to say next.

"I'm only tellin' you this next story because the polls are closed and nobody can say I'm trying to influence the outcome of your election, but every time Mayor Edwin Winslow has occasion to visit California there's a certain lady there he likes to see."

With his eyes on the road, Walker didn't see his father's face suddenly expand like a helium balloon.

"You see some lady in California, Daddy?" Walker asked innocently.

Joanna continued, "Now, this woman was once a bit player in the movies, but where she found real fame was —"

Win-Win shut the radio off fast. By kicking it right out of the dashboard.

The mayor prayed to God above that before Joanna Wells started shooting off her mouth in public his wife, Margaret, had been struck deaf, dumb, and blind. Maybe struck dead just to be safe.

Walker glanced at his father, wondering why he'd just busted up a new Hummer.

"You don't look too good, Daddy. You sure you don't want me to whip Laddy Johnson's ass for you?"

Thirty-six people in Tunbridge Square had to leap out of the way or they'd have been mashed flat when Walker Winslow screeched up in front of Laddy Johnson's campaign headquarters in the Hummer Gargantua. But Tiny Osgood, a six-foot-five, 322-pound videocam operator for

KYHA-TV had been looking the other way when Walker arrived in such a reckless rush. Tiny had been searching for a pretty-gal shot, a cutaway shot of the crowd that could be edited into the story later, ideally one that featured a pretty girl who'd be appropriately grateful to the camera operator who put her on TV. Tiny had just found himself a doozy, a little ol' gal with auburn hair, except instead of smiling at his camera her eyes went wide with fright like her daddy had just caught her 'n' Tiny doin' the nasty.

It was the girl's misplaced terror that finally woke Tiny up to the cacophony of the oncoming truck and the departing crowd. He turned to look and then like everyone else he tried to jump back. He didn't make it, not entirely. The Hummer ran over his right foot with both the front and rear driver's side wheels. The rear tire pinned his right foot and the rest of him fell over backward. Tiny was in shock but he knew his poor foot had been turned into turnip paste. He could feel it oozing around inside his Tony Lama boot.

But like the true professional he was he kept on shooting when Walker Winslow popped out of the huge truck, never noticing him lying there held fast to the pavement.

But Laddy Johnson had seen Tiny's predicament. He started Tiny's way to get into the Hummer and move it off of Tiny's foot. As Laddy was about to pass Walker, he looked at him and said, "You are a fucking loon."

Which made Tiny feel almost good enough to laugh.

Didn't tickle Walker any, though. He spun around like a windup Chuck Norris doll. Little fucker's kick caught Laddy just above the knee on his right leg. Right where the damn horse had kicked him. Laddy howled like he'd been the one who got run over. He bent down and grabbed his leg with his right hand. Walker, meanwhile, was still spinning.

Around he went again, faster than before. But this time Laddy was ready for him. He caught Walker's kicking leg at its skinny calf and held on. The miniature Winslow sack of shit yelped and hopped up on one leg.

Then Laddy reached out with his right hand and grabbed Walker's supporting leg, had him hanging upside down in nothing flat. Walker's cowboy hat fell right off his head. It'd just stopped rolling when Laddy roared and flung Walker headfirst straight through the window of the Johnson for Mayor campaign office. The effort was painful enough to make Laddy sit down on the sidewalk and once again hold the leg Walker and the horse had both kicked.

Tiny got the impression Laddy might have shed a few tears at how bad he was hurting if he hadn't had three cameras aimed at him. What with Laddy's experience in Hollywood, he knew better than to look right at any of the cameras or to turn away from them. He gave Tiny his profile and limited the expression of his pain to a tooth-grinding grimace.

A few seconds of Laddy's torment was all Tiny needed and he panned to Buck Musgrove and Eveleen Nellis going into Laddy's campaign headquarters. Tiny reckoned they were checking to see if Walker was okay, but, no, not five seconds after they'd gone inside, Walker came sailing right back out through the broken window and landed on the sidewalk with a thump. He flopped once or twice like a boated bass and then lay still.

This was the best damn footage Tiny had ever shot.

He wondered what would happen next.

Someone called out, "Hey, Mayor Winslow's in that Hummer."

Tiny swung his camera around and found he had an artful angle on Win-Win slumped over in the passenger seat, his tongue hanging out all deep purple with spots of black.

"Oh my god," a woman cried, "I think he's dead."

Right then, Tiny knew his career was made. He'd be doing interviews about this night until ... damn, his foot started hurting something awful.

"Could someone please help me?" he pleaded   .

Laddy Johnson hobbled into the driver's seat and did the honors.

Tiny Osgood got that with his camera, too. Right before he passed out.

Laddy soaked his throbbing leg in the whirlpool in the Roman suite at the Public Baths, the business his mother had owned and operated since coming to Gasoline six months before Laddy was born. Originally, the big tan stucco building had housed the Turkish Baths of Texas, an enterprise begun by an immigrant named Berker Ediz.

Berker was the eldest son of Ahmet Ediz the headman of the village of Erzurum in eastern Turkey, not far from the border with Iraq. When Berker was 12 his father allowed him to be hired as an assistant to a British geologist, Hadley Bliss, who was looking for oil in the area. With Berker acting as his native guide, Bliss spent three years looking for rock formations that would hint at the presence of oil. He searched high and low from the Iraqi border on the south to Lake Van in the north, all without luck.

Bliss would often tell Berker, "You Turks must be some deucedly bad Mohammedans for Allah not to have given you at least a little oil."

To which Berker would politely respond, "Perhaps,

esteemed sir, the oil is here but you have not found it because you are not the best of Christians."

The geologist had the grace to confess, "Perhaps I'm not, Berker. But I can tell you for a fact that other Christians are finding plenty of it." He pulled a crumpled newspaper from his pack. It had come from London. "Just last month a very respectable field was discovered in Texas by a fellow who was digging a well for water. Now there's a man upon whom Allah has smiled."

"Yes, esteemed sir, but is he a Christian?"

"In Texas, Berker, he very likely is."

The geologist had taken the boy's fragmentary English, expanded it and polished it to a high sheen. After three years of tutelage, Berker's accent was practically Etonian. In addition to the language lessons, Bliss exposed the boy to the disciplines of mathematics, geography, and philosophy. Gave him a proper English public school education in the wilds of Anatolia.

Every time the two of them returned to Erzurum for rest and relaxation, Bliss partook of what he considered to be the high point of Turkish culture: the *hamam*. The public baths. By age-old custom, the baths were open to people of every rank and station. But even those who were born to the hamam didn't seem to take as much pleasure from it as Hadley Bliss.

Which led Berker to ask one day, "Esteemed sir, do all the oil men of the West enjoy the baths as much as you do?"

His head lolled back, a warm wet cloth over his eyes, Bliss replied, "The civilized ones bloody well do."

The next day, the geologist gave Berker's father a parting gift of an extra six months' pay for his son's labors, said Ahmet had sired a magnificent boy, and departed for Iraq and the town of Mosul where he felt his luck in finding oil might improve.

Luck was something in short supply in Erzurum. An agricultural pest had taken most of the harvest for the second straight year. There would be seed enough to plant in the spring, but there would be little to eat through the winter. So a desperate plan was conceived.

According to Bliss's information, oil had been discovered in the town of Gasoline, Texas. And oil men all loved the *hamam*. So Berker, whose name meant dependable, and who spoke perfect English, would go to Texas. He would open a Turkish bath. It would prosper and Berker would send every spare dollar home to save his village.

So in the year of 1905, when Berker was 15 years old, he was sent to America, to Texas, with the prayers of everyone in Erzurum that Allah would favor him and his quest.

Laddy had fallen asleep in the hot swirling water, his head laying back against a thick white towel, a damp warm cloth over his closed eyes, in much the same fashion as Hadley Bliss had bathed over a century earlier. Laddy was unaware that he'd been joined in the opulent whirlpool — it was big enough for eight people — until someone took hold of his willie. Ordinarily, that would've been enough to snap him right out of his dream, kicking and punching, only he recognized the touch of that hand the moment he felt it.

Or had he felt it? Maybe his dream was just particularly vivid. Him getting hard, feeling the intimate embrace of the sleek, firm body settling down on him, it was all his imagination, the product of subconscious longing. But then ... then he smelled it: a new perfume. Not the one he remembered Joanna wearing. Not the one in his dream.

"Your momma gave me a key," he heard her tell him.

"She shouldn't a done that," Laddy murmured. "I'll have to revoke her business license when I'm elected mayor."

Co-ed bathing was allowed on the premises only by those couples who had a copy of their marriage license on file at the front desk. Several people who had divorced amicably had copies of more than one license on file so they could enjoy a friendly soak with a former spouse. But one license was the minimum required so as not to offend community standards.

"You'd sooner die than hurt your momma," Joanna told Laddy.

She had that right. Laddy removed the cloth from his eyes and looked at her. As much as he could through the steam rising off the swirling water. She didn't feel any different to him. But he hadn't seen Joanna naked in quite some time and he wouldn't have minded taking a look.

"So what brings you to my bubble bath, missy?" he asked.

She leaned her head on his shoulder, kissed his cheek.

"I heard Walker Winslow kicked you," she said. "Was it your bad leg?"

"You mean the one where your pert backside is currently resting?"

Joanna quickly removed her weight, but Laddy settled her back down.

"You never weighed much more than a feather pillow, and in this water, well, you're not even denting my goose-bumps. And to answer your question, yeah, the little shit got my bum leg."

"You think maybe I should take you to a doctor, get it checked out?"

Laddy shook his head. "That little cowpie Walker doesn't kick nearly as hard as a 1,500-pound horse."

Joanna accepted Laddy's decision and told him, "I'd offer to beat Walker senseless for you except he doesn't have any sense to start with, and you and Buck and Eveleen did such a good job on him he's in traction right now."

Laddy grunted. "And Win-Win?"

She put her arms around his neck. "Mayor Winslow has gone to confront his Maker."

"I thought he looked deader than any stiff I ever saw on a movie set," Laddy said.

"Me, too," Joanna said, wishing now that Win-Win's body had been taken away before she and the governor had arrived. The governor, though, had ordered the remains held in place for his viewing. He was about to jab his cigar snippers into Win-Win's body to make sure he was really dead before Joanna took hold of his wrist.

"You're right," the governor told Joanna. "Don't want to leave any confusing marks for the medical examiner to find."

"What killed Win-Win?" Laddy asked. "They know yet?"

Joanna said, "Autopsy hasn't been done, but speculation is a heart attack."

Laddy sighed. "Where's that leave the election?"

"Governor Freyman's impounded all the ballots. Says he's personally going to observe the counting of them. If you win, you're the mayor. If the dearly departed wins, there'll have to be a special election."

"Well, shit," Laddy said.

"Yeah," Joanna agreed. "Everybody figures Margaret Winslow will run in Win-Win's place."

Laddy's thought exactly. An eventuality that held no appeal for him at all. He'd rather have Tom Cruise drop him into a volcano or something.

Joanna chose that precise moment to tell him, "You know something, Laddy Johnson? My OB-GYN, tells me I'm still quite fertile."

Her statement was highly relevant to the way their bodies were positioned. Especially as Joanna's claim on him at that moment felt positively airtight; all the heated water swirling about their naked flesh was unlikely to affect things. All that mattered was —

The door to the Roman suite being flung open. Laddy's reflexes kicked in, which in this case meant he let his guard down with Joanna and climaxed. At the same time, Chief of Police Gunther Lomax burst into the room and shouted at him, "Laddy Johnson, you're under the arrest for the murder of Mayor Edwin Winslow! Lady, you get the hell offa that man so I can arrest him!"

Joanna was already well into her dismount and looking over her shoulder. To her great relief, while there were now three cops in the room, there was no photographer.

But one of the cops did recognize her. "Hey, that there's Joanna Wells!"

The joy of discovering a movie star naked in a whirlpool bath spread across the faces of both cops, but Chief Lomax only scowled.

Laddy looked at Joanna and asked, "Didn't you lock the door behind you?"

Not having a scripted reply, Joanna remained mute. Then in the interest of providing a common defense, she stood up and glared at the three cops.

"Get the hell out of here," she ordered, "or I'll sue all of you!"

Filling someone's life with lawyers was a fine Mexican

curse, and a threat to be reckoned with in L.A., but it didn't
cut any ice with Texas cops. They held their ground.

"Gunther," Laddy said, "what the hell are you talking
about? I never touched Win-Win. What I heard, he died of
a heart attack."

"You're damn right he died of a heart attack! Which you
gave him by challenging him to that fight. The district attorney says you're criminally liable!"

District Attorney Winton Earle had been as deeply in
Win-Win's pocket as Chief Lomax. No doubt, the two of
them had put their pointed heads together and concocted
this charge. It was ludicrous ... but so were many cases in
Texas that wound up with a man being executed.

That was when Joanna decided to muddy the legal
waters. First by laughing mockingly at Chief Lomax, which
none of the cops appreciated. And then by saying with
uncanny accuracy, "You say Laddy's challenge killed the
mayor? I say it was more likely he croaked when I told the
world he was close friends with the most famous madam in
Los Angeles."

The cops paid rapt attention to her, as much because
she'd addressed them naked from the waist up as for her
words. But they'd caught the gist of what she'd had to say,
too.

Chief Lomax smiled. "Now, that you mention whoring,
little lady, I don't suppose you and Mr. Johnson are married."

Joanna sat down.

"I didn't think so," the chief said. "Now, the two of you get
on out of there before I have to send my men in after you."

Laddy got out first. Then to the great consternation of
the two patrol cops, he held up a large bath towel to prevent
them from seeing any more of Joanna than they already had.

Lomax said, "I'll tell District Attorney Earle what you said, Ms. Wells. Maybe he'll want to file charges relating to the mayor's death against you as well. But I've certainly got the two of you on charges of public fornication."

Laddy said to Joanna, "You should have locked the door."

"Hell, everyone knows that," one of the cops agreed.

Everyone who'd grown up in Gasoline, that was.

Long ago, after Berker Ediz had failed to make a go of it running a proper *hamam* in Gasoline, he'd innovated and made his fortune by opening Texas's first adult waterpark.

Margaret Winslow sat in a dimly lit private room at Gasoline General Hospital and regarded her unconscious son Walker with a bleak expression. As always, her thick white hair was perfectly styled. He silk blouse and linen skirt were in the best of conservative good taste. Her low-heeled shoes were understated to the point of near invisibility. And the only sign that she was any more alive than her departed husband was the subtle rise and fall of her trademark pearls on the upper deck of her matronly breasts.

Walker stirred on his bed, his neck encased in an orthopedic collar.

"Momma," he asked groggily, "that you?"

"Hush," his mother told him.

"Yes, Momma," Walker said, closing his eyes and drifting away on a drug-induced cloud.

A nurse was supposed to check on Walker's condition every fifteen minutes, but Margaret had been in the room over an hour and no one had disturbed her visit with her son. Eventually, a doctor, spurred by worries of a malpractice suit, would work up the nerve to come by and examine the patient, but no nurse was about to intrude on the mayor's wife.

Men, she thought dismally. They were all such fools. Edwin having a fatal heart attack over the revelation that he had availed himself of the strumpets of Hollywood. As if she would have any objections other than to keep his indulgences private. It had been more years than she could recall since he'd last laid his great bulk on her, all sweaty and hairy, and she hadn't missed that experience at all. Not one little bit. No thank you, sir.

She'd given herself to Edwin a sufficient number of times to produce two healthy children: the lovely and brilliant Hayley and the difficult to explain Walker. Hayley had gone off to Yale and the London School of Economics and then had disappeared. Well, she had sent one last letter home, though it had been both brief and vague: *Dear Momma and Daddy. I have some important work to do. It may take quite some time. Please don't worry, and please don't look for me as that would likely complicate matters. All my love, Hayley.* Edwin, of course, had immediately gone to people he knew in law enforcement and demanded that the FBI, the CIA, and the Secret Service all look for his little girl. While Win-Win became hysterical, Margaret found Hayley's vanishing act thrilling and imagined that her daughter was working for one of the very intelligence agencies Edwin was trying to enlist to find her. Walker, then in junior high, came to Margaret with a request: Could he please go the Ringling Brothers and Barnum & Bailey Clown College in Sarasota, Florida? He wanted to become a rodeo clown.

His mother told him they would have that discussion later. Much later. She was very busy at the moment. Walker found out the source of his mother's preoccupation by snooping on a phone call his father was having with an FBI man. Hearing his sister was missing, he immediately wanted to go the FBI Academy in Quantico, Virginia and become a G-man. Raising that idea with his parents, he was told this was another topic that would be tabled for future discussion.

Thwarted in his first two choices for post-secondary education, Walker later took a job washing newly delivered trucks at Texas Rolling Stock. His mother frowned upon this choice, but Win-Win had said it was good honest work, and he paid his boy one dollar less per year than he paid his general manager, Norman Oklahoma. Walker used his salary to take martial arts lessons from a Korean master in Houston who, to Walker's great joy, was actually an inch shorter than he was.

In trying times like the present moment, Margaret wished that Hayley would come home. Failing that, she wished that Hayley would call and recruit her, asking Margaret if she would like to do something thrilling, dangerous, and far from Texas.

Her son's voice called her back to the here and now.

"Momma, could you give me a drink of water?"

Margaret rose from her chair, poured cold water from the pitcher on the bedside tray, and angled the straw in the glass so her son might sip.

"Thank you, Momma," Walker said.

She put the glass down and regarded her son with a measure of affection. He'd always been a sweet little boy. Dim but sweet. Never a bit of trouble. At least the kind that couldn't be managed. There had been little incidents with alcohol. And drugs. And girls. But always in the company of other youngsters whose parents were like the Winslows:

They, too, could go to the authorities and persuade them to overlook youthful indiscretions.

"How are you feeling, dear?" Margaret asked Walker.

"Like someone flattened the top of my head with a frying pan, Momma."

Margaret had seen the video of Laddy Johnson and his people flinging her son about, and it had made her blood boil. But she'd also seen that Walker had initiated the violence. Which meant that her vengeance would have to be indirect and after a certain interval of time had passed.

"Why didn't you bring your father straight to the hospital?" Margaret asked Walker. "The doctors might have been able to save him."

As far as Walker's orthopedic neck brace would allow, he shook his head.

"Daddy's heart blew up like a big-rig tire hitting an iron spike at 80 miles per hour. It was over and out, that's all she wrote, Momma I don't even want to think what Daddy's heart looks like, if they open him up."

Margaret Winslow didn't say anything, but she decided at that moment that however long it took to get even with Laddy Johnson she would make sure her vengeance was something truly and poetically vicious.

What she said to Walker was, "Dear, you're going to have to take over for your father."

"At TRS?" Even through the pain killers, Walker liked that idea.

"No, son," Margaret corrected. "As mayor."

"But what if that pri — What if Laddy Johnson wins?"

"There's always another election."

As Margaret saw it, with Walker married to the right woman, a girl she'd have to find for him soon, he could go as far as governor of Texas. Walker's son, with the right woman to guide him, could become president.

Walker, himself, wasn't thinking nearly that big. He liked the idea of selling monster trucks to rich people. That was as far as he ever wanted to go.

"Momma, I never went to school to be a politician."

Margaret Winslow stroked her son's brow.

"That's all right, Walker, neither did your father."

Arcelia Dominguez showed up at the Gasoline Police Department headquarters with her lawyer, Bartolo Bernstein, a tall, blue-eyed Sephardim, who knew the law from adoptions to zip-guns. They presented themselves to Desk Sergeant Waylon Gormly, who reluctantly asked, "Some way I can help you folks?"

Neither Arcelia nor Bernstein said a word. They just stared at Gormly.

Which made the cop uneasy. Lots of things did. Having been named after country-and-western legend Waylon Jennings, Gormly had taken up the guitar at an early age and with fair success. He also possessed a smooth baritone voice and a facility for evocative lyrics. He might have made a go of it in Nashville except strangers tended to make him nervous and the thought of standing on a stage in front of a big crowd terrified him. He'd made a CD of his music, and a friend said he could get it to Willie Nelson, but Gormly couldn't bring himself to hand it over. Not even to see if Willie might like to cover one of his songs. The possibility of success scared him, too.

He'd become a cop only because the job let him carry a gun. For a while there that had calmed him down. Until he started worrying that his gun might accidentally discharge and he'd shoot himself.

While on duty behind his desk, Sergeant Gormly kept his duty weapon in a locked drawer. He was thinking he might have to go for it, if these two people in front of him didn't start talking soon.

Just like she could read his mind, Arcelia told him, "You know who I am, Sergeant. You patronize my business."

Which had been true until his Winnie had left him last month. She'd gotten tired of him being so jumpy all the time. And the name Gormly had lost its charm for her. Like Winifred was any great bargain. He was working on a nasty little song about her right before these two came in.

"I have spent some time at the Public Baths," Gormly admitted, "yes, ma'am."

"And you are aware of who you have in your lockup, aren't you, Sergeant?" Bartolo Bernstein asked.

Gormly had watched the lawyer hogtie any number of his fellow officers in court. He knew he'd best answer truthfully. But his toes started tapping nervously anyway.

"Yes, I do know that," he said.

"So you know who we've come to bail out," Arcelia told him.

"Your son."

"And Ms. Wells," Bernstein added. "I've spoken to her attorneys in Los Angeles. I'll be representing their client until they arrive in town tomorrow morning."

"They?" Gormly asked. "There's more than one?"

"Six, to be precise. Three criminal defense attorneys; three civil litigators."

"What're the civil boys for?" Gormly asked.

Bernstein chuckled. "They do what they do, sue people:

the town, the chief, the department, the district attorney, pretty much anyone who's fucked with their client."

The way Bernstein was looking at him, Gormly knew that could include him. He glanced over at Laddy Johnson's momma. He'd heard the story about her and LBJ. He'd also heard that some of the most powerful people in the state still took a quiet interest in her welfare, and undoubtedly her son's as well. As far as lawyers went, she didn't need six of them, not when she had Bartolo Bernstein.

"We'd like to see my son and Ms. Wells, Sergeant," Arcelia said.

"More to the point," Bernstein added. "We're here to make bail for them and take them home with us."

Chief Lomax had firmly instructed Sergeant Gormly to let no one see the prisoners, and the subject of bail hadn't even been raised because murder suspects didn't get bail. Not in Gasoline or anywhere else in Texas. But officially, all Laddy Johnson and Joanna Wells had been charged with was public fornication. The murder charge was pending.

Even so, Sergeant Gormly knew he'd be looking for work in the morning if he let the two prisoners go. And unemployment scared him.

But not nearly as much as having Bartolo Bernstein and six more like him suing his lower-middle class backside. That happened, he'd be lucky to have a spare guitar string to his name.

"Can you tell us the amount at which bail has been set, Sergeant?" Bernstein asked.

Waylon Gormly shrugged like a man choosing the lesser of two evils.

"How's $500 a head sound?"

* * *

"Are you worried?" Joanna asked Laddy.

The two of them were sharing a cell, the only prisoners in the lock-up. Tuesday night, even on Election Day, was not a big night for hellraising in Gasoline. Well, it might've been if Buck had had his way and a posse of Johnson partisans had set out for Win-Win's headquarters.

Win-Win, Laddy thought. Hard to believe that big ol' sonofabitch was dead.

Thomas Wolfe might not have been right when he said you can't go home again, but it sure as hell wasn't easy once you got there.

Laddy was sitting in his underpants and boots. The Turkish towel that had covered Joanna as she was taken into custody was draped over her shoulders. Joanna was wearing Laddy's shirt and jeans, looking like a little kid swimming inside the folds of the oversized garments.

The cops had refused to let her retrieve her clothing before leaving the Public Baths, getting their cheap thrills at the thought of having a big Hollywood movie star all but naked in the back of their patrol car. They'd live off that story for the rest of their lives.

For his part, Chief Lomax hadn't objected to the treatment of his celebrity prisoner. He'd only told his men to make sure that Laddy and Joanna were booked for screwing in a public place and incarcerated. Then he left in his unmarked car — no doubt to confer with District Attorney Earle in furtherance of their scheme to frame Laddy, and possibly Joanna, for Win-Win's death.

Laddy and Joanna were booked and allowed to make their one phone call. They declined to be either fingerprinted or photographed. When Lomax's henchmen had insisted on these points, Laddy's reply had been blunt.

"You might as well shoot me now, boys, 'cause that ain't gonna happen."

"Me, too," Joanna added.

Every star in the Hollywood heavens remembered Nick Nolte's mugshots and none of them wanted to come anywhere near being immortalized in that fashion.

Laddy and Joanna also said they'd be sharing a cell, both of them fearing what might happen to Joanna if she were to be taken off by herself. Once their demands had been met — again by force of saying the cops' only alternative was to shoot them — Laddy had taken off his garments and given them to Joanna.

Laddy answered Joanna's question with one of his own.

"Why should I be worried? Governor Freyman said he's going to pardon me."

"For Win-Win's death?"

"Don't be silly. Nobody knew that was going to happen. He said he'd pardon me for beating the shit out of Win-Win. Turns out I didn't touch him. But if by some weird quirk in the law, Winton Earle can say I, or the two of us, contributed to giving Win-Win his heart attack, the governor will do the right thing."

But Joanna was remembering Governor Horton from *Desperate Hours* who wouldn't even pardon a man who'd been falsely convicted of murder because it would be politically ruinous. That plot device had always rung true to her. Now, she wondered if —

"Don't even think that way," Laddy told her.

"What way?" she asked, knowing full well he knew what she'd been thinking.

"That the governor would betray us. Politics is more a running gag with him."

Joanna snuggled closer to Laddy. He put an arm around her.

"I hope you're right," she said.

"About that, I have no worries."

"So what does worry you?" Joanna asked.

He was quiet a minute before saying, "One thing occupying my mind is what might be going on inside that fertile body of yours right now."

She looked at him with the big blue eyes that had made half of America fall in love with her. "You don't want me to have your baby?"

"Not if you're going to marry another leading man, and I don't get to see our kid but once a month."

He thought she might pull away from him, but she didn't.

"I'm done marrying other people," Joanna told him.

"Other people?" Laddy asked.

"Anyone but you."

Laddy nodded. "You have the date all set?"

"What date?"

"You know, for our wedding. Is it going to be at this new place of yours? You have the guest list made out? The caterer selected? I mean, you sure had the conception planned."

Now, Joanna pulled away, and he saw the answers to his questions on her face.

"You *do*, you have the whole thing planned out," Laddy said. "You were absolutely certain that I still love you so much that I'd go along with anything you want. Especially after we renewed acquaintances physically."

Anger settled like a storm cloud on Joanna's brow. Then she took Laddy completely by surprise. She slid off the bench on which they'd been sitting and went down on one knee in front of him, taking both of his hands in hers.

She looked up at him and said, "Ladbrook Johnson, will you please marry me? I'd dearly love to have the ceremony and reception at my new ranch; it's so beautiful. But you can have the clergyman of your choice. You can invite two guests for every one of mine. I'd like a California vegetarian cuisine menu, but we can serve franks and beans, if that's what you want. Please, Laddy, just this once, I'd like to marry the man I've been in love with ever since college."

He was tempted to ask if she'd had somebody write that speech for her, but he didn't want to push his luck.

"We'll live in Texas?" he said.

"Yes."

"You won't be gone more than four months a year making movies?"

"I won't."

"No fooling around with leading men?"

"Never again, Laddy. I'm thinking of making a radical change."

"What's that?"

"I'm thinking I'll start taking character parts from now on, even though I could play leads another year or two."

Laddy smiled. He pulled Joanna to her feet and sat her on his lap.

"You know," he said, "I'll bet you get your Oscar yet."

Joanna smiled and kissed him.

Then his mother's voice told him, "Well, give the girl her answer, son."

Laddy saw Momma and Bartolo Bernstein standing in the entrance to the lockup. Apparently, they'd been there long enough to hear Joanna's proposal. The lawyer was on his cell phone with someone.

Laddy turned to Joanna and told her, "Yes, Ms. Wells, I'd

be delighted to marry you."

Arcelia came to the cell door smiling brilliantly. "Congratulations!" She turned and added, "Now, let them out." Laddy finally noticed that Momma had brought Sergeant Gormly with her. He opened the cell door. Arcelia hugged her son and embraced her future daughter-in-law.

Bartolo Bernstein walked up and extended his hand to Laddy, "Congratulations."

Then he gave his phone to Joanna, saying, "A call for you from California. Lucan Thorn."

A hand fell on the singer's shoulder and gently nudged her as she dreamed. In a way, her dream was similar to the one everybody had about being naked at school. Only in the singer's dream she was standing naked in a room where a group of Middle Eastern men, and the president and vice-president of the United States, were going to torture her. Or so they thought. She didn't have anything up the sleeves she wasn't wearing, but in some inexplicable way, a weapon always came to hand when one of the men advanced on her. A pistol, a knife, nunchuks, a machete: she used each of them to lethal advantage. So far, the swarthy types had led the charge while the two Americans had hung back and urged the others on.

A voice asked, "Jazz, you hear me, baby?"

The singer's eyelids fluttered open. The dream receded and she remembered where she was: Nicosia, Cyprus. Then her legend clicked into place: Jazz Janssen. Strictly speaking, her cover identity should have been the first thing she thought of; ideally, she should have had a bit of trouble remembering who she really was. Maybe she'd been at the game too long. Her discipline was breaking down, and that was inevitably a fatal mistake.

She looked up and saw the warm brown face of Big Al, the tenor saxman who led her backup band. He was looking at her with concern in his eyes.

"You all right, baby?" he asked.

"Yeah, Al. Just getting a little old for all this late-night shit."

The musician laughed. "You what, 38 whole years old? Wait 'til you hit 66 like me."

The singer shook her head. "I'll never make it that long, Al. The time I'm your age, I'll be sitting on a beach somewhere counting my skin cancers, wondering was it really true I wasn't such a bad singer way back when."

Al laughed again. "Baby, you gonna die just like me. Onstage, after a third encore, the people's cheers still ringin' in your ears."

"Probably be tinnitus ringing in my ears," Jazz said. "You just stop by to chat, Al, or is that envelope in your hand for me?"

It was a red envelope. Just the right size for a Valentine card, but it was April not February.

Big Al handed it to her. "It's for you, same as the last two times. Someone left it in my saxophone case, and I never saw who."

Al was too much of a gentleman to ask for an explanation or to peek inside the envelope. All he knew was the first time it happened Jazz asked him to bring any future envelopes to her right away. For his troubles, Jazz always bought Al a meal at the best restaurant in town, wherever they happened to be, and poured wine for him until the sun came up.

"Thank you, Al," Jazz told him. "You're the best."

"Long as you know it," he said, leaving her alone.

Big Al was an expatriate American, as was Jazz. His parents had left Montgomery, Alabama for Chicago. Al had left Chicago for Paris, where he'd met Jazz.

Jazz's American origins were also southern. In her case, Gasoline, Texas.

These days, however, she carried a Cypriot passport. With Cyprus's 2004 admission into the European Union, she could roam the continent freely. She had been pretty much doing that anyway, since arriving at the London School of Economics, more years ago than she cared to remember. London was where she'd been recruited by the G. Which stood for the government of the United States, but didn't get any more specific than that. Made her a totally deniable covert agent. The things she did required total deniability.

She opened the envelope and learned that her father had died. A heart attack ... though there was some question as to what had precipitated Edwin Winslow's coronary event.

Jazz was being offered compassionate leave to attend her father's funeral.

Not that she could reveal her presence to anyone, including her mother and her brother. If she wished, there was space for her on an Air Force transport leaving that afternoon out of the British airbase at Dhekelia.

Hayley Winslow, a.k.a. Jazz Janssen, chose to fly commercial from Nicosia to Paris and from there to Houston, where she rented a car for the final leg of her journey.

Being back in Texas after so many years away seemed very strange, but also reassuring.

She wondered if she'd have to kill anyone while she was home.

In case her father's death had been caused by anything other than his own bad habits.

CHAPTER THREE

Laddy Johnson was living with his mother. He'd returned to his childhood home when he came back to Texas. He wasn't sure he was going to stick around if he lost the race for mayor, so he saw no point in buying a house and then having to turn right around and sell it. If he lost the race, and chose to remain in the Lone Star state, Austin was the logical place to live. That was where Californians went when they moved to Texas. Of course, Austin was just down the road from Joanna's new ranch, too.

She hadn't said she'd sold her Bel-Air estate, and he'd bet she hadn't. For that matter, he hadn't sold his house in L.A. It was being rented out by a friend's nephew who was just getting his career as a stuntman started.

If he did go back to California, it would only be part time. Scheduled to coincide with when Joanna was away shooting her movies. He suspected, and thought it reasonable, that Joanna would want the two of them to live at her new ranch. But he didn't intend to hang out there while she was off working someplace else. If it turned out he wasn't going to be Gasoline's next mayor, he'd go back to his profession. Maybe this time as a stunt coordinator, though. He was getting too old to do gags much longer.

As she did every morning, his mother had offered to cook breakfast for him, but momma cooked Texan and his palate had long ago turned Angeleno. He politely declined the offer of chicken fried steak with biscuits and gravy. He noted that his mother had kept her trim figure and never ate anything like the fare she offered her son. After momma went out to attend to her business, Laddy sliced up half a cantaloupe, toasted two pieces of whole wheat bread, and scrambled half-a-dozen egg whites, adding just a dash of salt. He washed it all down with a glass of cold spring water. Doing the dishes, he tried to remember when he last ate to please his taste buds instead of trying to keep his arteries clear until he was 110 and died in his sleep dreaming of pizza and beer.

Joanna was up at her ranch making preparations for their wedding. He couldn't say why, but that made him nervous. Which was crazy. He'd loved Joanna since he was 19. He'd wanted to have children with her for at least the last 15 years. She was one of America's biggest movies stars and she'd gone down on one knee — in a Texas jail cell, no less — to ask him to marry her. How many guys ever got that lucky?

It was just ... well, he was the one who felt like an actor now. And Joanna was the producer of an upcoming film in which he would star. She was putting all the pieces in place. She had her location all scouted out. And Laddy would bet his bottom dollar she would bring in her favorite cinematographer to film the ceremony. While she'd said he could write their vows, he'd bet she'd have a screenwriter, maybe that

Oscar-winning guy from *Desperate Hours,* called in to do a rewrite. She'd have a composer do a musical score. Floral arrangements would cost more than a skybox at the Super Bowl. A lighting crew would make the whole thing look like a fairy tale. But there'd be an army of security people and probably an anti-aircraft battery to keep the paparazzi at bay.

And at the moment he honestly couldn't recall if his mother and Joanna's momma and daddy got along. Laddy hadn't been engaged 48 hours yet and the whole thing was already giving him a headache.

But, to her everlasting credit, Joanna hadn't taken Lucan Thorn's phone call. She'd taken Bartolo Bernstein's cell phone and clicked the end button, breaking the connection. Returning the phone to the lawyer, she instructed him that she was no longer taking calls from Mr. Thorn. Laddy might have jumped with joy when he heard that, if his leg hadn't been hurting so bad.

When Joanna wasn't at the front of his mind, Laddy was preoccupied by the ongoing drama of the mayoral election. The counting of the ballots hadn't been completed yet. The longer it took, the more people on each side figured the election was being stolen by people on the other side. Nobody had threatened to sue yet if they didn't like the outcome, but it probably wouldn't be more than another day without a winner being declared before that happened.

Laddy's thought was that he'd bow out before he let things get to court. With Win-Win dead, if he dropped out, there'd have to be a new election called. Might turn out as close as this one, but he —

He saw a woman peeking in his window. He saw her just for a second and out of the corner of his eye, but he was sure that he wasn't imagining things. There she was again, at another window. This time the two of them looked right at each other. But she disappeared once more.

It was like seeing someone for the blink of a strobe-light.

"Hey!" Laddy called out.

He hopped away from the kitchen sink, favoring his good leg. He was moving gingerly toward the front door when he heard a car drive off. He hopped faster, got to the front door and yanked it open. To his left, at the corner of the block, he saw a gray sedan waiting for an elderly lady to clear the crosswalk. He couldn't tell from his vantage point whether a man or a woman was driving the sedan.

But he felt sure it had to be the woman who'd been peeking in the windows at him.

Thinking about it now, the woman's face seemed familiar. Someone he'd known at one time but hadn't seen since ... since he was a kid? If so, that made her someone local.

The elderly woman reached the curb and the gray sedan turned the corner.

Laddy got a glimpse of the driver's profile. It was the woman who'd peeped him, all right.

But he couldn't remember who she was.

Even so, he'd worked on enough films noir to be sure to get her license plate number.

"Señorita Wells, I am sorry to interrupt, but your former husband is here and he will not allow me to send him away. Not before he sees you."

Joanna was sitting out back of *La Casa de Buena Suerte*, The House of Good Luck, her new Texas home. The ranch was a 500-acre spread featuring hills, streams, meadows, and woodland. With her was her *feng shui* master, Hop Tu. They had already worked out the placement of the wedding bower, the guest seating, the dining area, the bandstand, and the dance floor. All was in harmony with nature, and nature in Hill Country was grand indeed.

Now, however, Joanna and Master Tu were addressing a far thornier problem: the visual appearances of the guests themselves, which could add to or subtract from the *feng shui* of the wedding party. Three potential guests had had their names stricken from the list of those to be invited by a simple shake of Master Tu's head, once he'd seen their photographs. Another six were receiving lengthier consideration before it was decided whether they would make the cut.

Anticipating such difficult choices, Joanna had left strict instructions with her personal secretary, Erindira de la Fuente, that she was not to be disturbed. Erin was a graduate of the Instituto Politécnico Nacional in Mexico City and the Harvard Business School. After receiving her MBA, Erin had gone home to marry her fiancé, German Padilla, the brightest new star in Mexico's business elite. It had been Erin's understanding that when she and German were married that they would be professional equals, building an empire that would bring a new prosperity to the Mexican people. Instead, German insisted that once they were married, Erin would start bearing his sons and stay at home and be their mother.

Erin broke their engagement in front of 300 of their closest friends who'd gathered at German's villa to congratulate the couple on their impending nuptials. Being so humiliated at a party intended to honor him was not an insult German could bear. The next morning he arrived at Erin's apartment, intending to beat a sense of respect, good manners, and obedience into her. She would become his wife and conduct herself in any manner he declared.

German did manage to throw the first punch, but it did not land. During her sojourn to the United States, Erin had studied Arnis, a little-known but brutally effective Filipino system of self-defense, the better to protect herself from Boston street thugs. She sidestepped German's blow and grabbed his arm, breaking it above the elbow. She also broke his jaw, and shredded all the ligaments in his right knee.

All of which took less than five seconds. Still, it was time enough for Erin also to sever her connection to her homeland. Once German regained consciousness, Erin knew he would have to destroy her to restore his honor. The eldest son of a vastly rich family, he would see to it she spent the rest of her life in the vilest women's prison in the country. Or he would simply have her killed. So she fled Mexico, flying business class to Los Angeles.

Once her tourist visa expired, her status in the U.S. became illegal, but friends from her Harvard days put her in touch with sympathetic figures in the entertainment industry, and ultimately Joanna Wells offered her employment, paid for her legal defense, and was developing a movie based on Erin's life.

Given the depth of their relationship, Joanna did not fire Erin immediately for interrupting the *feng shui* session, but simply asked, "Which former husband?"

"Me, baby," Lucan Thorn said, stepping out of Joanna's house. "You won't take my calls, I'll come see you in person."

Lucan recognized Master Tu from when he'd done the *feng shui* for the two times he and Joanna had gotten married. Damn Asian quackery hadn't kept them together.

"Planning a wedding, Joanna?" Thorn asked with a smile.

"Don't tell me you're finally getting together with that stunt-man of yours. Bit of a comedown, isn't it?"

"What do you want, Lucan?" Joanna asked quietly.

Thorn took a chair from the carefully arranged guest-seating area and turned it around and sat, knowing that would disturb both Joanna and Master Tu.

"I wanted to tell you the most extraordinary news," Thorn said.

"Tell me you're dying," Joanna responded.

Thorn asked, "How did you know?"

Joanna was taken aback, but only for a second.

"You're not dying. Not looking as healthy as you do."

Thorn grinned. "No, I'm not dying, but I was *told* I was. By a *team* of doctors. Given a matter of weeks to live. All because I'd taken a physical to be insured for a new film. I'd gone in for the usual poking and prodding feeling fine. The next day Beeb Bidwell called and sounded so awful I thought *he* was dying. But he told me he'd be by in an hour to take me to the doctor's office. The doc had something to tell me, and good old Beeb would be there with me when I heard it."

Despite their annoyance at Thorn, Joanna, Erin, and Master Tu, were caught up in the actor's story.

"We went to the doctor's office and I got the news: an aggressive form of cancer of the pancreas. Inoperable. I had-n't felt anything yet, but the pain would soon become unbear-able, even with medication, and the only consolation was that the agony wouldn't last long. But then neither would I.

"That was when five other doctors came in, while I was sitting there stunned, Beeb patting me on the back for moral support. They told me how my every remaining minute had been planned to turn down, at least a little, the flames of the hell I'd soon be enduring. They never even asked me if I might like to make any plans of my own. And that was when I thought of you.

"I wanted to see *you* again Joanna."

"Why?" she asked in a whisper.

"I asked myself the same thing. The only answer I came up with was that I was much more a shit to you than you ever deserved."

Thorn's words hit Erin harder than they did Joanna; Erin knew she'd never receive such a confession from German, not even if he was dying.

"I left the doctor's office alone," Lucan said. "I walked home. In L.A., can you imagine? I'd told the docs I'd submit to their dubious mercies once I started to feel the pain. Until then, I was simply going to think about things. I got two days of self-examination in before Beeb called again. There had been a mix-up in the lab samples. I was in perfect health; some other poor bastard was dying. Helluva thing."

Having learned that Thorn's mortality was not imminent, Master Tu was itching to return the actor's chair to its proper position.

But Joanna said, "So when you called me, that was after you knew you were all right?"

Thorn nodded.

"So why did you—"

"While doing my soul searching, when I thought I was dying, I asked myself what would I have liked to do for my second act, had I lived long enough. And again I thought of you. I felt you were ready for a second act, too."

Thorn got to his feet. Put the chair back precisely where it belonged.

"Having been spared," he said. "I thought the two of us

might wander the world together for a while, without the pressure of being married. See if something might occur to us how to occupy our time in a productive fashion. But I see you've made other plans."

Thorn gently kissed Joanna's cheek and he said, "Congratulations."

And then he left.

Driving away from Joanna's ranch in a rental Corvette, Lucan Thorn considered the performance he'd just given. All in all, he was pleased with it. It would've been too corny to play on screen or even onstage, but one-to-one with Joanna, and Hop Tu and the secretary for an audience, he felt it played. Worth every bit of the $25,000 he'd paid to have it written. The out-of-work screenwriter had been only too happy to dash it off for him — the fee being generous and the vague promise that Thorn might seek him out for future projects being even more enticing.

Thorn could have simply shown up at Joanna's new house and demanded that she come to her senses. Knowing how Joanna hated to be alone and that she'd purchased property in Texas, where his spies had told him Laddy Johnson had also relocated, Thorn had suspected she might have it in mind to marry her old college sweetheart. To marry so very far below herself. But hadn't she seen what happened to other successful leading ladies when they'd married ordinary guys? Why, they got divorced in short order. Which, admittedly, also tended to happen when an actress married an actor of equal station, but without the saturation publicity that advanced careers. Especially, the big post-divorce, courageous lady comeback story.

Joanna was too smart to have overlooked that, but Thorn knew she could be stubborn, willful. Determined to have her way even if it cost her professionally. Why, she might have slapped his face if he'd tried the direct approach, and then he would have had to slap her back. As they'd done in both of their marriages. This time, however, Thorn being an actor who prepared carefully for each role, worried that if things got physical, the personal secretary, Ms. de la Fuente, might intercede. Thorn had learned of the movie Joanna was developing about the woman's life. He'd even gone so far as to obtain copies of the post-beating photos of German Padilla, Ms. de la Fuente's former fiancé. Thorn didn't want her to do anything like that to him. Wouldn't be at all good for his image to have a woman beat the crap out of him.

Then again, Ms. de la Fuente had been the most moved of the three people who'd witnessed his little performance. He'd seen out of the corner of his eye that she'd especially liked his confession that he felt contrite about the way he'd mistreated Joanna. Would she have liked to hear the same words from Señor Padilla? Who could say? But she'd liked hearing the *mea culpa* from him, and that's what counted. It might be useful to seduce the woman, if only to pre-empt the possibility of receiving a beating from her.

Thorn had no doubt he could seduce her. A Hollywood star casting a spell over an average person was easier than taking candy from a baby. There ought to be a law against it, he thought, but if there was he'd be a serial offender. He gave Erindira de la Fuente some further thought. She wasn't at all bad looking, most likely passionate once you pierced her personal reserve, and undoubtedly she could be a useful source of information about Joanna. He decided to give her a call. Soon.

Meanwhile, he had to be out of Joanna's sight for the moment, but not too far away.

Might be worthwhile to go take a look at Laddy Johnson, see what Joanna was gettin herself into. Thorn had to laugh. He'd kept tabs on Laddy over the years. He knew the retired stuntman was running for mayor of a small Texas town. Wasn't that just perfect? Well, it would have been if the SOB settled down with some li'l ol' Takesus gal.

Not with his Joanna.

Thorn drove to Gasoline, but when he got to town he found his way blocked by a long funeral procession. Rather than be annoyed, Thorn studied the passing of the caravan of enormous SUVs. He was always on the lookout for local color, fresh vernacular, unusual faces with expressive tics. He sometimes thought of himself as a cultural anthropologist. One who made really good money.

From what he could observe, the deceased had been a person of some local prominence, but nobody looked particularly sorry that the guy had croaked, except one very angry white-haired woman and a little geek in a neck brace sitting next to her.

On impulse, Thorn followed along at the rear of the cortege, glad now that he'd rented a Vette, black of course, instead of a Porsche. He would watch the graveside service, see what he could learn about the people in town. Might pick up a scene he could put into one of his movies; might be really helpful if it gave him a clue as to how Laddy Johnson fit into the local tribal hierarchy.

The actor was so self-absorbed he didn't notice that he wasn't the only uninvited guest tagging along.

Twenty yards behind him, a gray sedan was also headed to the cemetery.

In it was a woman in her late 30s who was genuinely sorry that her father had died before she got to see him again. She was wondering who the dude in the Corvette was. Maybe someone who had something to do with her daddy dying?

Preoccupied as *she* was, Hayley Winslow, aka Jazz Janssen, didn't notice the pickup truck tucked into the stand of trees opposite the entrance to the cemetery.

Mary Sue Parker wore black and looked like just another mourner at Win-Win's funeral, except she had in her hand one of those tiny microphones Secret Service agents used. She wasn't talking with anybody else so she didn't wear an ear-bud. She was simply whispering into her digital audio recorder, a far more subtle way to cover the story of the mayor's death than if she'd brought a notepad and a pen.

So far, she'd given a description of the marble mausoleum in which Win-Win would be interred. There were no earthen graves in Gasoline. The town didn't want to foreclose the possibility of putting any patch of land off limits to oil exploitation. If at some future time it was decided that oil might be found under the Heavenly Wonders Cemetery, it would be available for recovery by directional drilling. And each of the families of the dearly departed resting above the new oil field would be receive a small but pleasing royalty.

But as big as Mayor Winslow's last resting place was, Margaret and Walker would be getting a windfall if oil was discovered beneath his crypt.

Mary Sue counted off and described the vehicles and the mourners passing through the cemetery gates. All the men wore dark suits and dark boots, but light colored Stetsons.

Wouldn't do to have a black hat show up at Mayor Winslow's send off. The younger women all wore sleek black suits, stiletto heels, and their hair down; the older women wore dark dresses that let them breathe easily, sensible shoes, and their hair up and bouffant. Everyone looked mournful but not particularly sad.

Norman Oklahoma, for example. He looked like a man who might need a new job soon, but certainly not like someone who'd lost a friend.

Even Margaret and Walker Winslow looked more angry than despairing to Mary Sue. Margaret's mood was as dark as the black Mikimoto pearls she wore for the occasion, and Walker appeared to be fighting a losing battle to keep his neck brace from swallowing his head. Both of them looked like they wanted to hit somebody.

For the sake of spicing up her story, Mary Sue fervently hoped that Laddy Johnson would put in an appearance, but no luck so far. Keeping her eye on the gate as the mourners gathered around the preacher standing at the head of Win-Win's casket, Mary Sue saw a black Corvette drive through the gateway. Other than the hearse, it was the only non-SUV in attendance. No, hold on a moment, a dumpy gray sedan pulled in after the sports car.

Mary Sue's breath caught in her throat when she saw who got out of the Vette. It took a hard swallow before she managed to whisper into her microphone. "Lucan Thorn, the movie star, has just arrived at Mayor Winslow's funeral."

Being an actor, Thorn always wore black, and thus was appropriately attired. When he put on his sunglasses it made him seem even more funereal. He started walking Mary Sue's way and her knees began to wobble. But then she had a thought that firmed her right up.

Lucan Thorn had twice been married to Joanna Wells. Joanna was Laddy Johnson's college sweetheart, had endorsed his candidacy for mayor, and had dropped the bombshell about Win-Win consorting with L.A. hookers. It couldn't be just a coincidence that Thorn was in Gasoline.

Damn, there was a great story to be had here after all. And she was going to get it. Mary Sue didn't bat an eye when Lucan Thorn stopped at her side.

Not even when he started staring at her cleavage.

The phone rang and Laddy hobbled over to the end table to pick it up. He was thinking it would be Joanna calling to consult him on some minor detail of the wedding plans, something to make him feel that his contribution to their wedding was more than saying, "I do."

Maybe Joanna was going to let him have a choice of appetizers. Like, "Honey, should we have Thai shrimp cocktails or Gulf shrimp cocktails?"

If it was something like that, he was going to say, "Let's go with the franks 'n' beans."

But it wasn't Joanna at all. It was a man's voice, local but not familiar.

"Hello, sir. I'm looking for Laddy Johnson. Have I got the right number?"

"Who's calling?" Years of living in L.A. had taught Laddy to be careful, even about something as innocuous as admitting your identity on your own telephone.

"My name's Tiny Osgood, sir. If you're Laddy Johnson, you drove Walker Winslow's truck offa my foot, and I'd like to thank you. Miz Dominguez over at the Public Baths give me this number and I sure hope I dialed it right."

Hearing that his mother had pointed Tiny Osgood in his direction, Laddy relaxed.

"You did, Mr. Osgood. How's your foot?"

"Not nearly what it used to be. Mashed all to hell, you don't mind me talkin' like that. An' please, Mr. Johnson, call me Tiny."

"All right, Tiny. My friends call me Laddy."

"I voted for you, sir. I mean, Laddy. I thought you'd like to know."

"Thank you, I appreciate that. Maybe we'll know before long if you backed a winner."

"I sure hope so. I never liked that sumbitch Mayor Winslow, God rest his soul. Never thought much a the rest of them Winslows, neither. Bought my truck up in Houston and got a better price on it than TRS ever offered me."

Gouge a customer, lose a voter, Laddy thought.

"Anyway, Laddy, thankin' you was just the first thing on my mind. I got somethin' else I think maybe you should know."

"What's that?" Laddy started to feel wary again.

"Well, I've got this cousin, name a Kirkly, little speck of a gal, don't go more'n 180. Seein' me with my videocam all the time when she was growin' up got her interested in takin' pitchers, too. Only she, and I hate to say this, her ambition is to be one a them paparazzi types. Kind that bothers famous people when they go out to eat and whatnot, know what I mean?"

Laddy said that he did, his uneasiness growing.

"Well, there's hardly anything at all for a snoopy photographer to do around these parts, so I wasn't too worried. But the other night Kirkly was in Tunbridge Square for all the commotion and she was just snappin' away. She's partial to still photos. She stuck around after you left and was there when the governor and Miz Wells arrived. That wasn't enough for her so she started snoopin' around some. An' someone small as her don't get noticed right off."

Tiny Osgood fell silent and Laddy knew he was about to deliver a blow.

"I hate to say this next part, Laddy, but Kirkly got pictures of you 'n' Miz Wells bein' hauled outta the Public Baths by them cops. She brought 'em to my hospital room to show me. I took the mem'ry stick right outta her camera, told her she wasn't gettin' it back and if she bothered you or Miz Wells anymore I'd bust her camera for her."

Laddy felt a wave of relief.

"Thank you, Tiny. We're more than even now."

"I'm afraid I got more to tell you, Laddy."

"What's that?" he asked, his leg starting to hurt.

"Well, us Osgoods, we're pretty stubborn. Kirkly followed Miz Wells up to this ranch near Austin. Now, she didn't trespass or nothin'. Just parked her truck behind some trees near the entrance to Miz Wells' ranch and decided to see who might come visit a movie star."

Laddy knew a cue when he heard one. "Who did, Tiny?"

"Another movie star, that fella called Lucan Thorn. Never cared for him much myself."

"Did he stay long?" Laddy asked, his jaw clenching.

"No, sir. Only twenty minutes or so, Kirkly said."

Joanna got rid of Thorn. Good for her, Laddy thought.

"But then Thorn come here to town," Tiny added. "Kirkly followed him."

"Lucan Thorn is here in Gasoline?"

"He's at Mayor Winslow's funeral. How d'you like that?"

Could Thorn have had a connection to Win-Win? Laddy

couldn't imagine what it might have been. Unless they both had patronized the same L.A. hookers.

"Anyway," Tiny continued, "Kirkly called me to see was it all right if she took pitchers a Lucan Thorn because she don't want me to bust her camera. I figgered I'd better check with you. So is it? All right, that is."

Laddy considered.

"Yes, it is," he said. "As longer as neither Ms. Wells nor I are in the picture. And, Tiny?"

"Yeah, Laddy?"

"Any pictures your cousin takes of Thorn, I want to see them first. I'll pay her for first looks."

Tiny laughed. "A first-look fee? Don't that beat all? Damn, I hope you're gonna be our new mayor."

The preacher wouldn't get cast as an extra on a soap, Lucan Thorn thought, but the Widow Winslow, now there was a sinister presence worthy of the big screen. The white hair, the black pearls, the blocky body, and most of all the voice of doom she had. They ever did another *Exorcist* sequel, she could pick up right where Mercedes McCambridge had left off.

The widow, whose name was Margaret, was standing at the head of the casket, crowding out the preacher. The little geek in the neck brace, a head shorter than mumsy, was her son, Walker. The stiff was Edwin Winslow, better known as Win-Win, late mayor of the town of Gasoline, and the opponent of challenger Laddy Johnson in an election that was still undecided, two day after the polls had closed.

Thorn had learned all this from the hot whispered voice of Mary Sue Parker, the young reporter with the nice rack and the accent that reminded him of Joanna before she took her French lessons. He'd listened to Mary Sue's story closely, fascinated by the facts that Laddy Johnson had challenged the deceased to a fist-fight, and that Joanna had revealed that Win-Win had been a client of his close personal friend Dina Cole, Hollywood's pre-eminent madam. Even as he'd listened closely to Mary Sue, another part of his mind had considered whether he should add her to his to-do list. Might be one woman too many, as he'd already committed himself to seducing Ms. de la Fuente. And, of course, recapturing Joanna. But when Mary Sue stopped whispering in his ear she stuck her tongue in it.

If she felt that way about things, Thorn decided, he'd just have to go the extra mile. But that would have to wait because Margaret had finished with the formalities, thanking everyone who'd come to see her husband off, and was beginning her soliloquy.

"My Edwin wasn't perfect, no angel certainly. But as I look around me now at all you good people I don't see anyone with a halo over his head. And if I had a mirror, I wouldn't see one over my own head."

"Might not even get a reflection, the old bat," a man near Thorn said none too quietly.

Being a professional, Thorn kept a stoic demeanor. But he would remember the line.

Margaret Winslow turned her head in the direction of the man who'd made the crack, and he withdrew behind a taller fellow with a bigger cowboy hat. Good God, Thorn thought, look at the malevolence in that woman's eyes. She really could be a star. Or a studio head.

Margaret continued, "For all his faults, though, the only thing I can criticize Edwin for is that he didn't take better care of himself. His heart gave out while he still had work to do. Our town is at a critical juncture. We must decide whether to try to cling to the past with no real hope of succeeding or to move into the future, adapting to new circumstances and prospering as we go. Edwin would have been just the man to lead us to that prosperous future."

The wise guy opened his mouth again. "Sure woulda, he coulda kept his pecker in his pants, 'steada stickin' it to some Hollywood whores."

This time everyone took notice, including Walker.

The younger Winslow tried to turn his head this way and that to see who'd insulted his father. The result was his neck brace crept up to his nose. But he still managed to demand in a muffled voice, "What sumbitch said that?"

Lucan Thorn pointed out the sumbitch. The fellow that the troublemaker had been hiding behind stepped aside and everybody saw who the culprit was. Walker's eyes bugged out above his neck brace. He forced it back down and cried out, "You!"

It was Ryton Safford, the grease-monkey from TRS that Daddy had fired and Walker had beaten up for revealing that Walker needed a booster seat to drive his truck. Safford thought he'd come to the cemetery and have himself some fun at Daddy's expense. Well, this time Walker would give him a beating he —

Wouldn't be getting right now. As soon as Walker took his first step in Safford's direction, Margaret yanked him back like a wayward chihuahua. She'd taken hold of his neck brace, and he felt a pain that made his toenails curl. He would do no brawling at his father's funeral.

But two of the biggest male mourners grabbed Safford by his arms and dragged him off. As he was led away, the lowlife fixed his gaze on his betrayer, Lucan Thorn, and called out, "I'll git you, you no-good ..." Safford's brow knitted. "Say, don't I know you from somewheres?"

He was flung out onto the sidewalk in front of the cemetery before he could receive an answer.

But now everyone was looking at Thorn. And Walker put the name to the face.

"You're Lucan Thorn."

"I am," Thorn admitted, removing his sunglasses. "But please don't let my presence interfere with this solemn occasion. I'll leave if you like."

"No, no. Don't do that," Walker said. "Daddy loved your movies."

Thorn smiled modestly. But he knew the decision wasn't the geek's to make. He looked at Margaret, who was studying him closely. After a moment, she nodded.

"Please stay," she said, "and thank you for your help."

With those words, Thorn knew he'd just been inducted into the Winslow camp in the battle against Laddy Johnson. His timing might have been better. He'd barely had time to offer the widow a gracious smile when a loud, female, countrified voice bellowed from the street, "Hey, y'all big news! The election's been decided!"

Everyone turned to see a strawberry-haired girl in jeans and a denim shirt.

"Laddy Johnson won — by *four* damn votes!"

Having delivered her news, the girl grabbed the camera with the telephoto lens that hung from a strap around her neck and started snapping reaction shots.

She began with Lucan Thorn.

CHAPTER FOUR

Buck Musgrove told Laddy, "There ain't no provision in the city charter for a recount."

Buck and Eveleen Nellis had driven out to Laddy's momma's house to give him the news.

"And Governor Freyman's got every minute of counting the ballots on videotape, so there's no room for disputin' anything," Eveleen added.

"Besides that, and I don't like to give that fella credit for much," Buck said, "the governor brought in as impartial observers a Baptist preacher, a rabbi, and a Texas Ranger."

Laddy laughed. "Leave it to the governor to turn my election into a joke."

"Weren't no joke," Buck countered. "The Texas Ranger he brought in was Nolan Ryan. You think anyone's gonna question Nolan's word."

"Not if he doesn't want a fast ball in his ear," Laddy conceded. "You're sure there's no recount provision?" he asked. "I could've sworn there was."

"You 'n' everyone else," Eveleen told him. "But the governor had the law checked out with a fine-tooth comb before he started the ballot count. He discovered that Win-Win and his butt-kissers on the Town Council passed the ordinance real quiet-like one Friday night when the rest of Texas was watchin' high school football, like God intended."

"That'd be the time for skulduggery all right," Laddy agreed.

Buck said, "There's all sorts of high-minded language in the law about efficiency, expeditin' democracy, and savin' the taxpayer's money, but in the margins some sumbitch hand-wrote: 'This'll save a lotta bellyachin' from anybody we don't like ever becomin' mayor.'"

"Win-Win probably didn't intend to videotape when his boys counted the ballots," Laddy said.

Eveleen snorted. "So they did themselves in," she said. "You're the mayor of Gasoline for the next four years, Laddy. And as you know, the mayor in this town can be overruled only by three consecutive and unanimous votes of the town council, each vote to take place at least one week after the one before it."

"Win-Win write that law, too?" Laddy asked.

Buck and Eveleen nodded.

It hit Laddy then how much power he'd gained. How the welfare of over 20,000 people would depend on his wisdom and honesty. How he'd been given a sacred trust.

"So what's the first order of business, Mr. Mayor?" Buck asked.

Laddy said, "First thing we do, Buck, is fire Chief of Police Gunther Lomax, and I mean right now. I'll write the termination letter today, but you take enough of your boys with you to take his badge, his duty weapon, and any other city property, and throw his backside into the street. Lock his files, his desk, and his office. Send some more of our people to seal Win-Win's office. If Winton Earle shows up at either Gunther's office or Win-Win's and tries to bully his way in, you tell him to back off or you'll arrest him."

"I'm supposed to arrest the district attorney?" Buck asked. "By whose authority?"

"Mine," Laddy told him. "Or your own. You're Gasoline's new chief of police. Just as soon as you take Gunther's badge from him, pin it right on your own shirt."

Eveleen laughed and rubbed her hands together with glee.

"This is better than a coup at the Kremlin," she said.

"Glad you like it, Comrade Nellis," Laddy told her, "because you're my new chief of the *secret* police."

"What?" both Eveleen and Buck asked.

"I'll give you the details later," Laddy said. "Now, Buck, you get going. Eveleen, I want you to make a list. On it, you put as near as possible the names of Win-Win's biggest supporters, financial, personal, whatever. Go on, you two. We don't have time to lose. Oh, and Eveleen, I want you to make sure from now on that City Hall and the mayor's office are locked tight outside of normal business hours. I don't want any laws being passed when we're not looking."

Buck and Eveleen stepped smartly on the way to complete their assignments, taking only the time necessary to glance at each other, the looks on their faces expressing exactly the same thought: *Who would've guessed Laddy Johnson could be so ruthless?*

Once he was alone, Laddy thought maybe it was just all his years in the movie business getting the better of him, infusing a sense of melodrama in what should be a routine transfer of civil authority. But he felt powerful forces were already gathering to destroy him and his new administration, that they would stop at nothing to restore the old order. Gunther Lomax and Winton Earle could launch the attack with that bogus public fornication charge of theirs. After that, who knew what might be next?

Just look at all the investigations that were thrown at Bill Clinton as soon as he arrived at the White House. Well, Laddy Johnson wasn't going to sit still for any of that crap. He was going to be more like ...

His daddy? Were LBJ's political instincts welling up in him? That might not be a bad thing. Long as he didn't get into a war with Vietnam.

Arcelia Dominguez had an iMac computer in her house. She thought it was much prettier than any of the other brands. Easier to use, too. She'd told Laddy she'd be happy to do a commercial for Apple, if they ever asked her. One of those spots with the two guys. She could be Mac's mom.

"And Margaret Winslow could be PC's?" Laddy asked.

Arcelia shook her head. "PC is a Window not a Winslow. He's a nice boy. He just needs a little extra attention. Maybe a new look too."

Laddy's mother used her computer for her business, for correspondence and for ... well, Laddy wasn't sure what else. His mother's personal files were password protected. He tried not to think what his mother could be up to that she felt she had to keep secret, and for the most part he succeeded. For the remaining part, he suspected Momma had something on her computer about ... about who his father was.

He sighed, pushing the thought aside and logged on to the Internet and then to the town of Gasoline's official website. He thought, having been elected mayor, he'd better see what the city charter had to say about his job. Having learned about the no-recount shenanigans, he wanted to make sure there were no other surprises in store for him.

And with one exception, there weren't.

His term of office was four years.

He would be paid a salary of $100,001 per annum, and received a pension and medical and dental benefits for himself and his family.

He would be provided an official vehicle and driver for his use 24/7, if he so chose.

He could spend $25,000 to redecorate his office, if he so chose.

He would appoint every top administrative officer in the municipal government, and none of his appointments was subject to ratification by the town council.

He could propose new town ordinances.

He could veto ordinances passed by the town council, such vetoes subject only to the infamous three consecutive and unanimous overrides by the town council.

He had the power to call special elections to the town council in the event a seat became unexpectedly vacant, or to wait for the next regularly scheduled election to fill the seat.

And then there was the kicker.

The mayor was required to maintain his residence within the city limits, and to spend at least five nights per week in that residence unless he was traveling on official business or taking personal vacation time, which came to four weeks per year.

Laddy reread that last provision looking for a loophole but didn't find one.

He was pretty sure Joanna wasn't going to want to spend

44 of the next 48 months living in Gasoline. And while he'd glanced at the real estate section of the *Gasoline Beacon* only a few times since he'd returned home, that was enough to see there were precious few houses on the market. Because each and every house in town came with the right to buy municipal gasoline at 25¢ a gallon. As long as the local economy was strong enough to keep unemployment low, the locals tended to stay put. So, how would Joanna like living in Gasoline *with her mother-in-law* for the next four years?

Probably about as much as going back to L.A. and living in the Valley. Laddy thought he'd better go visit his betrothed and have a little chat.

But before he could do that, the doorbell rang. He thought uneasily that maybe Joanna had come to see him. Maybe he could show her around the place. Promise if she moved into his old bedroom with him, he'd get rid of his boyhood single bed, the one he'd been sleeping on with his feet hanging over the edge, and buy them something roomier.

But when he opened the door, he didn't see Joanna. He saw the woman who'd been peeking through his mother's windows. And now that he got a good look at her, he recognized her, even though she'd changed her hair color. And her eye color, too.

"Hello, Laddy," she said.

Same voice, he thought. Sounded like music even when she was just talking.

"Hello, Hayley," he replied.

Hayley Winslow. Two years ahead of him at Gasoline High. An older woman to be worshiped from afar. Then to be held close, her Maria to his Tony when the school put on *West Side Story*.

Conor Farley had been the original choice to play Tony,

as he had a great singing voice. But it was a high tenor, almost an alto, and it was difficult to distinguish between his voice and Hayley's. Added to that was Conor's baby face; he didn't look old enough even to think about kissing a girl, much less dying for one. Hayley had prevailed upon Ms. Zanetakos, the drama teacher, to recast the part, after explaining herself to Conor first.

Ms. Zanetakos asked Hayley who she thought should play Tony. She pointed to Laddy, a mere stagehand in the production, and said, "Why don't we give that young fella a try?"

Laddy had never sung anywhere but in the shower before or since, but in those eight weeks rehearsing with Hayley, having her coax him and coach him, he'd somehow found the resources to go onstage and not embarrass himself or her. At the curtain call for their three performances, they'd held hands at center stage and bowed to the audience. The applause was overwhelmingly for Hayley, but it felt great to Laddy nonetheless. And each time the applause began to ebb, Hayley kissed his cheek and it cranked right back up.

She'd graduated two years ahead of him, just like Joanna had at UT. He must have had a thing for older women. Then Hayley went off to some fancy Eastern school, and he'd done his best to put her out of his mind.

When he met Joanna at UT, it felt natural to him to take up with another beautiful actress, one who made it easier not to think about Hayley all the time. One he came to love.

There was no question he loved Joanna, but over the years the thought would recur to him that he was surprised he'd never read about Hayley Winslow. He was sure she'd go on to achieve fame in some high-profile field of endeavor. And when he'd returned home he'd been certain he'd hear about her. She'd gone to law school, gotten married, was living with some rich guy in Dallas. Something like that. But he hadn't heard a word.

And now here she was.

"Been a long time, Hayley," he said.

"Sure has, Laddy," she said. "So you have anything to do with my daddy dying?"

Margaret Winslow not only knew about the no-recount law, she knew about its secret loophole, too. In fact, she was the one who'd made sure there was a loophole. Just in case.

"Damn, that was smart, Momma," Walker said after she explained it to him.

"Never cuss in front of a woman," his mother replied.

"Or a microphone," Lucan Thorn added.

The three of them were seated in the kitchen of Margaret's home. Win-Win had been properly filed away in the family crypt and bade godspeed by the preacher. By now, no doubt, he was trying to explain himself to St. Peter. Something he'd have a far easier time with than if he'd had to do the same with Margaret.

She truly didn't mind him carrying on with Hollywood floozies. If anything, she felt sorry for the poor girls, having that great lummox lie atop them. Margaret had been forced to double her bodyweight just to keep from being crushed by Edwin's bulk. That was an acceptable burden to bear to produce a child as magnificent as Hayley, but after Walker had been born it seemed certain to her that she and Edwin were on the downslope of their breeding cycle. She'd never had marital relations with him again, and had kept the weight on to discourage him from wanting sex with her.

She'd accepted that he'd look elsewhere. Had been

encouraged when he went out of state to plow his fields. Thought that meant he knew enough to be discreet about his affairs. That was all she wanted. But then Joanna Wells, damn her, she had to go and ruin everything.

Well, it hadn't helped that Margaret had let Edwin's health slip so badly. But how could she have nagged him not to overeat when she had deliberately kept herself hefty? Still, Edwin's heart attack had been a problem she hadn't foreseen, and Margaret Winslow definitely did not like it when she lost control of any situation.

If she died prematurely herself, why she'd never know what had happened to Hayley. And Walker, he'd never bother about becoming mayor. He'd take over TRS — and run it into the ground in short order. People would laugh at how low the mighty Winslows had fallen.

Margaret wasn't about to have that. She'd go on a diet immediately. Start exercising, too. Lose enough weight to look like a woman again, not a corn silo. Why, she'd even color her hair. And get rid of the damn pearls. Replace them with sapphires. Or rubies. Depending on how she colored her hair.

"Momma, you all right?" Walker asked, not liking the glaze in his mother's eyes.

Lucan Thorn understood, though. "I believe your mother is pondering her future."

Margaret Winslow looked at the actor and smiled. He was more than just a pretty face, this one. "Exactly what I was doing, Mr. Thorn. How did you know?"

"People in L.A. wear that expression all the time," he told her.

He didn't add that most of those people were self-delusional about their prospects. Margaret Winslow, though, was smart and ruthless enough to get what she wanted.

"And if I moved to Los Angeles, Mr. Thorn, what would you see me doing?" she asked.

Walker looked back and forth between his mother and Lucan Thorn. He didn't understand this turn in the conversation. Was Momma fixin' to leave Texas?

Thorn told Margaret, "I'd see you taking over a studio, Mrs. Winslow. Having everyone in town coming to you, pleading for you to let them make their movies."

Hot damn, Walker thought. That happened, Momma would for sure make him an action hero. And why not? He could move like the Chuckster. And with the lifts in his boots he'd be right about eye-to-eye with Sylvester Stallone.

"Perhaps I just might do that," Margaret said. "But first there are matters to attend to right here in Gasoline."

Thorn nodded. "Of course. What's a loophole for if not to use?"

Laddy decided to play it straight with Hayley Winslow. The two of them had gone for a ride in the country in her gray rental sedan. They were drifting up a farm-to-market road in the general direction of Austin with not another car in sight. Hayley had suggested the ride, and while Laddy didn't know what she was up to, he thought it might be better to find out somewhere other than his mother's house.

Because the one thing he did know was Hayley had asked him about Win-Win dying, and that was the subject that had caused her baby brother, that little weasel Walker, to kick him on his bum leg. Laddy didn't think he'd wind up having to throw Hayley through a plate glass window, but still and all he felt better having Hayley's hands and feet occupied driving a car.

He answered her question honestly. "I challenged your daddy to a fight after he publicly called me a bastard one too many times and hurt my momma's feelings."

Hayley looked over at him. Her eyes were an intense violet these days, like Elizabeth Taylor's were when she was young. Her hair was the color of Cherry-Ola Cola, cut short and spiky. Laddy knew all about tinted contact lenses. You saw them every day in Los Angeles. But Hayley's hair color and her cut, there was something foreign about them. You didn't see that retro-punk look even in New York these days. Might find it in London, if that's where Hayley'd been spending all her years away from home, but usually an American who'd lived in England for more than a month would feel she'd earned the right to fake an English accent. Hayley's inflections were as neutral as a network news anchor's.

"Any time you want to put your eyes back on the road," Laddy told her, "is fine by me."

She did and drove on in silence. Laddy contented himself with looking at her profile. Other than being paler than he remembered, she looked remarkably unchanged. A bit thinner was all. Like she'd gone to a vegetarian or vegan diet. Flushed away her toxins with eight glasses of spring water per day. Whatever her regimen, she didn't look bad for a woman pushing 40.

Five miles up the road, she asked Laddy, "You're not going to offer me your condolences on the loss of my father?"

"I'm sorry if you're hurting, Hayley. I can honestly say that. But what I'm thinking about is how not to ask you a million nosy questions."

She pulled off the FM road and onto a dirt track that wound its way along somebody's private property, passed through a pecan orchard, and up a little hill. At the crest, she got out, looked around in all directions, and then plopped down tailor fashion. Laddy saw tears stream from her eyes and down her cheeks, but she didn't move or make a sound.

He got out of the car and sat next to her, wrapping his arms around his legs. He felt the sun on his face, judging it to be warm enough to pink up Hayley's ivory complexion inside of twenty minutes. He had enough of a tan and natural melanin from his mother's side of the family, he didn't have to worry about short-term exposure to solar radiation.

His million questions had now grown by one. Was Hayley's grief genuine? He'd been exposed to too many actresses who could cry on cue not to wonder. If Win-Win had meant so much to Hayley, why had she been away from home so long?

He didn't ask. He stretched out on his back and covered his eyes with his right arm. He told Hayley, "Give me a poke if I start to snore."

He was pretty sure she let him drift off for a while, and then he heard her ask, "Did you put Walker in that neck brace?"

"After the little shit kicked me, yeah," Laddy answered, leaving his arm over his eyes. "And that was after he parked his truck on top of a guy's foot. I was on my way to move the truck when Walker kicked me."

He heard Hayley sigh.

Laddy sat up and looked at her. "Your father was in the truck's passenger seat at the time; he was already dead."

"Before you even got the chance to beat him up, huh?"

Laddy smiled. Hayley was no longer crying and he was

glad for that.

"I imagine Win-Win would've gotten his licks in, too."

"He probably would have," Hayley agreed and smiled back at him.

Laddy noticed that her eyes were their normal blue-green now. She'd either taken out the contact lenses or her tears had washed them away.

"Since you're too much of a gentleman to be nosy," she said, "I'll ask the question: So, Laddy Johnson, what have you been doing all these years, before you decided to run for mayor of Gasoline, Texas?"

Laddy gave her a look. Sure, he was no actual celebrity himself. But between appearing in 45 movies and being romantically linked to Joanna Wells every so often, his name and picture had appeared in both the mainstream and tabloid press. So where the hell had Hayley Winslow been hiding all this time, another planet?

But all he said was, "Mostly making actors look tougher than they are."

When the phone rang, Joanna Wells thought it was either her mother or father calling. Possibly to complain about members of her extended family not being invited to the wedding. When she'd first broken the news about marrying Laddy, her parents had been delighted.

Her father expressed his joy by saying, "About damn time you got it right. About damn time you got married in Texas, too."

Her mother, on another extension, had told her husband, "Now, Darren, you hush up. Joanna's going to be happy this time and that's what matters. Now, darling, how many of my

Jell-o molds are you gonna need for the reception? Well, I guess that'll depend on how many of the Wallersteens and the Norwoods will be coming, won't it? And you'll have to tell me what flavors your other guests might like."

That was when Joanna was forced to tell her parents that just Grandma Wallersteen and Aunt Patricia Norwood would be invited. After looking through her family photo albums, both Joanna and Master Tu had agreed that 99% of her relatives would seriously detract from the *feng shui* of the occasion. In other cases, a favored cousin or two might have been allowed in, but with no restrictions being placed on who Laddy might invite a margin of error had to be maintained. Not that this was how Joanna explained things to her parents. But she held firm: just Grandma and Aunt Pat. And no Jell-o molds.

Upon hearing this news, her father had told her mother, "Damnit, Birdie, if she wasn't marrying Laddy Johnson this time and right down the road from Austin, I wouldn't go myself."

The irony there was Master Tu had asked Joanna how she'd feel about having only her mother attend the ceremony. But Momma calmed Daddy down, and Joanna thought the matter was settled. Unless Momma was calling back just now to ask could she please bring at least one Jell-o mold for Grandma.

But when Joanna picked up the phone, neither of her parents was calling. A young woman said hello to her in a voice accented much like her own had once been.

"Miz Wells," the young woman said, "it surely is an honor speaking to you, and I won't take but a minute of your time."

Hollywood stars were not keen on giving away even a heartbeat of their time. Joanna's strategy when met with an unwelcome approach was to speak French.

"*Je suis désolé. La Madame n'est pas a la maison. Essai encore plus tard.*" I'm sorry. Madame is not at home. Try again later.

Joanna was about to hang up when the young woman with the country voice answered her in French. "*Quelle honte. J'ai des nouvelles importantes pour elle.*" What a shame. I have important news for her.

Joanna was astounded. Not by the claim that the young woman had any news whatsoever for her. That was a standard sales pitch. But the fact that a Texan knew French and could speak it with a pleasing accent, that was amazing.

"Who is this?" Joanna asked. "And how did you get my phone number."

Joanna hadn't bothered to have her Texas phone number unlisted; she'd thought that putting it in the name of J. Wallersteen would suffice.

"Miz Wells, my name is Kirkly Osgood, and I'll tell you straight out I'm a paparazza."

Damn if the girl didn't know her Italian, too, getting the gender and number of her noun right. But the thought of an ambush photographer working ranch land Texas struck her as hilarious. Until it occurred to her that this creature might have learned about her wedding and then her blood ran cold.

"What do you want, Ms. Osgood?" Joanna asked with ice in her voice.

"First, I want to put you at ease, Miz Wells. My cousin, Tiny, told me no pictures of you. So there won't be any from me."

"My thanks to Tiny," Joanna said, wondering who Tiny might be. It never ceased to amaze her how stars picked up strangers faster than black linen picked up lint.

"Yes, ma'am. I'll be sure to let him know. What I wanted to ask was, is it all right if I take pictures of Mr. Lucan Thorn. I asked Tiny to check that out with Laddy Johnson, but I haven't heard back yet."

"Mr. Thorn is nearby?" Joanna asked.

"He was in Gasoline, the last I saw him."

The bastard, Joanna thought. Lucan was planning to make trouble for her. So she smiled at the thought of siccing a paparazza on him. "Yes, by all means, feel free to take pictures of Mr. Thorn. Take as many as you like. He doesn't mind at all. In fact, he likes to walk about his living quarters at night in the nude."

"*Ma'am?*" came the startled response.

"Oh, yes, he's quite the exhibitionist. Thinks he has a magnificent body."

There was a pause before Kirkly asked in a quiet voice, "Well, does he?"

Joanna said, "You'll have to see for yourself. Form your own opinion."

"Um, okay, sure. Does he ever, like, step out onto a balcony in the altogether?"

"He's more discreet than that," Joanna said. "But he does like to make love by candlelight with a window or a door open so the light flickers. You might want to adjust your camera for low-light shooting."

"Yes, ma'am, I'll surely do that. And thank you very much."

"You're quite welcome," Joanna said.

"May I ask you one more thing?"

"Off the record?"

"Actually, it's more like something I want to tell you, but asking a question's the way to get at it," Kirkly said.

"Go ahead," Joanna allowed.

"Do you know Hayley Winslow?"

"I know the Winslow family name, of course," Joanna said. "But I don't know Hayley. Who is she?"

"She's Mrs. Winslow's older child, her daughter."

"And that's what you wanted to ask me about?" Joanna said.

"Yes, ma'am. Because she and Laddy Johnson went to Gasoline High together. Not in the same grade, mind you. Hayley's two years older. But they were in a play together, *West Side Story*."

Joanna was thunderstruck. This was harder to believe than a Texan speaking French. Laddy Johnson onstage? He'd never mentioned that to her. Never uttered the name Hayley Winslow in her presence. Never ... Wait a minute. *West Side Story?*

"Miss Osgood," Joanna asked hesitantly, "would you know the part Mr. Johnson played?"

"Yes, ma'am, I checked the newspaper clipping. He was Tony. Ms. Winslow was Maria."

Laddy playing the lead in a *musical?* Joanna just couldn't get her mind around that. But having spent years in L.A. and in and out of divorce court, she knew the next question to ask.

"Miss Osgood, is there a reason you're bringing all this up right now?"

"Yes, ma'am, you being so nice to me and all, I thought I should let you know I saw Laddy Johnson and Hayley Winslow driving off together, heading out into the country-side, oh, an hour and twenty-one minutes ago."

"*Merde*," Joanna Wells said.

Kirkly Osgood knew just what she meant.

* * *

Walker Winslow held a news conference in the main showroom of Texas Rolling Stock to announce that he was demanding a recount in the mayoral election, was contesting the results, and when the election got thrown out for lack of a clear winner, he'd be taking his daddy's place on the ballot. He made this pronouncement against a backdrop of new SUV models from Ford, Chevy, and Hummer, artfully arranged from left to right in red, white, and blue. Couldn't get any more American than that.

What Walker had failed to recognize was that by standing in front of three monster trucks, he had given himself the stature of a Mouseketeer. Norman Oklahoma who'd set the stage for Walker, had seen immediately how diminutive Walker looked, but who was Norman to criticize his new boss's ideas? He just bit his tongue to keep from laughing.

With Lucan Thorn to introduce him, Walker had drawn a crowd of TV and print media from as far away as Dallas and San Antonio. What little space was left over was filled by TRS employees who had been instructed to cheer and clap whenever they saw Norman Oklahoma do so. More than one reporter noticed the employees staring at Norman and ignoring Walker.

As far as nudging the media in the right direction went, Mary Sue Parker was there to get the ball rolling. She'd been promised an introduction to the general manager of the Fox TV station in Houston for her help. After making his statement and opening the floor to questions, Walker turned to Mary Sue first.

"Yes, Miss Parker," he said, "you have a question?"

Mary Sue nodded. "I've heard from a source in the

Johnson campaign that the Town Council had passed a no-recount ordinance. Doesn't that mean that Laddy Johnson's four-vote margin of victory in the mayoral election against your late father stands up, and there's nothing you can do about it?"

Unbeknownst to anyone present, Mary Sue's source in the Johnson campaign, her former lover Ben Musgrove, had slipped into the showroom at the back of the media contingent and stood just ten feet behind Mary Sue. No one was paying him the least bit of attention at the moment. Had Margaret Winslow been present at her son's announcement, she might have noticed an enemy in their midst, but Margaret was in Win-Win's old office at TRS just then meeting with former chief of police Gunther Lomax and District Attorney Winton Earle.

Margaret had told Walker all he had to do was stick to the talking points she'd prepared for him. Don't say anything else. Since Momma had agreed to let him run TRS if she stayed in town, and would make him a big movie star if she moved to Los Angeles, Walker had sworn to do just that.

But Walker hadn't known at that time what Ben Musgrove was about to ask him.

"What do you mean you've been fired?" Margaret Winslow asked Gunther Lomax.

Margaret didn't play chess, but she still felt like one of the big pieces had been grabbed right off her board. That horsy piece, the knight. Laddy Johnson snuck right in and stole him. Margaret Winslow's feelings about horse thieves were Texas traditional: They ought to be hanged.

"What I mean, Miz Winslow," Gunther said, "is Buck

Musgrove barged into my office, with a letter from Laddy Johnson saying I was fired, and a pair of Texas Rangers sent along by Governor Freyman to make sure nobody argued the point. They took my badge and my gun and Buck said I was lucky they let me keep my hat and boots. Buck's the new chief of police."

Winton Earle leaned forward and spoke in a low voice. "Even more important than taking Gunther's badge and gun, Margaret, the Johnson people also now have his files."

"Yeah, but we don't know they're gonna be readin' em," Gunther said.

Margaret Winslow turned two icy blue eyes on the former chief of police.

"You wouldn't have left anything embarrassing lying around, now would you, Gunther?"

"Well, ma'am ... there might be one or two things," he replied, feeling a sudden urge to pee. He wanted to raise his hand like a schoolboy, ask could he go to the bathroom. But he knew he wasn't going to get away that easy.

"That was very careless of you, Gunther," Margaret told him. "I surely hope any embarrassment to be suffered will be limited to you."

The district attorney looked bleakly at his former partner in law and order.

"Oh, I'm sure it will be, Margaret. My office, as you know, doesn't believe in plea bargains. A man commits a crime, he's going to do his time."

"Now, Winton," Margaret said to the D.A., "we don't know that Gunther's done anything *illegal*. He may have just been scratching his backside, so to speak. And maybe that will escape notice if he tidies up after himself."

"And if he doesn't," the D.A. said, "if he tries to lie his way out of trouble by throwing dirt on somebody else, I'll make sure he goes to prison until Jesus comes to save him."

Gunther Lomax realized that he'd just been good copped/bad copped. Margaret Winslow had told him he better break into his old office and remove any incriminating documents he'd stupidly left behind. And his old buddy Winton Earle had told him if he tried to sell out people with a lot more pull than he had, he'd spend the rest of his life behind bars.

Of course, Winton was thinking Gunther might go to the FBI or something. But maybe the way for Gunther to save himself — and he could hardly believe he was thinking this — was to go to Laddy Johnson. See if he could make a deal with the new mayor.

But what Gunther told Miz Winslow and that sumbitch Winton was, "Don't neither of you worry one little bit. I'm the last person's ever gonna embarrass you."

Walker's face turned beet red. Half-a-dozen video cams and a dozen more still cameras captured his anger both for posterity and immediate distribution. Up until just a minute ago, everything had been going fine, too.

The new standard-bearer of the Winslow clan had answered Mary Sue's question: Wouldn't everyone just have to live with Laddy Johnson being Gasoline's new mayor?

Walker shook his head, as much as his neck brace allowed. "The governor and the rest a them folks countin' the election votes were workin' with what you'd call your incomplete documentation. That is, they knew the law, but they didn't know *all* of it."

"What's that supposed to mean?" an Austin reporter

asked.

"Just what I said. There's a no-recount law, all right. But after it was passed the Town Council added a "clear winner" amendment. Says for the no-recount rule to apply, you've got to win the election by 5 percent or better of the vote. Not just four, maybe-they're-legal-maybe-they-ain't, votes like Laddy Johnson got. He's not a clear winner. We've got to vote again, and this time he'll have to run against me."

Walker grinned wickedly.

"Why didn't the governor take the amendment into account when he supervised the ballot count?" a TV guy from San Antonio asked.

"Maybe he didn't know about it," Walker replied innocently. "He'd've checked with the mayor's office, he'd've found out. It was on file there all the time."

"The mayor was dead," a snot-nosed gal from Galveston pointed out.

"His secretary isn't," Walker snapped. "Millie Birdwell woulda told them, they'da bothered to ask."

"Would Millie have told them about the amendment if Win-Win had lived and he'd won by four votes?" the guy from Austin asked.

The newspeople all laughed, and all the TRS employees looked to Norman Oklahoma to see if they should join in. He shook his head, and bit his tongue even harder.

"A course she would," Walker said with a glare. "You sayin' Millie's not honest?"

"Far be it from me," the Austin reporter replied.

A Dallas newsman asked, "Mr. Winslow, do you have documentation for this "clear winner" amendment? Something we can show our readers?"

"Darn right, I do." Momma'd be proud of him, Walker

thought. He'd almost said "Damn right, I do." But cussin' wasn't in his talking points.

Norman Oklahoma stepped forward holding a leather folio bearing the official seal of the town of Gasoline: a gushing oil derrick set behind crossed six-shooters. Below that was the town's motto: *In oil we trust*. He handed the folio to Walker, who opened it as if he was holding the original copy of the Declaration of Independence.

"See there," Walker said. "You thought I was kiddin' you, think again."

He let everybody take their pictures and get a good look. He was in control now. Cruising.

Until a voice at the back of the room asked him, "You still boning Mary Sue, Walker?"

That was when Walker turned red and snapped the folio shut.

"Who said that?" Walker asked.

"That'd be me," Ben Musgrove answered. Every camera in the room turned toward him.

"I was the source in the Johnson campaign Mary Sue mentioned a moment ago, the one who told her about the no-recount law. The part of the law that was on file at Town Hall, not hidden away in the mayor's office like the clear-winner amendment. Mary Sue, she was real grateful for me playin' my part in this little scam you got goin' here. She asked me would I like a little token of her appreciation for helping her out. I told her not if you were still boning her."

The cameras swung around to focus on Mary Sue. To her credit, she held her chin high and let the ghost of a smile lift the corners of her mouth. After allowing Mary Sue her moment, Ben continued, drawing the cameras back to him.

"She didn't answer me, so I thought I'd tag along and get

a look for myself. See if I could tell who she was giving her favors to. But I don't think you're getting any from her these days. Then I noticed Mr. Lucan Thorn, the movie star, over there. *He* looks like he could be getting some, or soon will be. And that'd explain why a bigshot sumbitch like him is introducing a little dog-turd like you."

The cameras swung around to Thorn and he dazzled them with a big-screen smile.

With almost everyone's attention on the actor, and no talking points relevant to Ben Musgrove's personal attack on him, Walker lost control and charged Ben. But Norman Oklahoma was only a step behind Walker and grabbed him around the waist with one arm. Norman outweighed Walker by a hundred pounds and had no trouble carrying him off to his momma.

The cameras swung again to capture the departing Winslow scion trying to kick his way out of Norman's grasp, but they didn't stay on him for long. They darted from Lucan Thorn,to Mary Sue Parker to Ben Musgrove.

The media pack had divided priorities and clumps of reporters set about shouting out questions to each of the principal players. It was as good a news conference as anyone could remember. In Gasoline or anywhere else.

CHAPTER FIVE

Hayley Winslow pulled her rental car to a stop in front of the Public Baths and looked over at Laddy Johnson. The more time she spent with him, the happier she was that she hadn't felt the need to kill him. She'd accepted his explanation of the events leading to her father's death. Daddy never should've called Laddy a bastard in public. It was wrong. Especially for him. Miss Joanna Wells, on the other hand, didn't have to tell the world about Daddy's philandering.

Hayley sighed. She was so jet-lagged and blue over Daddy's death all she wanted to do was crawl in bed somewhere and go to sleep for a week.

"Laddy, will you do me a favor?" she asked.

"If it's not illegal, immoral, or something I'll get caught for," he said.

Hayley smiled. She'd always been drawn to Laddy. She remembered the two of them onstage as Tony and Maria. Him dying in her arms. Her kissing his lifeless lips and whispering, "*Te adoro, Anton.*" Him playing the scene straight the first two times, but in the final performance giving her a fleeting grin only she noticed. Their little secret.

"I haven't seen my mother yet," Hayley told Laddy. "Will you keep it to yourself that I'm back in town?"

"Sure," he said. "But Gasoline *is* a small town. Remember how fast news spreads."

She nodded. "I just need a little rest before I see Momma. I'll find myself a hotel room out on the highway somewhere."

For the first time since he'd seen Hayley again, Laddy had to ask two questions of her. "You going to be okay?" And, "You want to come inside and take a bath?"

Despite her fatigue and her sorrow, Hayley managed a small laugh. "The new mayor bathing with a Winslow? Wouldn't that cause a scandal?"

Laddy smiled. "Yeah, it probably would. But I was thinking you could have your own suite while I was soaking with the governor."

Governor Freyman, having reached Laddy on his cell phone, had summoned him to the baths. After informing Laddy about the newly discovered clear-winner amendment, he said they needed to talk.

"Thank you, Laddy," Hayley said, "but all I want now is to go to sleep."

He took a key off his key ring and handed it to her. "This is to my mother's house," he said. "It's a five-minute drive from here. You remember the address?"

"I remember the house; I remember how to get there," she told him.

Back in high school, Hayley had driven Laddy home after rehearsals.

"Go sleep in my bed," he instructed. "The sheets are clean and my mother will be home before I will, so we'll have a chaperon. I don't want you out on the highway and falling asleep behind the wheel."

Hayley didn't have the strength to argue.

She kissed his cheek and whispered, "*Te adoro, Anton.*"

Governor Fryman was naked except for his hat, his cigar, and the drink in his hand.

"You got yourself one little pisser of a town here," the governor said.

Laddy replied, "It's as crooked as a no-bid contract, but we like it."

The mayor-elect had declined to bathe with the governor and sat outside of the hot-tub fully clothed. The governor blew a cloud of smoke at the ceiling and chuckled.

"Have to admit," he said, "I wouldn't mind having the legislature pass a few laws in the dead of night that I could pull out of my sleeve when I needed 'em."

Laddy shook his head. "You'd have the feds breathing down your neck in no time."

The governor dipped the unlit end of his cigar in his drink and stuck it back in his mouth. "Yeah, you're right about that. You know, if nothing else, I expect I'll get enough material out of four years of being governor for a platinum album."

"The rewards of public service," Laddy said.

"There oughta be some," the governor replied, "because the pay ain't all that great. Now, I'm gonna call one of the cuts on my new album 'Getting Tanked in Gasoline.'"

Laddy laughed. The governor grinned around his cigar.

"Thought you'd like that. So I asked you to come by and help me with the lyrics. This 'clear-winner' amendment that little shit Walker pulled out of his ass may, in fact, be legal. But that don't mean I can't have the Attorney General investigate how it was passed and who was in on the gag. And the funny thing about investigations is, they're liable to find all sorts of evil-doing completely unrelated to their original purpose. I don't think Walker, his momma, or anyone else is gonna holler too hard if I suggest they tear up that amendment of theirs and step the hell out of your way. But I thought I'd check with you before I did, as your decision will directly affect how I write the chorus of my song."

The governor took a sip from his glass as Laddy thought about things.

He said, "I'd want to know right off what other tricks they've got in store for me."

"Any sensible man would," the governor agreed.

"If I agree to a new election, I want it to be next week."

"No chance for them to think up any new devilment. That's smart," the governor said.

"And everyone who votes has to do it verbally, right out in public."

The governor, who'd been slouching comfortably, sat up straight, spilling half his drink into the swirling water. He blinked twice at Laddy. He took the cigar from his mouth and guffawed.

"That'd make it damned hard to steal votes, wouldn't it? Hell, we'll *televise* everyone announcing his vote. 'Dear Sir or Madam, looky right there at the camera and tell the world who's the best sumbitch to run this town.' People could keep track of the score right at home." The governor returned his cigar to his mouth. "A course, it'd be a mite embarrassin' if you lost to Walker that way."

Laddy snorted. "Yeah, I might have to do something

drastic like retire from politics."

Joanna and Laddy's momma, Arcelia, arrived at Arcelia's house from opposite directions, but at the exact moment. Arcelia was at the wheel of her new red Honda Civic Si Coupe. Got thirty-two miles to the gallon, highway, but took off like a rocket. Needed to use high-test fuel but in Gasoline, premium grade was 25¢ a gallon, too, so what the hell? Joanna was driving a black Saab 9.2X all-wheel-drive. Probably weren't more than a dozen of them in Texas, but there was a dealership in Austin to take care of all her maintenance needs.

Each woman gave the other and her car a look. Then Arcelia swung into her driveway and Joanna pulled in at the curb behind a nondescript gray sedan. Arcelia and Joanna exchanged a polite hug. Both of them refrained from a full-out embrace. Arcelia liked Joanna well enough, even thought she was a fair actress, but was of a mind she should have married Laddy long ago, and made a grandma out of Arcelia. The older woman hoped things would work out well now, but she had to wonder if Joanna, with her marital history, kept a divorce lawyer on retainer. Would a big star like her be content to stay married to her son? Arcelia'd had all these thoughts run through her mind not long after bailing Joanna out of jail.

For her part, Joanna withheld herself physically and emotionally because she knew exactly what Arcelia was thinking and didn't blame her one bit. Also because Joanna was wondering if Laddy was already cheating on her, before they even got married.

Two could play the cheating game, of course, but Joanna

wanted to put that kind of thing behind her. She wanted a real marriage this time. One that would last and make her happy. Let her be indifferent to when she started getting gray and wrinkled because her husband would love her for who she was, not how she looked or whether she could still open a movie. In all the world, Laddy Johnson was the only man she could imagine feeling that way about her. If she couldn't realize her dreams with him, she was lost.

Which just might be the case if Kirkly Osgood had it right about Laddy and Hayley Winslow. Ever since hearing that awful news, all Joanna could think about was Laddy's comment that she might be pregnant. Driving down to Gasoline, she became certain that she was. Which was a ridiculous way to think. How could she know so soon if she had conceived? You heard stories that some women knew immediately. She hadn't, though. For her it took a phone call from a stranger implying that her fiancé was fooling around.

Arcelia moved back a step and looked at Joanna. "Sweetheart," she said, "you've always been beautiful, but now you are radiant. Glowing. And I like your car, too."

See there, Joanna thought, even Laddy's mom could tell she was pregnant.

"You look great, too, Arcelia, and so do your wheels."

Arcelia linked her arm through Joanna's. "We are two very fashionable women. That is all there is to it. Did you come to see Laddy?"

Joanna nodded. "I was hoping we could talk."

"I'm sure he'd love that, but he's not home."

Joanna's paranoia kicked in: Was Laddy still out with Hayley Winslow? Would his mother cover for him with some lie? She asked Arcelia, "Would you know where I might find him?"

Arcelia looked at her wristwatch.

"I think he should still be at the baths."

Arcelia's words were innocent enough and they rang true to Joanna, but they also immediately conjured up a distressing picture in her mind: Laddy and Hayley Winslow in a whirlpool together, doing exactly what she and Laddy had done. Oh, God! She hoped Hayley was on the pill. Or sterile. Something.

To Arcelia, she said, "Laddy hurt his back or something? He needed a soak?"

Arcelia looked up and down the street, as if to make certain no one would overhear what she was about to say. The precaution only heightened Joanna's anxiety. She was sure Laddy's mother was about to confide his assignation with Hayley Winslow to her.

"*Chica*," Arcelia whispered, "he is with the governor. On business, you know. Politics. The election and all that. I don't think they want anyone to know. So I don't ask."

Joanna's knees went rubbery with relief. She might have fallen if Arcelia hadn't had hold of her arm. And in that instant the older woman knew exactly what had been bothering her.

"Joanna," she said, "there is no one but you for my son. He has never even introduced another woman to me since he met you."

Which was the truth — despite Arcelia's frequently urging Laddy to find himself a good woman and settle down, and give her a grandchild or two. But now she was going to do her best to make sure Laddy's marriage to Joanna was happy and lasting. Joanna would have no trouble from her mother-in-law, that was certain.

"Come inside, Joanna," Arcelia said. "We will have a cup

of that awful green tea Laddy likes drink now and wait for him to come home."

"You're very kind," Joanna told her.

"I am a good mother, that's all. Perhaps someday you will be the same."

Joanna smiled. She liked to think there could be a happy ending for her.

Arcelia opened her front door.

"*Mi casa es su casa,*" she told her prospective daughter-in-law as they stepped inside. "Laddy will make you very happy. Of this, I am sure."

Joanna fervently hoped Arcelia was right.

But just then the two women heard a disturbing sound. Somewhere in Arcelia's house, someone was snoring.

Margaret Winslow was mad. Men, damn them, were all the same: every last one of them a rutting dog. She glared at her son and took only the slightest satisfaction in seeing him cower. The Winslows, mother and son, were by themselves at home with the curtains drawn.

"You were sleeping with this reporter floozy, Mary Sue whatever her name is?" Margaret asked Walker.

"Daddy said I could," Walker whined. "In fact, he was the one suggested it."

Margaret, who'd been pacing, came to a sudden stop. Her voice dropped to an iron whisper. "Did he indeed?"

"Yes, Momma," Walker said, taking his cue from her and speaking quietly.

"Walker ... did you ever get the feeling your father had passed this creature on to you after having her himself?"

Walker's face scrunched up. "Daddy giving me his sloppy

seconds? Eeeyew, no!"

But thinking about it now, Walker remembered that Daddy had spent a lot of time in his office alone with Mary Sue. Just talking, he'd always thought. Wasn't that right? Walker applied his power of reasoning to the question. Sure, he decided, talk was all they was doing. If Daddy and Mary Sue had been going at it, everyone at TRS woulda heard, the way Mary Sue carried on. And Daddy, big as he was, he got to bouncin' on Mary Sue he woulda busted up some furniture for sure. Not to mention Mary Sue's backbone.

"No, Momma," Walker repeated. "It wasn't like that at all. Mary Sue was just with me."

"And Ben Musgrove, apparently," his mother said without mercy.

Walker appeared to shrink. It got any worse, his neck brace would be resting on top of his boots. "Well, yeah," he finally admitted, "but that's 'cause she was just, you know, spyin' on Laddy Johnson's campaign. For us. For me. She had to gain their trust."

Walker was all but begging his mother to cut him a break.

Instead, she said, "It must make you proud, having a girlfriend so devoted she'll sleep with another man for you. Why, right now, I'll bet she's doing you another favor. Sleeping with Lucan Thorn so he won't go lend his name to Laddy Johnson's campaign."

At that moment, for the first time in his life, Walker Winslow wanted to hurt his mother. Only two things stopped him. His neck was still hurting way too bad to do his special Chuck Norris spin-kick. And if Laddy Johnson could pitch him through a window, he'd bet Momma could do it, too.

"Walker," Margaret said, "from now on you will see no young woman without my permission. In fact, you will see *only* the young women I present to you. And you will treat all of them like a gentleman. And when the time comes you will marry the girl I choose for you. We will have no more trouble in this family with Winslow men making fools of themselves over women and embarrassing me. Do you understand?"

Momma was towering over Walker when she asked this question.

To his credit, Walker took a step back so he could look her in the eye without having to bend his neck, and said, "No, ma'am, I do not. I will make my own choices. I'm a grown man. Grown as I'll ever be anyway. I'll see who I want and do what I want."

Margaret did not relent. "You have no home, you have no savings, and if you cross me, you'll have no job. I'll put you out on the street."

Walker knew his mother wasn't bluffing, but he didn't care. He straightened his spine and stood taller than he ever had before. Maybe five-five.

He said, "My truck's all mine, free and clear. I got maybe $500 in my pockets. Lots of men made their fortunes starting out with less than that. I'll see you 'round, Momma."

He turned to go, hoping mightily she didn't smack him a good one from behind.

"Walker, you get right back here," Margaret ordered. "You come back here this instant. Walker, you get back here. You'll *starve* without me. You'll die penniless in a month. Walker, you are *not* a man!"

Walker closed the front door of his parents' house behind him with Momma still hollering curses at him. He closed the door gentle-like. The way, he was sure, Chuck Norris would do it.

He got in his truck and started it up. He knew it was too late for him to go to clown school; the Ringling Brothers had shut the place down some years back. But he could try to make his mark in Hollywood. Why not? Laddy Johnson had. And look at all the short guys who'd succeeded out there. Hervé Villechaize, Verne Troyer, Danny DeVito. Heck, what'd any of them have that he didn't?

Still, it wouldn't hurt to have an introduction.

Walker went looking for Lucan Thorn.

Lucan Thorn had decided that Texas was the world's largest open-air loony-bin. He'd thought he'd seen every kind of madman in creation on the streets of New York. Hell, there were colonies of lunatics living *under* the streets of New York. But Texas was a whole new ballgame. It was like the last place left after a nuclear holocaust. A society formed from characters Tennessee Williams had left over from the plays he never got to write: the beautiful, the bestial, the cunning, and the damned.

And this was where Joanna had come to live. Where she'd *returned* to live. The place she called home. Thorn had pursued her for only one reason. Of the half dozen women to whom he'd been married, and the hundreds he'd bedded, Joanna was the one he'd chosen to bear his child. That was why he'd been so upset when she'd come back to Texas; he'd known that was where Laddy Johnson had gone. No leap of imagination was required to think that the two of them would reunite. That's what people did: They retreated to the comfortable and familiar.

Especially once they reached the age where risk-taking ceased to be exciting and became threatening. If you played life hard and fast long enough and had an ounce of brains in your head, you knew you'd pay a high price. So you checked your rear-view mirror, put your turn signal on, and eased out of the fast lane. Maybe you even looked for the exit ramp at some sublime locale where you could stretch out on a sunny beach, enjoy a tall, cool drink, and laugh at all your wicked memories.

The capper, though, was to successfully reproduce. To have a son, maybe a daughter, who would carry your genes forward. Remind people of you. Have your offspring produce yet another generation. And in some distant time when the scholars traced your line they could point to you and say, "This is where the dynasty began."

But none of that would be possible if you chose the wrong mate. The offspring would suffer. And insanity, of course, was hereditary. Which was an important consideration if Joanna, of her own volition, wished to live in this crazy place. He hated to admit it, but maybe she was better off with Laddy Johnson after all. As for Thorn himself, he'd have to go back to his Rolodex and select the next most likely mother of his children.

Thorn's reverie was interrupted by an elbow to his ribs.

Mary Sue Parker told him, "If this is what you call foreplay out in California, it's a little slow for me."

Thorn looked to his right. He saw the reporter for the *Gasoline Beacon* in her natural state. Well, the bikini wax was a token of artifice, but the rest was all youth and firmness and pleasing proportions. Her face was a showcase of symmetry. The eyes burned with intelligence and ruthless ambition. All of which Thorn found compelling. He might, impetuously, have moved Mary Sue to the head of his list of procreative possibilities if she, too, hadn't resonated with the twang of Texas lunacy.

The product of commingling their genes might be James Dean on one hand or Charlie Manson on the other. But neither result would happen from their coupling that day. Thorn had made Mary Sue show him her packet of birth-control pills — and he'd counted the empty slots to make sure she was up to date. As for STDs, they'd simply have to take each other's word that neither of them was at risk.

"What is it you want?" Thorn asked Mary Sue.

She shot him a look. "We're in bed. We're naked. What do you think I want?"

She grabbed hold of the object of her desire in case he was a slow learner. She was relieved and even pleased at his quick response. She hadn't realized how old Thorn was until he took his clothes off. The guy was middle-aged at least and maybe more. Yeah, he dyed the hair on his head and his crotch, but he forgot about under his arms. How the hell old did you have to be anyway before your pits went gray? And then he just lay there next to her like he'd fallen asleep with his eyes open. But now, having him up and running, she knew just what to do and pulled him down on top of her.

But he still didn't get on with it.

He wanted to talk some more.

"What do you want other than sex, Mary Sue? Fame? Money? Adulation?"

Mary Sue simplified things for him. "I want *everything*. If something doesn't taste good, I'll spit it out."

It must have been the right answer, because finally — finally! — she felt him come home to momma. She was having sex with a movie star. Now, it was just a question of how she could parlay things from there.

Mary Sue would have help in that matter. As Joanna Wells had said, Lucan Thorn liked to leave his windows open, and in a tree outside the third-floor hotel suite where Thorn and Mary Sue were knotting their limbs, tongues, and private parts, Kirkly Osgood had the lens of her camera poking through the foliage. She was snapping away, alternating her composition between the artful and the graphic. There were different markets to be served, she reckoned.

In her own way, Kirkly was as intently occupied as the couple in the bed.

Which was why she didn't notice Walker Winslow on the sidewalk below, staring up at her with eyes and mouth both wide open .

Hayley Winslow's mouth hung open as Joanna and Arcelia watched her sleep from the doorway to Laddy's Johnson's bedroom.

Joanna had never seen the room before, but she immediately realized who it belonged to from the picture on the wall of Laddy in his Gasoline High School football uniform. The punk-rock chick with the purplish hair lying in the single bed was a complete stranger. Could this really be Hayley Winslow, the girl who'd once played Maria in *West Side Story?* Joanna would have cast her as Magenta in *The Rocky Horror Picture Show.*

Arcelia knew just who she was looking at, and the expression of disapproval on her face was far more stern than the one Joanna wore.

"*¡Despierte, chica!*" she ordered. Wake up, girl! "*¡Despierte ahora!*" Wake up now!

The figure on the bed responded in the blink of an eye, not only sitting upright but pulling a handgun from under the pillow and pointing it straight at the woman who had so rudely awakened her. Neither Arcelia nor Joanna had time to be frightened because in the next heartbeat Hayley recognized Laddy's mom and tucked the weapon into a pocket of the jacket she was wearing. It was almost like a magic trick. Now you see the gun, now you don't

She gave Joanna a momentary glance and then returned her attention to Arcelia.

"What are you doing here, Hayley?" Arcelia asked. "Here in my son's bedroom."

"Nice to see you again, too, Miz Dominguez." Hayley smiled. Not at the situation, but at the way her voice had automatically reverted to childhood inflections.

"I told you to stay away from Laddy," Arcelia continued, her anger unabated. "I told you after I see you kissing him."

Every muscle in Joanna's body tensed when she heard that newsflash.

Hayley saw Joanna's reaction, and looked at her, still smiling. "Miz Dominguez means a hundred years ago. Onstage. During curtain-calls. Three performances. A little peck or two on the cheek each time. To get the crowd revved up, you know. Or maybe you don't, Miz Wells, if you've only done movies."

Joanna had started to relax until she heard that last little dig. "I've done theater," she told Hayley.

"Then you know. It was no big deal."

"It was a very big deal to me," Arcelia told Hayley.

"Really?" Hayley asked. "I thought maybe the statute of

limitations had run out."

She stifled a yawn, as if bored with the conversation.

Arcelia shook a finger at Hayley. "You come into my house uninvited; you sleep in my son's bed. I do not like this."

Hayley nodded at a key resting on the nightstand. "Laddy invited me. Told me to let myself in. Bunk out on his bed."

Joanna tensed once more, and this time Hayley offered no comforting reassurance.

Arcelia frowned. Started to speak but reconsidered her words. Finally, she said, "You are a grown woman now, Hayley. I cannot tell you what to do. But I can tell you I do not want you in my house. And I hope my son has the sense to stay away from a woman who carries a gun."

Hayley stood up. She'd gone to sleep with her shoes on, so she could be right on her way. But she did pause to tell Arcelia, "I have a permit for the weapon."

"Please go," Arcelia responded. She stepped back, as did Joanna, to give Hayley room to exit.

"Not very Texan of you to disrespect a person's Second Amendment rights," Hayley said.

"Do not come back here, not ever," Arcelia told Hayley.

"At least you're making seeing my own mother seem easier," Hayley answered.

She stepped past Arcelia and Joanna and waved goodbye with her back to them. Joanna watched Hayley go. Evaluated her. Hayley's strangely colored and oddly cut hair she took to be a requirement of some role she was playing. No post-adolescent woman would choose that look because she thought it was flattering. The color certainly didn't go with Hayley's aquamarine eyes. As for the rest of her, she had good shoulders, slim hips and long, toned legs. She walked with an understated fluidity that spoke of dance training or maybe martial arts and pilates. And she carried a gun. All very mysterious and exotic. Sexy, too, damn her.

And Arcelia's vehement treatment of Hayley, that was out of character. There was more behind it than the few little pecks on the cheek Hayley had mentioned.

Had Laddy had a full-blown teenage romance with the daughter of the town's leading family? Had Arcelia found out and put a stop to it before there could be any retribution from the Winslows? And ... oh, God, could Laddy and Hayley still have feelings for each other after all this time?

Joanna had never done a soap opera, but just then she was waiting for a swell of minor-key music from an electric organ and a voice-over announcer saying, "Be sure not to miss our next exciting episode."

CHAPTER SIX

Buck Musgrove glared at Gunther Lomax and suspected a trick.

"Where'd you get them files?" the new chief of police asked the old chief of police. "I've got your office, I mean, my office sealed tight. So where'd you get'em?"

Gunther held a stack of files under his arm. The one Buck didn't have in his grip.

The former chief said, "These are copies I made. For my own protection. Case the ones I kept at work went missin' or somethin'."

Laddy Johnson sat behind his desk at his campaign headquarters. He'd decided not to move into Win-Win's old office until any question of his right to do so had been resolved. He'd dropped by the campaign office to see if Eveleen, in her new capacity as chief of his secret police, had gleaned any intelligence he should have before going home. But she was out, and when the phone rang he had to answer it himself, taking a disturbing call from his mother. Then Buck had come storming in, dragging Gunther along with him.

Buck looked at Laddy and asked, "Is that a crime, Laddy, copying official documents?"

Laddy said, "Xeroxing without a permit? I don't know, Buck. We'll have to ask the city attorney for an opinion."

"That'd be my cousin, Delbert," Gunther said, helpfully.

"God in heaven," Buck exclaimed, "we got a powerful lot of housecleaning to do."

Laddy took a shorter term point of view. "What's in those files that would interest anybody, Gunther? Buck, turn him loose so he can sit down."

Grunting, Buck followed orders and Gunther took a seat, put his files on his lap and rubbed the arm Buck had been squeezing.

The former chief of police leaned forward to confide in the new mayor, "These files are what your prosecutors would call a smoking gun. Only I can't take 'em to Winton Earle on account a he's in these files, if you catch my drift."

Laddy sighed. He'd played the stunt double for a number of villains in legal thrillers and he tried to recall the dialogue for this kind of scene. "Are you saying you have documentary evidence that the district attorney and possibly other elected or appointed officials have committed crimes while in office, even using the powers of those offices to enable the commission of those crimes?"

A look of wonder appeared in Gunther's eyes. "I din't know you was a lawyer," he said.

Laddy shook his head. "I'm not. I just got killed as one in the movies."

Buck said, "Ask him, Laddy, is he one a the other officials in them files."

Laddy looked at the former chief and said, "Gunther?"

Gunther had to clear his throat to try to get the words out. After his second and third attempts at speaking failed, Buck slapped him upside the back of his head.

Wincing, Gunther had no trouble saying, "That there's police brutality."

"We plan to send Buck to an anger management program," Laddy assured Gunther. "But I have to admit my patience is wearing thin, too. Speak your piece, Gunther, or we'll go take a look at the original files in your old office."

"Okay, okay," the former chief said. He plopped his files down on Laddy's desk. "What you'll find in there, written down in black and white, is we was stealing the town blind. Have been for years. I brought my files in to you because I'm afraid Winton and some others will try to make it look like the whole ball a wax was all my doing. It wasn't, so I'm looking for a deal."

"What others?" Buck asked.

"What kind of stealing?" Laddy wanted to know.

Gunther looked from Laddy to Buck and back, not knowing who to answer first. Hoping his instincts were right, he went with Laddy.

But he answered with a question of his own. "Well, what do we have around here that's worth stealing?"

Laddy blinked and said, "You mean oil?"

"Damn right, I do. We've been robbing from the Municipal Field."

Buck drew back his hand to clip Gunther another good one, but Laddy shook his head.

"How much have you stolen?" the new mayor asked.

"Well, we been at it a long time and ..." Gunther had trouble going on. Laddy nodded to Buck who gave Gunther another slap. "Ow, damnit! That hurts."

"How much, Gunther?" Laddy asked.

"I don't know the 'zact amount. But we done filled a lot of tanker trucks."

Hearing that, Buck clenched his fist, but Laddy held up a hand to stop him.

"Let's get to Buck's question," Laddy said. "Who else is involved?"

Gunther hung his head. "Well, there's me, as you might have suspected. An' there's Winton Earle, as I already let on. An' some folks at the field an' the refinery. Their names're all in the files."

"Win-Win?" Laddy asked.

Gunther lifted his head and gave a crooked grin. "You really think he made all that money sellin' trucks? Hell, how you think he got TRS started?"

"Walker?" Laddy asked.

Gunther laughed at that. "Hell, no. Was only a few years ago that boy learnt to take a pee without someone holdin' his wiener for him."

Buck had to choke back a laugh. But Laddy wasn't amused. He wasn't done exploring the extent of the Winslow family's larceny.

"Margaret?" he asked.

Now, Gunther's expression became sly. "Well, the lady is a bookkeeper, ain't she?"

That left only one more person to ask about, and now Laddy was the one who had trouble getting the words out, but he did. "What about *Hayley?*"

That question took Gunther by surprise. Buck, too.

"*Hayley?*" Gunther said. "Nobody's seen hide nor hair of her in years. Her disappearin' was the only thing I ever saw to make Margaret Winslow cry. No, Hayley's not involved."

Gunther reflected a moment. "She had been, smart as she was, I bet we woulda got away with it."

Having raised that thought, Gunther lapsed into a regretful silence.

"Lock him up," Laddy told Buck, "but don't rough him up."

"What're you gonna do?" Buck asked.

"Call the governor. Have him put me in touch with the attorney general or some other prosecutor who doesn't have a finger in this pie." Laddy sighed. "What a mess."

Buck said, "Could be worse."

"Yeah, how's that?" Laddy wanted to know.

"You coulda taken after your daddy an' become president. Think a the shit-piles them suckers in the White House have to clean up."

Buck dragged Gunther off to jail, not having cheered Laddy even marginally.

He picked up the phone and called his mother back.

Walker Winslow was waiting for Kirkly Osgood when she climbed down out of the tree outside of Lucan Thorn's hotel suite. He'd watched Kirkly taking her pictures. At first, he wasn't sure what she'd been photographing. But then he'd heard a familiar moan, followed by a rising shriek, sounds that had once given him goose bumps. Mary Sue. He'd know her bedroom aria anywhere. He'd never felt like more of a man than when he'd heard Mary Sue yip 'n' yelp. Except now she was doing it for someone else. Louder than she'd ever done with him. Which was when Momma's words about Mary Sue giving herself to Lucan Thorn came back to his mind.

Walker knew that Thorn had checked into the Gaslight Castle, the town's only deluxe hotel. That was why he'd come by: to ask Thorn who he should see in L.A. about starting his career in the movies, and to ask could he please have a letter of recommendation. It didn't seem like that big a favor to Walker's way of thinking. After all, the actor had already endorsed Walker for mayor.

Thinking on the present situation a moment, Walker decided it'd be in his interest not to get mad at Thorn for putting his brand on Mary Sue. Instead, he'd seize the camera from the girl in the tree. Then he'd give Thorn back one of the pictures where he had his hindquarters in the air. Walker was sure Thorn would be real grateful for that. He'd be happy to help Walker start his movie career. And every so often, Walker could hand over another picture, and Thorn would be happy all over again.

Why, they'd become the best of pals. Maybe even make some movies together like Newman and Redford. Wouldn't that be great? Walker would show Momma how wrong she was about him.

Except when the girl jumped down from the tree and was standing right there next to him on the sidewalk, he saw she had to be eight inches taller than him and outweigh him by 40 pounds. It seemed damned unfair to Walker that even the girls these days were getting so much bigger than him. Stealing the camera, especially in his current condition, with the damn neck brace and all, was out of the question.

So he tried to buy it from her, saying: "I'll give you $500 for that camera and all the pictures you got in it."

Kirkly laughed at him. "The camera costs $900 by itself; the lens is another $2,000; and the pictures, my God, with what I get for them I just might buy me a ranch, put in my own little lake, and go fishin'."

Walker took all that to mean she was refusing his first offer. "I'll throw in my truck," he said pointing to the shiny new Hummer Gargantua.

Contrary to what Walker had told Momma, the Gargantua was still on the books as belonging to TRS. But he was sure Daddy would have wanted him to have it.

Kirkly gave the Hummer a glance. "It's a nice enough truck, but I'll probably buy one like that for my servants to fetch the mail and groceries."

But having dismissed the offer, Kirkly took a second look at the Hummer and then turned her gaze on Walker, studying him head to toe.

"How'd you get your neck hurt like that?" she asked.

Walker was not about to answer. Instead, he focused on the camera being held casually in Kirkly's left hand. He was trying to decide if he could snatch it and get to his truck before she could catch him.

As Walker pondered, Kirkly asked another question, "Are you the little sumbitch who ran over my cousin Tiny's foot? He said Laddy Johnson grabbed hold a the runt that did that and tossed him through a storefront window. An' then someone else threw him back outside. That'd explain your neck bein' in that plastic wrapper, now wouldn't it?"

Injured or not, Walker realized he better forget about stealing that camera and get ready to defend himself. But first he tried a bluff.

"Girl, don't you know who I am?"

"The little sumbitch who ran over Tiny's foot?"

Walker honestly had no idea what she was talking about. All he remembered about the awful night that Daddy died was racing into to town to kick Laddy Johnson's ass. Only

Laddy an' Buck Musgrove tossed him on his head a couple times and he had no recollection of anything else.

"I'm Walker Winslow," he said.

"Yeah, so?" Kirkly responded.

"My daddy was Edwin Winslow, the dead mayor."

Kirkly looked closely at Walker and started to grin.

"Yeah, yeah. Now, I see it."

"Most folks in town know the Winslows," Walker said.

"I'm not from here," Kirkly informed him. "I'm from over in Blessing. I just moved in with my cousin Tiny last month on account a I don't like Momma's new boyfriend. Him saying I should be posing for pictures 'stead a taking 'em. An' wouldn't I look cute without all my clothes on?"

Hearing that, Walker looked at Kirkly from a new point of view. Most times, he took after women who were no taller than him and who wore heels on their shoes shorter than his. But having the idea planted in his head, he had to admit to himself Kirkly would look cute nekkid as a baby in bathwater. Yeah, the two of them in a whirlpool over at the Public Baths, wouldn't that be fun? Just swimming around her, seeing the sights, it made him want to holler.

Even better than that, her words gave Walker one of his rare useful ideas.

"So this step-daddy a yours — " he started to say.

"Momma hasn't married Daryl, and I pray the sweet Lord she never will."

"Fair enough," Walker allowed. "But the man is still a sleaze, wanting to see you bareass while he's keeping your momma company."

Kirkly gave a grudging nod to that description.

Walker continued, "An' yet there you are up a tree taking pictures of two other people naked and having at it. Now, you could say a big famous celebrity like Lucan Thorn's got it coming. It's a part of his job description."

Kirkly frowned and asked, "How'd you know who I was shooting?"

Walker stood as tall as he could. "This is *my* town. I know what's going on around here. Now, like I said, embarrassing a movie star's one thing, but how about that poor young girl he's with up there? Is she all that much different than you? An' isn't what you just done to her the same as what your momma's boyfriend wanted to do to you?"

The realization that maybe she was as big a shit as Daryl hit Kirkly like a thunderclap.

She thought maybe she could PhotoShop the girl out of the pictures, but, no, that wouldn't work. It'd just leave Lucan Thorn look like he was having sex with the invisible woman. Might be good for a few laughs. *Hey where'd ol Lucan's peter disappear to?* Kirkly couldn't draw the dang thing back in. It was inside the girl; she got PhotoShopped out, it did, too. And a naked star screwing without a girl or a dick, who was going to buy that?

As Kirkly pondered her problem, Walker gave her something else to think about. "That young lady up there, her name's Mary Sue. She used to be my girlfriend." Walker hung his head. "Until Lucan Thorn stole her away."

Hearing those words positively inspired Kirkly. She picked Walker up and kissed him on the lips.

Rising so suddenly into the air and being kissed harder than he ever had in his life, made Walker's head swim. But he still had the self-possession to say, "Hey, put me down!"

Kirkly did, but she led Walker by the hand over to the passenger side of his truck.

"Gimme the keys an' git in," she told him.

Walker obeyed without hesitation. Any woman who could lift him off the ground like that was not to be messed with. Kirkly ran around to the driver's side and slid in behind the wheel. For an awful second, Walker thought she was kidnapping him. But then she handed him her camera and told him not to drop it. Being given such a position of trust reassured Walker.

Kirkly fired up the engine and looked at the gas gauge. "Full tank," she said, "good. An' that $500 of yours, you got it on you?"

"Yeah," Walker said tentatively.

"Good," Kirkly said, pulling away from the curb, "that'll get us where we're going."

"An' where's that?" Walker wanted to know.

"To sell your story. How a heartless movie star stole your woman from you. You, a poor bent-up little crippled fella. We'll get at least a quarter-million dollars for it, maybe a half-million with the pictures an' all. An' what we'll do about Mary Sue, it just come to me. We'll blur her face up is all. So nobody can see what she looks like. That okay with you, Walker honey?"

A half-million dollars was just fine with Walker. Made him want to turn a cartwheel. But Kirkly had the truck already doing 60, and he was wearing his damn neck brace, so he just buckled up his seatbelt instead.

"Sounds good to me," he told Kirkly. "But where we gonna sell my story and your pictures?"

"Boca Raton, Florida. Home of *The National Enquirer*," she told him. "Let's start working on your story right now. We spice it up right, we might get a nice round million."

And so with visions of new-found wealth dancing in his head, Walker Winslow, the heir to the mayor's office, left the town of Gasoline, Texas.

Before going home to face her mother, Hayley Winslow stopped by the Magic Comb to have her hair trimmed and colored. The shop looked the same as the last time she'd seen it, right down to the sparkly linoleum on the floor. And Fleeta Wallis was still there cutting hair.

Fleeta was as blonde as ever though she had to be 60 by now. She was still chewing her Nicorette gum and still wiry-slim at five-nine. But she'd upgraded her breast implants a cup size or two. She recognized Hayley the minute she stepped through the door.

"They always come back," Fleeta said with a grin. "How you, Hayley?"

"In need of help," Hayley said. "You have an opening?"

"So happens I do." Fleeta cast a critical eye on her prodigal client. "I can give you a cut no problem. But I ain't got no grape sody-pop, if you want me to match that color you're wearin'."

"Do you remember my original color?" Hayley asked.

Fleeta sighed. "I remember every follicle I've ever clipped and dipped. Sometimes it keeps me up nights, wonderin' 'bout the way I've spent my life. Come on over to the sink. I'll see if I can't scrub some a that motor oil out of your hair."

Hayley's present haircut including the Tahitian Sunset coloring had cost her 500 euros in Rome. But telling Fleeta that would only make Hayley the butt of jokes throughout town. Just showing her face in the shop was akin to broadcasting that she was back, which was a violation of her orders. And that meant, de facto, that she'd retired from being an undercover agent for the government. Goodbye,

Jazz Janssen. Welcome back, Hayley Winslow.

Thing was, you wanted to leave the company she'd been working for, you were supposed to spend a year, maybe two, at a *retreat* so the currency of any information you carried in your head was devalued. You just up and went off the reservation ... well, she'd never heard of anyone who'd actually done that. Tough luck. Let 'em take her to court.

And if she had to sleep with a gun under her pillow, well, she was doing that anyway.

Fleeta asked, as she was vigorously shampooing Hayley's head, "So what you been up to, darlin', these past twenty years or whatever it's been?"

"Making the world safe for plutocracy," Hayley said.

Fleeta gave Hayley a funny look, but then nodded in understanding. "That's right, you went off to one a them fancy Yankee colleges, din't you?"

"Unh-huh," Hayley said.

"You been home yet?" Fleeta suddenly put a sudsy hand to her chest. "Oh, my Lord, do you know about your daddy?"

Hayley nodded. "I do."

Fleeta said, "Win-Win was a real nice man. I voted for him. I woulda been at the cemetery to see him off if I didn't have a cut 'n' a curl right then. Your daddy, he gave me a great deal on my GMC Suburban last year. Said he wouldn't let nobody but me cut his hair, or Walker's or your momma's. Hey, have you seen your momma yet?"

"Thought I'd get gussied up first," Hayley replied

Fleeta nodded in appreciation of Hayley's wisdom and rinsed her hair.

"You won't have to go home to see Margaret, you know," the stylist said.

"Why not?"

"Well, she'll be here in thirty minutes. Told me she wants her hair colored red."

Hayley sat bolt upright and stared at Fleeta.

"Surprised the daylights outta me, too," Fleeta said. "But don't worry. She don't mean a purply-red like yours. This one's a color I got in stock."

When Laddy called home, Arcelia told him, "Son, you better get home in a hurry. I know I dragged you back here to become the new mayor an' all, an' you're doin' important work, but this is your life I'm talkin' about now an' it really won't wait."

Laddy tried asking once more the question he'd put to his mother the first time she'd called, "Momma, is this about Hayley?"

His mother got all stiff and formal on him as she had before when he'd mentioned Hayley's name. "Ladbrook, I told you I won't discuss this matter on the phone. Now you git on home right now."

Being a dutiful son he did just that. And that was when he saw Joanna's car parked out front. So he was going to have to talk to both of the women in his life about his old friend Hayley. Wouldn't that be just fine and dandy? His only consolation was that the rental sedan that Hayley had been driving was nowhere to be seen. So she would not be directly involved.

Laddy opened the front door of his mother's house. For the first time in his life, he wished that he could have a stunt double stand in for him. Maybe he could give Lucan Thorn a call.

He tried to start things off with a little humor, doing his

best Desi Arnaz impression and calling out, "Luuuucy, I'm hooome!"

Sounded good to him, but when his mother and Joanna appeared from the kitchen neither of them was smiling.

Laddy tried for a laugh once more. "Honest, sheriff, it weren't me; it was that other fella."

Nothing. Not the slightest hint of an upturned lip. Laddy could now sympathize with all the stand-up wannabes who tried open-mike nights at comedy clubs. He might've broken out in flop sweat. But he got mad instead.

Who were these two women, he thought, to give him any grief? His mother had recruited him to come back to Texas and try to get elected mayor. And once he'd run that gauntlet, Joanna had popped up out of the blue and all but assaulted him in a Jacuzzi. He didn't need to take any guff from either of them.

His mother said, "Well, what do you have to say for yourself, Ladbrook?" Both she and Joanna had their arms folded across their chests.

"You mean about Hayley and me?" Laddy asked.

The two women nodded in unison.

Laddy shrugged. "Guess it was just fate. You know, the two of us playing star-crossed lovers onstage."

"And *singing*," Joanna said, her voice filled with incredulity. "That's the part I can't get over: you in a musical."

Laddy said, "It was just the one time, dear. Didn't mean a thing, and I never did it again."

They still didn't laugh, but Laddy did. He liked that last little riff, and still chuckling, he slipped past his two interrogators into the kitchen and pulled a longneck out of the fridge.

"Anyone else care for a beer?" he asked politely.

No one else did. He sat down at the kitchen table and waited. If they joined him, he figured there might be some hope. If they remained in the doorway standing and staring at him, he'd finish his beer and go pack his bags.

Momma sat down first, then Joanna. They both sat on the other side of the table.

"Hayley was sleeping in your bed when we got here," Arcelia told Laddy.

"Mmm-hmm," he replied. "She was tired and I gave her a key."

"You didn't come here with her?" Joanna asked.

Laddy shook his head.

"So she was here all alone?" Joanna followed up.

Laddy looked around the kitchen, craned his neck to get a view of the front of the house. "Doesn't look like she had a party before you two found her."

Arcelia pursed her lips, still unamused. She folded her hands in front of her, took a breath, and told her son. "I never told you this, Laddy, but I spoke to Hayley a long time ago. After the two of you were in that play. I told her to stay away from you."

Any hint of humor now deserted Laddy's eyes. "Well, Mom, she did a real good job. You ought to be proud of her. She stayed away from the time she graduated high school until just yesterday. I hadn't seen her, heard from her, or corresponded with her." Laddy turned to look at Joanna. "And you, sweet thing, you ought to be the last to rush to judgment, seeing you haven't thought it was worth telling me your two-time ex-husband has come to town."

Joanna winced, and Laddy said, "Yeah."

He finished his beer and stood up. "Hayley is my friend," he said. "That's all she is, and for me that's been plenty. She's never made a move on me and I've never made one on her. There are times I honestly can't figure out why not. From my point of view, I guess, I respect her too much. I think she feels the same. That explanation doesn't satisfy either of you, too damn bad."

It seemed things hadn't worked out so well after all, Laddy thought, as he left his mother's house and got in his car. He drove away not knowing where to go. Maybe the best thing to do was see if he could find Hayley. Hope to hell she hadn't up and disappeared again.

Maybe they could get past this mutual respect thing.

CHAPTER SEVEN

Taking the chance that Hayley might have gone back to her childhood home, and that Margaret Winslow wouldn't shoot him dead when he rang her doorbell, Laddy crossed the garden path to the Winslow house. To avoid the vengeance he'd imagined Margaret might wreak on him, he used the knocker instead of the doorbell. The knocker was a somewhat smaller than full-size replica of a Lincoln Navigator.

The knocker was Texas tacky, but it went with the house. The place had to be 10,000 square feet, the facade a mix of pink brick, fieldstone, and redwood. The windows were large and might have flooded the house with natural light but all of them were covered with thick draperies. There was a mansard roof with a madly misplaced turret at one corner of the house, as if the contractor had misplaced his blueprint and grabbed whatever was handy.

The only touch of grace was the landscaping. Someone with an eye for grass, trees, flowers, and shrubs, and how they should be arranged, had been given a free hand and a big budget to work some natural wonders. It was almost enough to distract a person from looking at the house itself.

When Laddy was growing up, though, he had thought the place looked great. No other house in town came close to it in the estimation of a teenager whose only other exposure to architecture was Houston, and nothing up there had knocked him out. But now the only thing Laddy wondered about was how much oil Win-Win and Margaret had to steal to build and maintain this place.

Laddy lifted the knocker and let it fall one more time. Looked like nobody was home. He tried to remember if the Winslows had any domestic help. Seemed like with a place this big and the money the Winslows had, there ought to be someone to answer the door, but nobody came. Laddy turned to go back to his car, wondering where else Hayley might be. He got as far as the end of the garden path when he heard the Winslow's front door open.

He turned to see a gray-haired man wearing a hand-tailored suit standing in the doorway. The guy didn't look like a Winslow or even a Texan to Laddy's eye. He looked like one of those New York money-men who'd sometimes appear on the location of a movie that was going wildly over budget. Those guys were all refined as hell, spoke almost in a whisper, but they were able to put the fear of God into even the most egomaniacal of directors.

Laddy had always wondered how they did that.

The man said to him, "Mayor Johnson, what a happy coincidence. I was just about to call on you. Won't you please come in?"

The guy even sounded like a New York money-man.

"And you are?" Laddy asked.

The man smiled. His teeth were somewhat pointy but

otherwise as perfect as Lucan Thorn's. "My name is Herbert Prescott. I'm an attorney."

"From New York," Laddy said.

Prescott's smile took on a gleam of sincerity. "Why, yes. We're off to a good start. We recognize each other."

The guy seemed too sure of himself and Laddy didn't like that. Didn't like not knowing what his game was. So he asked, "Is Hayley at home, and can she come out to play?"

The question made Prescott blink twice before he regained his balance. Score one small point for Laddy. Prescott told him, "I'm sorry but I've never had the pleasure of meeting Ms. Winslow and, no, she's not at home."

"So who is at home?" Laddy asked. "Mrs. Winslow, Walker?"

"Just me," Prescott answered.

This was all getting very strange. A complete stranger, a lawyer from New York, knew who Laddy was, never having met him, and was alone in the Winslow house, and had invited him in for a chat. If this was a movie and Laddy went into that house, he'd never get out alive.

Laddy asked, "You don't moonlight as a burglar, do you, Mr. Prescott? You do have permission to be in the Winslow home?"

The lawyer nodded. "Of course, I have permission. Technically speaking, though, I don't really need it. The late mayor was a tenant at this address. His wife still is. I represent the corporation that owns the property."

Laddy was dumbfounded. "The Winslows were *renters?*"

"Only recently," Prescott answered. "Our purchase was finalized just last month."

"But why'd they sell?"

Prescott said, "It was part of our deal with them. As you're the new mayor, I was sent to your charming town to strike a new deal with you."

The New York lawyer swung the front door wide and bade Laddy to enter.

He smiled once more and now his teeth seemed pointier than before.

Lucan Thorn and Mary Sue Parker were still in bed in his suite at the Gaslight Castle when Joanna Wells barged in on them. She hadn't bribed her way in; she'd simply announced herself to the manager, said she understood her former husband was in residence, and wished to speak with him. The manager, a fan of many years, who fell in love with Joanna each time she appeared in a new film, said he'd be happy to escort her to Mr. Thorn's suite. And would she be so kind as to give him her autograph? Made out to Emilio, *por favor.*

Life was too easy for a Hollywood star.

Except for one caught in bed with another woman by his wife. Or even his ex-wife.

Thorn had been sitting up in bed, supported by a cluster of pillows, thinking his thoughts when Joanna entered. Mary Sue lay sleeping peacefully next to him, but to be fair she had done most of the work during their exertions.

The outraged wife and the philandering husband was a scene Joanna and Thorn had played all too often in the past. Thorn knew what was to follow wouldn't be pleasant; even so, he wanted to invite Joanna to join him and Mary Sue in bed. At his age, two women might be more than he could handle, but the true artist, he felt, never shrank from a challenge. And at that moment he felt no sign of shrinkage whatsoever.

At least not until Joanna held up a finger in warning and told him, "Not a word, Lucan, not a goddamn word."

Thorn shrugged. A real actor didn't need dialogue to express himself.

But Mary Sue stirred and mumbled, "Who's that? You order more room-service, baby?"

Joanna grimaced. They all called him baby. Every last one of them. She hated that.

She pointed her finger at Mary Sue now. "You, too," she said, "zip your cocksucking lip."

But Mary Sue was as much a Texas girl as Joanna and she raised herself up on one elbow and replied, "Hey, who the hell do you —"

Joanna leaned over and her hand shot out with ophidian speed. She grabbed Mary Sue's cheek between thumb and forefinger and twisted. Mary Sue shrieked. She fell back on the bed, her eyelids fluttered and then she lay still.

Thorn, who always enjoyed a catfight, and had been getting worked up at the prospect of seeing one, was stunned. He stared at Joanna with an open mouth.

"Jesus," he whispered, "did you kill her?"

That made Joanna almost mad enough to slap him, but she didn't want to go too far with the physical violence.

"I pinched her cheek is all," Joanna said. "It's this Filipino thing Erin taught me. She'll wake up in a minute or two and remember not to give me any more sass."

Lucan Thorn felt himself shrivel as he imagined Joanna doing that killer pinch to his private parts. She did it down there and it might well be fatal. And if Joanna had learned this Asian martial arts stuff from Erin de la Fuente, Thorn was certainly going to forget any notion of trying to seduce the woman. But ...

But then Lucan Thorn put two pieces of a puzzle together.

Joanna was developing a movie on Erin's life; and Erin was teaching Joanna self-defense techniques. Prepping Joanna to play a part.

Thorn said, "You're going to play Erin de la Fuente in the movie you're developing."

Joanna looked at him as if he was a simpleton. "Gee, you think?"

It hadn't occurred to Thorn that with Joanna's Yellow Rose of Texas appearance she would play a Latina. But why not? She'd been brilliant as the gray-haired, wrinkled, doughy Marilyn Kendricks in *Desperate Hours*. Why not play against type again? She could very well win her Oscar this time around. Assuming Meryl didn't have the lead role in a drama again.

Thorn told Joanna, "You know, I think you'd be great in the part."

She hadn't come to be flattered by her former husband; she'd come to confront him. To threaten him. To cast him off. Be that as it may, she still respected him as an artist, and when it came to hearing praise from him, she had no defense.

"Thank you, Lucan," she said. "I appreciate that, even if you are a bastard."

Thorn grinned, and he'd always had a killer grin.

"Lucky for you I am," he said, "because I've done a bit of snooping on Erin's story, of course, and I know that her ex-husband was a bastard, too. She beat the hell out of him, I heard, and that's why she had to flee Mexico. Now, I know you're mad at me, Joanna, and you have every right to be, but, honestly, who would be better in the part of Erin's husband than me?"

Joanna had to laugh. Of all the *chutzpah*. She catches him in bed with another woman, after she knows he's come to Texas to make trouble for her, and he turns it into an opportunity to pitch himself for the co-starring part in her new movie.

"I don't think so, Lucan," she told him.

Not the least deterred, he gave her another grin. He even took one of the pillows from behind his back and put it over Mary Sue's head. Not the most considerate thing to do to Mary Sue, but a peace offering to Joanna nonetheless.

"Think about it, Joanna," he said. "We've got the chemistry, we've got the anger, and in the end you get to beat the shit out of me. What could be more fun than that?"

Maybe nothing, Joanna had to admit to herself.

That was, if she wasn't pregnant with Laddy's baby ...

And if Laddy was going to dump her for Hayley Winslow ...

And if getting together with Lucan a third time didn't make her certifiably crazy.

She said, "Maybe, Lucan. That's as far as I can go."

Joanna sighed and headed for the door. Things hadn't gone at all the way she'd planned. Before she left the suite, she called out, "Get the pillow off that poor girl's face before she suffocates."

Thorn flipped the pillow off Mary Sue, but he was already calling his agent, Beeb Bidwell, to tell him to push Thorn's participation in Joanna's project as hard as he could.

"You tell anyone else you're back in town?" Fleeta Wallis

asked Hayley Winslow as she applied chestnut hair coloring to Hayley's hair. Hayley thought her natural color was somewhat darker than that, but she honestly couldn't remember.

"No," Hayley lied, "you're the first."

Hair-dressers were naturals at hearing notes of duplicity in their clients' voices, but Hayley had been lying to people in life-and-death situations for almost 20 years. If she couldn't fool the experts, she'd have died in some Middle Eastern dungeon years ago.

"Then you don't know Laddy Johnson's back?" Fleeta asked.

"Back?" Hayley said, continuing her deception. "Where'd he go?"

Fleeta paused in her work to look Hayley in the eye. "You don't know he went to Hollywood? Became the most famous stuntman since ... well, whoever the hell a famous stuntman is." Fleeta went back to work while regaling Hayley with stories of Laddy's career. She made it out to be far more colorful than Laddy's own modest description of how he'd kept busy.

What interested Hayley the most was Fleeta's depiction of Laddy's thwarted romance with Joanna Wells. Hayley had actually seen one of Joanna's early movies, *Honeymoon for One*. The story was about a young woman engaged to be married whose fiancé died in an auto accident on the eve of their wedding. After the funeral of her beloved, she decided to go on the honeymoon trip to Hawaii they had planned and paid for. On the flight to the Islands, she was seated next to a charming guy who was sensitive enough to realize she was hurting and not hit on her. They simply shared a pleasant conversation. Once in the tropical paradise, though, she was approached by all sorts of men, both tourists and locals.

By dealing with them, she learned who she wouldn't be looking for if she ever got over her broken heart. In the end, it was the beauty and the renewal of nature, and the hope that her lost love was now a part of the "bigger picture" of fantastic sunsets and blue ocean that helped her heart begin to heal. On the plane ride home, of course, she was again seated next to the nice guy she met on the way out. And this time maybe they would be able to carry their conversation a bit farther.

Hayley could see how Laddy could have fallen in love with someone like that. Except the woman in the movie was a fictional character, grieving but flawless, and larger than life. The Joanna Wells that Hayley had seen at Arcelia Dominguez's house was mundanely real: insecure, jealous, and smaller than Cinemascope.

But who was Hayley, with all her faults, to criticize anyone? Joanna Wells probably didn't have any blood on her hands. At least not more than metaphorically. Having spent years on a rollercoaster ride through hell, Hayley's warped judgment was that Laddy should've killed Lucan Thorn for coming between him and Joanna.

Of course, thoughts like that were among the reasons that had abruptly pushed her out of the covert agent business. She might have to become a Catholic just so she could find someone to whom she could confess her sins; someone to ask God if maybe he could, please, forgive her.

"You know," Fleeta told Hayley with a wistful smile, "I've thought about you over the years, wondering what you'd got up to. And most of the times I thought of you, I thought of Laddy right along with you. The two of you in that play. You 'n' Laddy. Tony 'n' Maria."

Romeo and Juliet, Hayley thought. A love that just

wasn't going to happen.

"Oh, look," Fleeta said, "here comes your momma."

Laddy sat in the living room of the Winslow house, not really caring for the Texas Ostentatious décor, and asked Herbert Prescott, "Is that how much you paid Win-Win?"

The New York lawyer had just offered Laddy a staggering amount of money to get behind big oil's effort to buy the town's oil field and refinery. Prescott was sipping scotch neat from a piece of the Winslow's cut crystal. He'd asked Laddy if he'd like a drink, but Laddy had declined. He was pretty sure he could take the lawyer if they got into a physical tussle, or at least break free from his clutches and get outside where he could yell for help. But relying on his movie background, Laddy knew that characters like Prescott were never above slipping a mickey to the gullible.

Prescott answered Laddy, "It would be impolitic of me to discuss our business dealings with Mayor Winslow. Each offer a business makes is done within a specific context. While one situation might be similar to another, no two are identical."

Laddy grinned. "Makes comparison shopping tough."

"Yes, it does," Prescott admitted with a smile of his own. "But you needn't worry that you're being shortchanged. My offer to you is not only comparable to the one Mayor Winslow accepted, it's actually a bit higher."

"Even with buying Win-Win's house thrown into the bargain?" Laddy asked.

Prescott responded, "We'd be happy to give you a very good price for your house in California."

Which was the lawyer's way of letting Laddy know how

closely he'd been checked out. Prescott undoubtedly had already been authorized to pay a high enough price for Laddy's house that he couldn't reasonably refuse. Come to that, Prescott probably wouldn't have taken Laddy as a serious bargainer if he hadn't raised the issue.

"Thanks, anyway," Laddy said, "but I've always liked that house, and I know it doesn't have termites."

"So do we," Prescott responded, showing off a little now. He got up to freshen his drink.

Laddy looked at the cut of the lawyer's suit. It showed no sign of a bulge that would reveal the presence of a gun. But an experienced tailor would know how to cut a suit to hide a weapon. What was much harder to do was walk around carrying a gun and look like you weren't. An FBI agent who'd been a technical advisor on one of his movies had taught Laddy the signs to look for. Far as Laddy could tell, Prescott wasn't packing. Not a gun, anyway.

He might have a knife up his sleeve. The FBI guy had raised that possibility, but before he could give Laddy a lesson in knife detection a guy like Prescott had come along and cut the movie's budget, laying off the technical advisor.

His drink replenished, Prescott went back to his seat opposite Laddy.

"What about Walker?" Laddy asked. "He's demanded a do-over on the election, and I said okay. What if you pay me and he becomes mayor? Your deal with Win-Win hold for him, too?"

"Young Mr. Winslow has had a change in career plans," Prescott informed Laddy.

For one horrible moment, Laddy thought that Prescott had had Walker killed. Not that the twerp wasn't likely to die young in any case, but his demise ought to be the result of a street fight. Not from a cold-blooded assassination.

Prescott read the concern on Laddy's face and explained, "Walker Winslow only recently left town in the company of a young woman by the name of Kirkly Osgood."

Tiny's cousin, Laddy remembered.

The lawyer continued, "The two of them were discussing with great animation how much money they would make from selling photos and a story of the actor, Lucan Thorn, having sex in a suite at the Gaslight Castle. A tabloid newspaper in Florida was mentioned as a potential buyer."

Concern still filled Laddy's face but now the reason was different.

"Who was Thorn having sex with?" he asked.

"Young Mr. Winslow said it was his girlfriend," Prescott answered.

For a crazed moment, Laddy had wondered if Walker and Joanna had ever ... Nah, not Joanna. She never took up with anyone who wasn't already a household name. Except him, of course. And Walker, he was tight with that girl reporter from the *Beacon*, Mary Sue Parker.

"Mr. Johnson," Prescott said, interrupting Laddy's reverie. "Do you think we might conclude our business?"

Laddy stood up and looked at the lawyer. He had to give Prescott credit. If he knew all those details about Walker leaving town with Kirkly, he was running some full-press, high-tech operation here. He was probably recording every word Laddy had said inside the Winslow house. Probably on video, not just audio. But Laddy hadn't done or said anything incriminating, so a fat lot of good that would do him. And Prescott didn't know that Hayley had come back to town. So while the lawyer was good, he wasn't perfect.

"I've got some thinking to do, Mr. Prescott," Laddy said.

The lawyer also rose to his feet. "I'm prepared to offer an additional 10 percent if you sign the papers right now."

Laddy shook his head.

"Very well," Prescott conceded. "Then the original offer stands, but only until midnight tomorrow."

Laddy said, "I see."

A noncommittal statement at best. The lawyer tried to reassure him. "You would be exposing yourself to no legal jeopardy, Mr. Johnson. You are not yet sworn in as mayor. You would simply be acting as our advocate."

"Your shill is more like it, Mr. Prescott.

The lawyer shrugged. "As I've already indicated, we're willing to pay you quite handsomely. And I've discovered over the years that Texans are a pragmatic lot when it comes to balancing financial rewards with qualms of conscience."

Laddy said, "We've had our share of crooks, that's for sure. You'll have to excuse me now, Mr. Prescott."

Laddy left then, feeling greatly relieved when Prescott didn't pull a knife and stick it in his back. But by the time he got behind the wheel of his car he had only one thought in mind: Where could he find Hayley Winslow?

"Mother," Hayley said, "are you all right?"

Fleeta stood next to Hayley, alternately beaming at one Winslow and then the other.

For her part, Margaret had taken one look at her daughter and done a fine imitation of Lot's wife, Edith, after she peeked back at the city of Sodom and was turned into a pillar of salt. With Margaret's white hair and all the blood drained from her face, the resemblance was uncanny.

Hayley stepped forward and caressed her mother's cheek.

It felt cold beneath her hand, and Hayley saw her mother's eyes glazing over. Margaret was clearly going into shock. Not knowing what her mother's underlying health was at the moment, Hayley didn't want to let the condition deepen. She gathered a fold of her mother's skin between her thumb and forefinger and, using the same technique Joanna Wells had used on Mary Sue Parker, she gave a sharp twist.

Margaret Winslow reacted as if she'd been struck by lightning: she went up on her toes; her arms shot out; her mouth grew round; her eyes bulged; and her hair stood on end.

Fleeta Wallis thought Hayley had just killed her mother and said, "Sweet Jesus, save us all!"

The 21st century being New Testament times, God had more mercy on Margaret than he'd had on Edith. Salt no more, she settled back into her shoes and said, "Hayley, is that really you?"

Hayley nodded. "It's me, Momma."

Margaret smiled warmly. For all of one second. Then a snarl entered her voice.

"You *abandoned* me, Hayley. You left me to contend with your father and Walker all by myself. Now your daddy's dead, and Walker's run off. All hell's busting loose. And you finally come back to say howdy-do. All these years, I worry about you being dead, and now you even take that away from me. Where have you been, girl?"

"Keepin' the world safe from plutockersy," Fleeta said, trying to be helpful.

The look Margaret directed at the hairdresser drove her from her own salon, leaving the two Winslow women to sort out their reunion by themselves.

"What did she mean by that?" Margaret demanded.

"It was just a little joke I made," Hayley answered. "Not the usual one. Mostly what I say when people ask what I do is, 'I'll tell you, but then I'll have to kill you.'"

"Are you threatening me, young lady?" For all her bluster, there was a note of fear in Margaret's voice, and her cheek, where Hayley had pinched her, still hurt like the dickens.

"No, Momma, I'd never do that. You want the truth, I was doing what a lot of young Americans have been doing these past few years. Bumping off foreigners for Uncle Sam. I just came back on compassionate leave to see Daddy tucked away in his box. Only getting back to America, and to Texas, I suddenly realized I could use a long spell of not killing anybody, so I'm going to retire from the business."

Margaret was stunned by her daughter's confession, but also somewhat pleased.

"You were an assassin?" she asked.

Hayley nodded. "That and a whore. A drug dealer. An arms runner. A jazz singer."

Except for the singing part, Margaret thought of how many times she could have used someone with Hayley's résumé over the years.

Still, the little bit of maternal instinct Margaret had left in her made her ask, "Why, Hayley, why?"

Hayley looked her mother straight in the eye and replied, "I guess things started going south for me back when I learned that big secret you and Daddy were keeping."

The list of secrets Win-Win and Margaret had kept would run the length of the state, but she knew just which one her daughter meant. Once again, Margaret stood stock-still. Only this time Hayley didn't pinch her.

She went to a sink, rinsed her hair, and toweled it off. Most of the new color had taken, but there were still streaks of Tahitian Sunset here and there. Not exactly what she'd been hoping for, but maybe she'd start a new look: mostly normal with moments of insanity.

She left the shop without saying goodbye to her mother.

Unable to find Hayley after an hour of searching their old high school haunts, Laddy went to the mayor's office to attend to city business. If Herbert Prescott's information was correct and Walker had left town with Kirkly Osgood to pursue a career in yellow journalism, Laddy had to figure he would be the next mayor of Gasoline, Texas. That being the case, he had to start acting in the town's best interests. Assuming he could figure out what they were.

He called his new chief of police, Buck Musgrove, and his new chief of the secret police, Eveleen Nellis, and told them to round up everybody who had been involved in any way, shape, or form with the looting of the Municipal Field and have them brought, forcibly if necessary, to the Town Council chambers. That space had a maximum occupancy of 300 people, but when the town's high school football team, the Oil Barons, had won the sectional championship and was given the key to the city and a day off of school, they'd packed 502 fans into the room.

Laddy sincerely hoped the number of people stealing the town's natural resources from their neighbors didn't exceed that number. It didn't, but it came close.

There were three shifts of workers from both the oil field and the refinery, every cop in town above the rank of sergeant, soon-to-be-former D.A. Wynton Earle, three of his assistants, the board of trustees of the Municipal Field, the CEO of the independent accounting firm that audited the field's books, and six of his underlings, and thanks to Eveleen's meticulous snooping, three mistresses of crooked bigshots who were cut in on the pilferage by their sugar-daddies.

Laddy looked at the sorry collection of thieves from the mayor's chair, centrally positioned behind the horseshoe shaped desk at which the town council deliberated. Half of his fellow elected officials were not sitting adjacent to him because they, too, were seated among the larcenous, but with Laddy voting they still had a quorum. The exits from the room were guarded by resentful patrol officers who'd lacked the seniority to be included in the crime. They were in the mood to shoot any selfish bastard who tried to escape.

Buck strode over to Laddy and bent over so they could speak quietly.

"That's all of them," Buck said, "except for you know who."

Laddy gave him a look. "Margaret Winslow's on the lam?"

Buck shrugged. "She's not at home, not at TRS, not shopping anywhere in town. She had stopped into the Magic Comb, but she left before Fleeta could color her hair."

The very notion amazed Laddy. "Margaret Winslow was going to color her hair?"

"Well, Fleeta was going to do it for her," Buck said, "make it bright red."

Laddy couldn't believe it.

"I know," Buck agreed, "it'd be like seeing Willie Nelson with a crewcut. And that's not all. Your old girlfriend Hayley Winslow's come back to town. She was talkin' to her momma at the salon. Fleeta stepped out to give them their privacy. When she come back, they was both gone."

Laddy closed his eyes and took a deep breath. Hayley's meeting with his mother had been less cordial than the siege of the Alamo; he could only imagine how forgiving Margaret would be of her prized daughter's mysterious 20-year absence. He let his breath out and opened his eyes.

"You feelin' okay?" Buck asked.

"Just dandy. How many cops you got left patrolling the streets of our fair town?"

"Six," Buck said. "They was the only ones left that wasn't crooked, and I thought we better have somebody with badges out there on the streets. 'Specially, when folks get wind of what the bunch in here has been doin'."

Laddy nodded and said, "Okay, this is what you do. Station one cop at the Winslow home, one at TRS, and one at the Gaslight Castle. Any of them sees Margaret, he's to arrest her immediately. And don't let any of these boys be bullied by her. They're to cuff her, read her rights to her, put her in their car, and bring her straight to me. She's not to be allowed to talk to anyone, not even a lawyer, not until she sees me. Are we clear on all that?"

"You care to tell me what you're thinkin'?" Buck asked.

"There's a New York lawyer named Herbert Prescott in town. We do not want Margaret talking to him."

Buck decided to leave it 'til later to ask why not. Instead he asked, "You want me to leave my three remaining cops on regular patrol?"

"No. Have them check out every bar in town. Even the dives. Maybe Margaret's having herself a drink somewhere."

Seeing Margaret Winslow as a barfly was beyond Buck's imagining, but then so was picturing her with red hair.

"Things are getting real crazy around here," he said, straightening up.

"Yeah, and just wait 'til the price of gas goes up," Laddy replied.

Joanna Wells was back at her ranch, *La Casa de Buena Suerte*. While Laddy had been looking all over town for Hayley Winslow, Joanna had been looking for him. With an equal lack of success. Stars who could open a movie on the strength of their names were not used to chasing down the objects of their affection. Well, not most of them. And every last one of them got highly irate when their desires were frustrated in any way. By the time Joanna stormed through her front door, she was ready to break pottery. Preferably over Laddy Johnson's head.

Being denied that pleasure only irritated her further. She clenched her fists at her sides, drummed her heels into the parquet, threw her head back, and shrieked. This tantrum produced two results: it rid Joanna of all manner of negative energy, and it drew an audience.

Erindira de la Fuente stood in the doorway of the living room, looking at her employer with a calculating eye: Was Joanna in pain, or merely behaving as a spoiled child?

Deciding it was the latter, Erin said, "You have frightened the staff."

Thinking of the household domestics as so many mice timidly peering around corners gave Joanna a moment of amusement and she smiled.

Erin shook her head and added, "And undoubtedly you have disturbed Master Tu's serenity."

That wouldn't do. Hop Tu was the only person she trusted to do *feng shui* for her.

"Please go to him and say I'm sorry. And tell him I'll have

a plane chartered for him within the hour to take him back to Hong Kong."

Erin stayed right where she was, giving her employer a dubious look.

"The wedding's off," Joanna said.

"*¿Por que?*" Erin asked. Why?

"I don't wish to discuss it," Joanna replied.

Erin took a seat at one end of a long sofa in the living room. She waited no more than five seconds before Joanna sat at the other end. Maybe another five seconds before the star started to spill her guts. This wasn't the first time Erin had helped Joanna through an emotional crisis.

"Laddy's been cheating on me," she said. "With an old girlfriend."

"You have seen this for yourself?" Erin asked.

"I've seen the girlfriend in his bed." Joanna recounted the story of finding Hayley Winslow in Laddy's bed at Arcelia Dominguez's house.

"So this old girlfriend was in the bed alone," Erin said. "Then she left. After she was gone, Mr. Johnson came home. He said nothing had ever happened between the two of them, and —"

"That's what men do: They lie," Joanna proclaimed.

"Most, perhaps," Erin conceded. "Most women, too. But you, while you were living with Mr. Johnson, you left to make a movie and came back engaged to *Señor* Thorn."

Joanna stiffened and asked, "And your point is?"

Erin said, "Perhaps you simply suspect Mr. Johnson of doing what you have done."

Joanna got to her feet and glared at Erin. "I've been very good to you, Erin. Generous to a fault. I'm going to make a *movie* about your life. And this is how you thank me?"

Erin remained seated but in no way overshadowed. "I show my gratitude, Joanna, by being the only person who will be honest with you." She frowned. "No, that is not quite right. I'm sure Mr. Johnson is honest with you, too. And you must like that or you would not come back to him."

Joanna reddened with renewed anger. "I did *not* come back to Laddy Johnson. I came back to Texas. But I'm done with that now. I'm selling the ranch."

Erin nodded. "Very well. I will buy it from you."

Joanna continued her rant. "I'm selling the Bel-Air estate, too. I'll move to Manhattan; buy a summer home in the Hamptons."

Erin examined her manicure. As a martial artist, she could never have long nails, but she liked to keep her cuticles neatly trimmed and covered with a clear polish. Beyond that, looking at her nails was a clear signal to Joanna that she was bored.

So the star adroitly changed direction. "What do you mean you'll buy the ranch?"

"I like it here," Erin said. "I'll give you a fair price."

As her personal secretary, Joanna paid Erin $2,000 per week. A nice income, but hardly enough to buy 500 acres and a large house just outside of Austin.

"How will you pay?" Joanna asked.

"With the money I make from our movie," Erin replied.

"The movie hasn't been shot," Joanna said. "It hasn't taken in dollar one at the box office. And who's to say I won't just shelve the project?"

Erin stood up, took Joanna's hands, sat the both of them back down so their knees were touching. She said, "I want you to play me in the movie. You are the best actress for the role. You have come to know me, to understand what hap-

pened to me. But, *chica*, if you do not do it, I will find someone else. You must remember that if *for any reason* you let
more than one month go by without making substantive
progress in completing the project, I can buy the screenplay
from you for 25¢ on the dollar and set up my own deal."

With everything else going on in her life, and primarily
thinking of Erin as her employee, Joanna had forgotten she
was also her business partner and a Harvard MBA. Erin had
been the one who'd drawn up the contract between them for
the project, and Joanna had blithely signed it without running it past any of her business people. Joanna had a copy of
the agreement, but Erin had the original. Jesus.

"Beeb Bidwell has already called," Erin told Joanna. "He
is pushing for *Señor* Thorn to play German. He is trying to
get on my good side, so I will persuade you to let your ex-
husband play my ex-husband. If I buy the script from you,
Mr. Bidwell will help me set up my own company to make
the movie, no?"

Joanna thought, Yes, he would, the bastard. "Is the ranch
the only thing you want, Erin?" she asked. "Or do you want
a pound of flesh, too?"

"You are skinny enough as it is, *señorita*. What I want is
for you to be happy. If Mr. Johnson has been with another
woman, forgive him, and win him back. After all, by agree-
ing to marry you, he has already said that he forgives you. I
have no hope of reconciliation with the man I once loved.
You are much luckier than me."

Joanna felt her eyes moisten.

"I ... I just don't know, Erin. Laddy and me, we get so
close, but things never seem to work out. And every time I
think I've put Lucan behind me forever, here he comes
again."

Erin was tempted to say the devil is always like that, but she only told Joanna, "You must decide, of course, but if I can help in any way, I will."

D.A. Wynton Earle was the only person at Laddy's gathering in the Town Council chambers wearing both handcuffs and leg irons. Neither of these indignities kept him from standing and threatening the mayor-elect.

"You better get your laughs in now, Laddy Johnson," Earle said, "because soon enough the worm will turn and you'll be the one in irons and I'll be the one putting you in prison for a long, *long* time. I'm still the district attorney around here, boy."

Earle was a year younger than Laddy, so calling him boy was not only politically incorrect, it was an affront to an elder, too. In rebuttal, Laddy turned to his chief of secret police and said, "Eveleen, will you bring in our star witness, please?"

Eveleen, delighting in the theatrics of hardball politics, had that witness at the ready. She opened a door at the rear of the room and dragged in former Chief of Police Gunther Lomax. He was in cuffs and leg restraints, too. She let everyone get a good look at him and then shoved him offstage and shut the door, a prop to be used and then put away.

Laddy opened a leather-bound notepad in front of him.

"You might want to sit down now, Wynton," Laddy told the D.A. "What I'm about to say might weigh on you more than all that county jewelry you've got on."

The prosecutor tried to hang tough, but lasted only a few seconds. He knew that bastard Lomax had ratted him out. Him and everyone else, most likely. He took his seat.

Laddy cast his gaze on those gathered before him and began, "The way I understand it, people in law enforcement, when they're after a criminal enterprise, like to start by getting a little fish to tattle on a bigger fish. They take things a step at a time until they get the kingfish at the top. Well, this time things didn't work out quite that way. This time one of the bigger fish started talking first and gave us the other big fish and a whole lot of smaller ones. All in all, it's still a good deal from a lawman's point of view. At least that's what the fella I talked to in the state attorney general's office told me."

The mayor-elect now directed his attention at D.A. Earle. "You should be particularly worried, Wynton. They tell me crooked prosecutors don't do well behind bars."

Laddy's words hit the D.A. like a kick in the teeth. He jumped to his feet, jangling his chains, and whined, "I know more than that damn flatfoot Lomax. I kept records. I can help you convict everybody here. I want a deal!"

A refinery worker seated behind Wynton Earle spat and hit the prosecutor in the back of the head with a loogie that was composed in equal parts of chewing tobacco and brown phlegm. It clung to Earle's hair and everybody got a good laugh. But Laddy tapped his gavel and quieted them down. He didn't want things getting out of hand.

He had an officer take Earle out of the room to get cleaned up, but promised him nothing for his offer of cooperation. It was good to know, though, that a second paper trail of the whole rotten scheme existed.

He said to the remainder of his audience, "You can already see how things will go. Rats will desert the sinking ship to try and save themselves."

The blue-collar guy who'd just given up his chew stood and told Laddy, "Yeah, and you'll take all the big-shot rats, let them make deals, and put us poor folks in the slammer."

Laddy sat back and just looked at the guy. Wondered if he should give him a George Clooney stare, a Viggo Mortensen stare, or even a Johnny Depp stare. He'd done stunts for all those actors — had to scrunch down some to pass for Depp — and they all had great stares. In the end, he just went with his own cold-eyed scrutiny. Didn't take 15 seconds before the refinery worker looked away and sank back to his seat.

Laddy asked, "Is there anyone else here who wants to cry poor after he's been ripping off his friends and neighbors for years and years?"

Every head save one bowed down in shame. That improbably red-haired bouffant belonged to one of the floozies who'd been hauled in with her corrupt boyfriend. She looked right at Laddy and raised her hand like a school-girl. He acknowledged her with a nod.

She stood up and said in a piping voice, "I'm Merrilee Tompkins, and I didn't steal nothin' from nobody. I was workin' check-out in the Baytown Wal-Mart up 'til last month and I just got here. If I'da known Sherman was a big crook ... well, you can bet I woulda got somethin' outta him worth gettin' locked up for, 'cause he sure ain't no bargain in the sack. Even with his damn Viagra."

Laddy laughed along with everyone else, except Sherman Myerson, the CEO of the accounting firm that was supposed to audit the Municipal Field's books. Teach him you didn't want to value shop for your mistress. Or your Viagra.

With another rap of his gavel, Laddy calmed things down again.

"Okay," he said. "that's enough comic relief. What I want to know now is how much oil the sorry lot of you stole and how much is left. In other words, at the current rate of consumption, how much time do we have before Gasoline, Texas becomes Out-of-Gas, Texas? Is there someone here who can tell me that?"

Sherman Myerson forced himself to his feet and gave a glum recitation of the numbers. The Municipal Field after three-quarters of a century of exploitation for local use had been down to 50% of its proven reserve. Then back in the early '80s when the looting of the field started, the rate of depletion became far more acute. It wasn't so bad at first, but when people started getting a taste for the extra money they were hauling in, the pressure to steal more increased. Greed had proved to be as addictive as heroin.

"So how much oil is left?" Laddy demanded.

"Maybe enough to last five more years, we all keep driving big SUVs," Myerson said. "And we stop stealing, of course."

"Yeah, well, you can count on that second part," Laddy told him.

The mayor-elect took a moment to give everyone time to repent their misdeeds, and to try to figure out a thing or two for himself. He'd been back in town long enough to see that it hadn't changed all that much since he was a kid. The chain-stores had gone from Woolworth's to Best Buy and the like. The high-school had a new football field and bleachers. But other than that the infrastructure hadn't been upgraded much. The housing stock was much the same; precious few McMansions had been built. There were new trucks parked in driveways but there were no big motorboats and not even that many Harleys. How the hell had all these people been spending their ill-gotten gains? Laddy didn't see them all salting it away in Swiss accounts.

To help solve the mystery, he said, "You know, whatever else happens to all of you in the way of punishment, you're going to have to give back the money you stole, every last penny, and there'll likely be fines to pay, too."

Laddy's words caused a wave of fear so strong he could smell it. People looked at one another with dread on their faces, and some of them began to weep.

"What?" Laddy asked. "Please don't tell me you spent it all. I've seen damn few signs of high living around here."

Hank Knackman, a trustee on the Municipal Field's board of directors got unsteadily to his feet.

"There's some money left," he said. "Maybe it could go to paying some fines, but there's not nearly as much as you might think."

"Why not?" Laddy asked.

Knackman had a hard time trying to force the answer past his lips. Finally, he said, "We all thought that we shouldn't start buying so much stuff we'd set other folks to wondering where we got our money from. You know, if a whole group of people in town started spending like kings, their neighbors would be bound to notice and start talking. So we thought the safe thing to do would be to invest our money as a group."

"And?" Laddy asked with a sinking feeling.

"And we did," Knackman said. "Invest the money."

"In what?" Laddy asked, praying it was anything but —

Hank Knackman said the very name he feared: "Enron."

CHAPTER EIGHT

Laddy supervised the loading of all the oil thieves into buses the governor had sent from the state Department of Corrections. The only exception was Merrilee Tompkins; she was sent home to Baytown to see if she could get her job at Wal-Mart back. She hadn't receive any considerations of value that couldn't be attributed to Sherman Meyerson's legitimate income, and by her own testimony she hadn't gotten "that poor little limp thing a Sherm's into any place the law might object to." All the others would be locked up down in Victoria — hometown of wrestling superstar Stone Cold Steve Austin — pending their arraignments and further processing through the criminal justice system.

The governor had agreed with Laddy that getting the wrongdoers out of Gasoline might be the only thing to prevent them from being lynched once word of the theft got out. As Laddy and Buck Musgrove watched the buses and their escort of Texas Rangers disappear to the south in the dark of night, the mayor-elect felt greatly saddened.

He shook his head and said to Buck Musgrove, "*Enron.*

If that isn't just perfect, I don't know what is."

"Big fish eats the little fish," Buck agreed. "Big crook swindles the little crook."

"Five more years, everyone around here will be riding bicycles," Laddy opined.

"More likely paying, what, five or six dollars for a gallon of gas like the rest of the country," Buck countered. "Gas gets too high, though, bicycles might start looking good. We can change the town's name to Ten-Speed, Texas. Raise us a crop a new Lance Armstrongs."

Buck clapped Laddy on the shoulder. "Those're worries for another day. You want me to put such cops as we've got left around here back on regular patrol?"

"Yeah," Laddy said, "the ones that don't need to go home and sleep."

"What're you gonna do?" Buck asked. "And what about Margaret Winslow? I can keep looking for her, if you want."

Laddy said, "Just go over to the Gaslight Castle. There's nowhere else in town the likes of Herbert Prescott would spend the night. Camp out in the lobby and stay between Margaret and Prescott. Don't let them talk. That's all I want for now."

This time Buck asked, "You gonna tell me why?"

Laddy answered without getting into details. "The future of this town might depend on those two being kept apart."

Once Buck drove off, Laddy tried to think where he should go. He didn't want to go to his mother's house. Didn't want to sack out in Win-Win's old office. Eveleen might have a sofa-bed she could let him use, but that didn't appeal either. He felt dispossessed in the place of his birth. What held the most appeal was sleeping in his own bed in his home in the San Fernando Valley — but that was a helluva long drive, he had renters in his house with another six months on their lease, and there was unfinished business for him to attend to right there in Texas.

Such as working things out, or breaking things off, with Joanna. The latter, of course, would be a lot harder to do if she turned out to be pregnant with his child. Given his own history, Laddy didn't feature being an absentee father. More likely he'd smother his son or daughter with so much attention they'd move to Australia just to get away from him.

But he didn't want to talk to Joanna right now when he might lose his temper and do or say something stupid just to bleed a little pressure off his brain. When he talked to her, he wanted to be cool. Dispassionate. Loving, if he could manage that.

So he got into his car and went looking for Hayley Winslow again. He thought maybe she went to take a look at Texas Rolling Stock. Hayley'd be able to appreciate the irony. Win-Win selling trucks that needed an oil well apiece to keep their tanks full at the same time his thievery was sucking the Municipal Field dry.

The lights were all on when Laddy arrived at the glossy truck dealership, pennants stood high in a freshening breeze, and the biggest passenger vehicles on the planet gleamed in row after orderly row, but it was after business hours and the doors were locked. Laddy rattled the front door in frustration as much as in the hope that anyone would let him in. But he drew the attention of Norman Oklahoma who came out of his office and did let Laddy in.

"One a your police officers already come by," Norman said. "I haven't seen Margaret, and you want to look at my bank account you'll see I don't have one red cent I didn't earn."

"That's good to hear, Norman," Laddy said, "the part about you being honest."

"Didn't need to steal," Norman said. "Win-Win paid me fair because I work hard and he knew he could trust me."

"Best résumé a man could have. By any chance, has Hayley Winslow stopped by?"

Norman smiled and nodded. "She was here for a minute 'bout an hour ago. Was a real surprise to see her again after all this time. She didn't stay long, though. Just shook my hand, told me she hopes my family is well, and said you couldn't give her one a these trucks to drive." Norman's smile widened and he added, "I always did like that gal."

"Me, too," Laddy agreed. "She say where she might be heading next?"

"Back to town. Said she wanted to circle the bases before she headed home. Didn't know she played baseball, but that's what she said."

Laddy thanked Norman and headed back the way he came. As far as he knew, Hayley had never played baseball. But having attended UT and graduated from UCLA, Laddy knew a thing or two about metaphor. Hayley, he was guessing, was making contact with local touchstones before she went back to wherever she'd been hiding out all those years. Once again, he felt like Tony in *West Side Story*, racing around, hoping to see Maria one last time.

It might break his heart if he didn't.

There were no museums to visit in Gasoline. There were two art galleries, but they closed even earlier than TRS. There was, however, a handful of bars with live music, places where new bands honed their acts before they took a crack at playing in Austin. And besides that, there was —

The place on his right that Laddy would have passed if he hadn't been cruising so slowly. He turned into the driveway and found a parking place. He looked at the name on the building. For good or ill, you couldn't find a more American icon: Wal-Mart.

The same chain where Sherm Meyerson had found his Merrilee in Baytown. Proof positive you could find just about anything you needed in a Wal-Mart. Thinking about it some more, he realized that even though Hayley had expressed her disgust with the monster trucks her father had sold, she'd still gone out to TRS to take a look at the place. If in all her years away, Hayley had lived outside the country, in some distant land yet untouched by the colossus of Bentonville, she might feel compelled to visit. If only to march up and down the aisles and emerge having refused to buy anything. A point of pride she could carry back to her hideaway.

Just when Laddy thought his logic was compelling, he remembered what Hayley looked like now. She had purple hair. Spiky purple hair. People who looked like that didn't shop at —

He saw her come out of the store. Her hair looked different. Somewhat. And she had a bag in her hand. She'd bought something. Laddy still had his engine on and he drove straight over to her. She smiled when she saw him.

"You know," she said, "I'm really glad you kept this old Mustang. This is what a car should be, isn't it?"

"Yeah, it is," Laddy said. "Hop in. I'll give you a ride."

She nodded and went around the front of the car. He popped the door open for her and she climbed in and tucked her bag between her feet. She slammed the door shut and asked, "How'd you know where to find me?"

"Lucky guess," he said. "What'd you buy?"

"Some Clairol hair color and a hair dryer."

He noticed now that only streaks of purple remained in her hair and the spikes had been brushed out. She looked more like the way she had when he first knew her, and he wasn't sure if that was good or bad.

"I'd never been in one of those places before," Hayley told him. "Thought I'd take a look and see what all the fuss was about. Apparently, other people like to just walk around in there and look at things, too. I met this woman named Susan, said she was a teacher. She goes to Wal-Mart to relax, if you can imagine that. I accused her of being the store detective, but she said, no, it just made her feel good to see how orderly things were compared to her working environment. I could identify with that a little bit."

Sounded to Laddy like Hayley had given him a cue, let him know he could ask how she had passed her time, but he decided to wait on that. "Whatever gets you through the night," he said.

"I wasn't going to buy anything," Hayley told him, "but I saw myself in a mirror and I thought I could use a little help."

Some cues you just couldn't ignore. "You could wear clown makeup and look great." Before she could respond, he added, "Is there somewhere we could go and talk, just the two of us?"

Hayley squeezed his hand and said, "Sure. Let's go to my place."

They drove back to the place out in the country with the

pecan orchard. There was an old but well-maintained house past the hill they'd visited the last time. It was a small frame structure, just two bedrooms, a nice enough kitchen, a small living room with a fireplace, indoor plumbing for calls of nature, but only a tin shower stall with water that never got warmer than cool. The nickel tour didn't take five minutes, but it was long enough to see that the place had received loving care since the day it was built.

There was a porch out front and at night a view of a million bright stars shining down out of the Texas darkness. Laddy and Hayley sat on wooden chairs at least as old as the house. Each of them had a cup of coffee with a knock of Scotch in it. Single-malt stuff, a brand Laddy'd never heard of — Glengyle Reserve — that Hayley told him could be purchased in only one shop in Edinburgh.

They both had a lot on their minds as they sat and sipped and stared at the sky. Hayley was the first to give voice to her thoughts. "Do you love Joanna?"

Laddy nodded without looking at Hayley. "Sure do. Ever since I first met her up in Austin. College party. I hadn't even intended to go, but I had this friend, Roy Gristly, he asked me to go with him and knock him out if he tried to drink a fourth beer."

"Roy have a drinking problem?" Hayley asked.

"He was worried he might, his family history and all, and he thought a few loose teeth or a mild concussion were preferable to letting it get any worse."

Hayley asked, "You follow through on your commitment? Sock your friend a good one?"

"Didn't have to. Ten minutes after we arrived, he hooked up with the only co-ed I met at UT who was a teetotaler, a Baptist girl from Anniston, Alabama, name of Sheree

Northrop. She laid the old line on Roy that lips that touched wine would never touch hers."

"And that worked?"

"They got married a year later and after graduation they moved to Brazil as missionaries, intent on wresting the whole of South America from the clutches of the Vatican. I haven't heard from them since, so they must still be busy."

"And you met Joanna at this party?" Hayley asked.

"Having no further need of my services, Roy introduced me to Joanna. He'd shared with her the story of my being willing to work as a guardian angel. Joanna asked if I might do the same for her as sometimes she got overly giddy at parties and she'd heard rumors there were male students at UT who would be inclined to take advantage of a young woman in such a condition."

"And the rest was history?" Hayley asked, turning to look at him.

"Unh-huh," Laddy said.

"You, yourself, never took advantage of Joanna in a state of giddiness?"

"I wouldn't say never," he admitted. "But the first time anything happened was a month after we'd met. We were both sober, but somehow we found ourselves in the coldest creek in Texas without our bathing suits on. Damn near proved impossible to do anything, though, cold as that water was."

"Still, you prevailed," Hayley said.

"Yeah, we did," Laddy said, and smiled at the memory.

The two of them went back to looking at the stars a while. Then Hayley asked, "What're you thinking?"

Laddy said, "I was just wondering if you've got a creek on the property."

Hayley laughed, put a hand on his arm, and kissed him. On the cheek.

Laddy smiled and said, "It's always been like that between us, hasn't it? A kiss on the cheek, not a dip in the creek."

"Yeah. Have you ever wondered about that?" Hayley asked.

He looked her in the eye. "Maybe once or twice or a million times."

"Me, too." She sighed and said, "Until I finally had to do some snooping. Some of which I did before I left home and a great deal more I did after I went away."

Laddy told her, "It bothered me a long time that you left without saying goodbye. Still does when I let myself think about it."

Hayley kissed him again, this time on the lips, but still holding back.

"Stay right here," she said. "There's something I have to show you."

Hayley went inside. A light came on in the living room, throwing illumination through a window and onto the front porch. Laddy sipped at his scotch-laced coffee and wished he'd put more single-malt in his cup. Hayley was back quickly with a manila envelope in her hands. She sat next to Laddy once more, but didn't look at him. Her eyes were fixed on the manila envelope she held. It wasn't like her not to face a problem straight on, but right now she was nervous.

So feeling a bit anxious himself, Laddy asked, "What've you got in there?"

She looked at him and asked, "How do you feel about secrets, Laddy? Should they always be revealed or sometimes are they better left alone?"

Hayley's question did nothing to soothe Laddy's nerves. He said, "I guess it's all a matter of whether you're going to feel better or worse once you know."

Hayley nodded. "Trouble is, you can't always know which it will be."

Laddy sucked it up and extended his hand. Hayley gave him the envelope. He opened it and took out an 8x10, black and white, glossy photograph. In the light from the house, he recognized the image of his mother immediately. She was a teenager in the picture, but her face was already formed in its adult likeness. Directly behind her stood an icon of American history, Lyndon Baines Johnson, and having studied Texas history in high school, he recognized the former governor, John Conally, too.

"Have you seen this picture before?" Hayley asked.

Laddy shook his head. "But I've heard about it enough that I feel like I have." He laughed without humor. "It does look like LBJ has his hand on Mom's ass."

Hayley had no comment on that.

He looked at her and asked, "Are you telling me that you've found out for sure that the president was my father?"

"Actually, Laddy, I'd feel a lot better if I could tell you that," Hayley said.

"What do you mean?" he asked.

"I mean, what I found out, first by overhearing a hellacious argument between my momma and daddy, and later by doing my own investigation, was who took this photograph."

Laddy was puzzled. "Why's that important? But since you raise the subject, who was it?"

"The photographer," Hayley said, "was a young local man just getting his start in Texas business and politics."

"So?" Laddy asked, still not understanding.

"The young man was being given a leg up by the swells because he'd been a Texas college football hero." Laddy was about to say so what again, but he started to see where Hayley was going. And then she added, "The young man starred at A&M. He was an All-American Aggie."

It clicked into place for Laddy. "Your father?" he asked. "Win-Win was the photographer?"

Hayley nodded. She waited for him to make the next jump. But it looked to her as if his mind had just put up a wall, high and wide, against the thought it was forming.

Hayley prodded him. "Laddy, why would my mother get furious, and stay angry for years, at my daddy if he only took a picture? Why would my parents and your mother warn me never get involved with you? And why would we, despite how we feel about each other, always shy away from getting too close?"

"Oh, Jesus," Laddy moaned, "you're my sister. Win-Win was my father."

He drained his cup, took Hayley's and finished hers, too.

Still seeking denial, he looked at her and asked, "Do you know that for sure?"

Hayley shook her head. "My evidence is circumstantial. I know that Daddy was the photographer. I know that besides the president he also put up the money to buy your momma her business and set you up here in Gasoline. I know that when I simply hinted at the matter to my mother today she went catatonic, and this was after she blithely dismissed a confession I made that should have shocked her."

Seizing on the opportunity to distract himself from his own situation, Laddy finally had to ask Hayley what she'd been doing. "What could you have to confess that's so shocking?"

She used exactly the same words she'd used to tell her mother.

"My God," Laddy said, "all the years I was playing make-believe in the movies, you were out there doing it for real."

Hayley nodded. "Still think I'm someone special, Laddy Johnson?"

He didn't miss a beat. "More than ever," he said. It was a sentiment that led him directly back to his own problem. "So what you've just told me is, my momma might've been with either Win-Win or LBJ, and no one knows for sure which of them was my daddy."

"I was hoping my mother would confess," Hayley said, "but she didn't. There are, however, a couple of ways to find out."

Laddy realized immediately what the first one was. "DNA," he said. "If we're siblings, we'll have enough markers in common to make it obvious."

"Yeah," Hayley said. "You figure out the other way, too?"

Laddy shook his head.

Hayley took his hand and led him inside. "We go to bed and see what happens."

"Oh," Laddy said.

CHAPTER NINE

They lay in the same bed, but they hadn't even been able to get naked, and their only physical contact was holding hands. For a long while, they just looked up at the ceiling in the dark, listening to the crickets and the cicadas. The open window let in a warm breeze, but they kept the top sheet over themselves for modesty, even though Laddy had his drawers on and Hayley wore her bra and panties.

Even so, they were exquisitely aware of one another. If the lights had been on and they'd dared to look, they could have counted each other's goosebumps. But if there was one force equal to the urge to propagate the species, it was the taboo against procreating too close to home. Incest was just too damn creepy.

Hayley finally said, "We can't take a chance, can we?"

"No," Laddy said.

"We shouldn't even be here like this," Hayley opined.

"No, we shouldn't," Laddy agreed.

"Do you want to go sleep in the other bedroom?"

"No, I don't," Laddy said."

"I could go," Hayley offered.

He held tight to her hand. She didn't try to pull free.

"I know," Hayley said, "this is quite a predicament."

"A dilemma," Laddy said.

"Good thing we're not kids anymore; we probably wouldn't be able to help ourselves, if we were." And with those words, Laddy understood why Hayley Winslow hadn't said goodbye to him all those years ago.

He squeezed her hand and then let go, saying, "Take off your undies."

She let go of his hand and asked, "Are you sure?"

"I hate to say this, but trust me," he told her.

She did, and removed her bra and panties, while Laddy pulled off his undershorts.

"And now?" Hayley asked.

"Turn on your left side," he said.

She did, and as he felt her weight shift, he turned on his right side and scooted up against her. They lay touching at their shoulders and along the lengths of their spines. Hayley's heels came to the bottoms of Laddy's calves. A shudder passed through each of them.

"Does this mean what I think it means?" Hayley asked.

"Yeah," Laddy said. "I've got your back."

"My backside, too."

They both laughed and after a minute they drifted off to sleep ...

Awakening in the morning only when Margaret Winslow entered the room, saw them in bed together, and shrieked loudly enough to crack glass.

Lucan Thorn had let Mary Sue Parker spend the night.

She was simply too young and comely and supple to cast away without enlarging their acquaintance. There had been many others who were as attractive as Mary Sue, and Thorn had let them go after one brief sampling. But Mary Sue had something the others didn't: a winning wickedness. When she'd come around after being pinched into unconsciousness by Joanna, he could see from the moment she opened her eyes that she was scheming to get even, just as he would have been. They were two of a kind. Of course, their sexual encounters would become less frequent, each of them taking other lovers as whim dictated, but on a personal level, he could see them being intimates for a very long time.

He would hold the upper hand initially, but he was sure there would come moments when power devolved to her. And when it did she would make him pay cruelly. Which was perfectly fine. He believed in penance, and even mild degradation, as a way to relieve his guilt. Every emotional twist and turn was a tool he could bring to a performance.

Mary Sue looked up at him from the room-service breakfast they were eating in his suite. She was wearing a terrycloth robe provided by the hotel. Her skin glowed from a scrubbing in her morning shower, and her long dark hair had been brushed straight to air-dry. To his eye, she looked like she could pass for 18. She still ate like a kid, too. Two fried eggs over easy, bacon, hash-browned potatoes, a glass of whole milk, toast with grape jelly. Well, let her enjoy it while she could, he thought. He'd make do with his decaf and raisin bran.

She asked him, "So when are you going to take me to the mountaintop and show me the kingdoms of the world?"

Thorn laughed and said, "You think I'm the devil?"

"Well, you did a good job playing him in that movie,

Turn Up the Heat."

"There were those who said it was type-casting," he admitted. Without saying so, he was pleased that she knew his work. He asked her, "You know what the problem about making deals with the devil is? You get what you want, but it's never quite what you expected."

"Let me worry about that," Mary Sue told him. "I told you I want money, power, and fame. But what I really want? I want people to be scared of making me unhappy. You understand?"

"Of course, I do," Thorn said.

"So you think you could help me get what I want?" she asked.

"Wouldn't I be scared of you, too, if I did?" he replied.

"Sure you would," Mary Sue said, "but you'd like to have me scare you."

He laughed again. The little hellion was really something. "And all this is your way of saying you'd like me to be your entree to Hollywood."

Mary Sue was tempted to say, "Why else would I sleep with an old shit like you?" But even she allowed for some restraints on her candor. So she told Thorn, "I figure I'd have more opportunities there than here."

"And you want to act, I suppose," Thorn said.

"Not on your life," Mary Sue replied. "How many actors have real power at any one time? Five or six? Sure, you're one, but it's a real small club. Besides, I like to work behind the scenes. Be able to go out without getting hassled all the time."

Thorn always found it refreshing and a little reassuring when young people told him they didn't want to perform on camera. To his way of thinking, the urge to be an actor was far too common these days. It was a more original impulse to want to labor outside the limelight. And it also cut down on the potential competition for him. He wanted to be the first actor to remain a leading man until he was 100.

He told Mary Sue, "It might be a good idea to sic you on Beeb Bidwell, start you on your road to conquest as a talent agent. You'd probably have to skimp by on $500,000 a year for the first year or two, but you'd be learning the business, and after that you could make real money and acquire all the power you had the wits and the nerve to grab."

Mary Sue's eyes gleamed at the prospect.

"But as they say in my line of work," Thorn continued, "what's my motivation?"

Mary Sue opened her robe and led the actor back to bed.

"Tell you what," she said. "By the time all your actor buddies are mainlining meth to keep their peckers perky, you'll still be able to get excited just by thinking about me and all the things I've done to you. And all those fine ladies out there in L.A.? They'll give you one a those ..."

Mary Sue frowned. She couldn't put her finger on the phrase she wanted.

"Lifetime achievement awards," Thorn suggested.

"That's the one," Mary Sue said.

And with that she started proving her worth. Lying back and feeling the bliss, Thorn said, "Well, fair is fair."

Without missing a beat and displaying a talent worthy of a ventriloquist, Mary Sue handed him the phone and said, "Call this Beeb guy and tell him I want a real nice office."

"Where the hell did she come from?" Laddy asked.

"Momma?" Hayley replied. "She's from Galveston."

Laddy should have known; they were already cracking bad jokes like an old married couple, one where ma and pa didn't have sex and might be consanguineous. Laddy had made griddle cakes for breakfast. Hayley said she knew how to cook but most of her recipes ran to saffron and goat. She did, however, brew a fine pot of coffee. Each of them was on a second cup at the breakfast-lunch-and-dinner table in the kitchen of Hayley's rustic retreat.

"I meant," Laddy said, "how did she know we were here, and how did she even know this is your place?"

Hayley sipped her coffee and then said, "On that first part, I'd have to say she just tried her luck and stopped by. On how she knew, my guess is she and Daddy must've done some looking for me when I disappeared, and if they checked all the property records in the area, they probably spotted the name of an absentee titleholder: Susan Evers."

The latter half of her explanation drew a look of puzzlement from Laddy.

"Come on," Hayley told him, "you're the movie guy."

Which gave Laddy enough of a clue to say: "A character from a film; you used that for a pseudonym."

She nodded. "Momma named me after Hayley Mills, so I ..."

"Became one of her characters for the purpose of owning this ranch."

"Right. Hayley played twins, Susan Evers and Sharon McKendrick, in *The Parent Trap.*

Laddy remembered the movie but not the characters' names. It was just their luck that the two of them, a stone's throw from middle-age, got caught by the real-life mother of a fictionally named daughter the first time they went to bed. Still, it gave Laddy a notion.

"You know," he said, "I'm just about positive I'm not related to either Susan Evers or Sharon McKendrick. I should probably check with my mother first to be absolutely sure, but it's another way we could look at things."

Hayley said, "You're definitely not related to Jazz Janssen, and I like that name better."

"Who's that?" Laddy asked.

"That was me when I was doing awful things for the G."

Laddy mulled that one over and said, "We went that way, I'd probably become someone you'd wind up throwing under a train. Maybe we better just play it safe."

"Yeah, damnit," Hayley conceded.

"You know where your mother ran off to?" Laddy asked.

Hayley said, "Open a window. You can probably still hear her screaming. But what's the point? You want to tell her we were just rubbing fannies?"

"Don't think I didn't enjoy that, but no. Your mom's wanted for grand theft."

It was Hayley's turn to wear a blank look, so Laddy told her of the great Municipal Field oil heist and how a caravan of Gasoline's leading citizens had been hauled off to the clink.

Hayley shook her head in wonder. "Well, you remember what Balzac had to say about that: '*Derrière la fortune toujours grande se trouve un grand crime.*'"

"Sure," Laddy replied, "I remember that; it's the translation I forget."

"Behind every great fortune lies a great crime," Hayley told him.

"Well, he got that right, old Balzac did, but I'm sorry to say the word's out on Margaret Winslow and the cops are looking for her."

Hayley frowned. Laddy took it to be the normal concern of a child for her on-the-lam desperado mom until she said, "It could be awkward if they catch her. I'm afraid I confessed to her, as I did to you, some of the crimes *I* committed for the G. I've become a real blabbermouth."

Laddy understood the potential leverage Hayley had given Margaret. If the matriarch of the Winslow clan was ever brought to trial, she could cause the federal government some serious discomfort by revealing what her daughter had been up to. Of course, the government might want to head that off and the charges might be mysteriously dropped. Which would be okay as long as no Woodward or Bernstein came along to dig up the real story. All in all, it would be better if Margaret was never taken into custody.

The situation made Laddy shake his head.

"I think I'm the one who should be doing that," Hayley told him.

"Feel free to join in," he said, "but I'm taking this as a cautionary tale for me."

"How's that?" she asked.

He told her about the offer he had pending from Herbert Prescott, good until midnight, to get the townspeople to sell the Municipal Field. He concluded with, "This is an oil deal that's got tar-baby written all over it. Touch it even with your pinky, you're stuck with it for good. I wasn't going to take any money for myself, but I was thinking of letting Prescott's buyers believe the field has a lot more oil in it than it does. That is, I wasn't going to tell him about all the oil that's been stolen. But now I think even doing that would come back to haunt me."

"No doubt about it," Hayley said. She thought for a minute and then added, "But maybe I can help you find a better way to work all this out."

Just the idea of working with Hayley made Laddy smile.

"Long as it doesn't involve putting you in trouble," he said.

"No but that's the other thing," Hayley told him. "When I'm done helping you, I might have to go away again."

Laddy felt a pain greater than the time that damn horse kicked him.

"Why?" he asked.

Hayley sighed and said, "Well, if the law catches up with Momma and she tries to blackmail her way out of trouble, she's going to have a lot harder time of it if I'm not around to lend credibility to her story."

"Goddamn," Laddy said.

"At the very least," Hayley agreed.

Erindira de la Fuente, per her duties as Joanna's assistant, answered the phone at Joanna's ranch. "*La Casa de Buena Suerte*," she said. The house of good luck. The name was corny, Erin thought, maybe even risqué, if you wanted to take it that way, but she liked it nonetheless.

"*Hola, amiga,*" a gringo voice said. The caller's accent was atrocious but at least he got the gender of the noun right. "Do you know who this is?"

"*Señor* Thorn," Erin replied without elaboration.

"*Sí, es mi,*" he said.

"*No, es yo,*" she instructed.

"I stand correctado," he said with a laugh.

"*Corregido.*" The language lesson was getting tedious for Erin. "*La señora no está aquí.*"

"Joanna's not home? Where is she? Riding her *caballa?*"

Erin's employer was, in fact, riding a mare, so she couldn't even dispute Thorn on getting the gender of horse wrong.

"Would you like to leave a message, sir?" she asked.

"I would," he said. "Please let Ms. Wells know I'll be stopping by at noon."

"Has an invitation been extended, sir? I don't have you in my appointment calendar."

Lucan Thorn laughed again. It was a sound that countless movie fans knew and loved. To hear Thorn laugh was to know that all was right with the world. It left Erin cold.

"Really, sir, I don't have an appointment for you."

"Erin, sweetheart, I'll bet you a Ferrari to a farthing Joanna will see me, but as a courtesy, please let her know that I called first."

The actor hung up on her still laughing.

Erin did not like the man. He was nothing but trouble for Joanna. Worse, the way Joanna refused to put him out of her life diminished the actress in Erin's eyes. Joanna needed to be *mas fuerte.* Stronger. True, Thorn was still a handsome man, wealthy and adored by millions. But Joanna was every bit his equal in beauty, riches, and popularity.

What both of them lacked, sadly, was a seriousness of character.

Erin thought this did not bode well for her partnership with Joanna. But maybe this time *la señora* would surprise her and scorn her former husband, shame him if that was possible, and drive him away, which was always possible for a strong woman. Even Erin's former husband, German, had learned that lesson. Though she was sure he still waited for the day when he could kill her.

She'd just finished composing the message that Thorn would be visiting when the phone rang again. Please, she thought, please, please ...

"*La Casa de Buena Suerte*," she said, answering the call.

"Hello, Erin. This is Laddy Johnson."

Not *Señor* Thorn. Her prayer was answered. "Good morning, Mr. Johnson."

Erin took it as a good sign that Laddy was calling, that seeing his old girlfriend was just a momentary thing, if anything at all. Laddy was the man for Joanna, Erin felt. If Joanna could not see something as obvious as that, how could Erin trust her to make business decisions in their production partnership?

"Is Joanna available?" Laddy asked.

"She's out riding, Mr. Johnson."

"Well, do you think she might have the time to see me today? And if I'm not being too nosy, do you think she'd care to see me today?"

"I know she has the time, sir. As for her inclination, I can not say."

"Which horse is she riding?" Laddy asked.

"Betty Boop," Erin answered.

"A mare," Laddy said. "She still have a gelding?"

"Yes, sir."

"Well, if she's not riding that one, I'll take my chances. When's a good time?"

Erin smiled to herself. "Twelve p.m. would be perfect."

"High noon, it is," Laddy confirmed.

Just before Laddy left Hayley's little ranch house to drive to Joanna's *casa grande*, she said to him, "You mind if I ask you a question about your mother?"

She was sitting on an old black-and-white plaid sofa that

looked like somebody had bought it at Sears about 1968. Despite being dated, the couch was in tip-top shape like everything else on the property. Laddy sat next to Hayley, close but not quite touching.

"Coming from anybody else," he said, "that'd be a risky question. Coming from you, why should I object?"

"Might not be that great coming from me, either. But I've been trying to work something out in my head, and you're really the only one who can give me an answer."

Laddy squared his shoulders. "Okay, go ahead."

Hayley said, "Let's agree that any young person, male or female, could get swept up in the charisma of somebody famous."

"Yeah," Laddy agreed, thinking for the moment they had veered onto the subject of him and Joanna. You were a former spook like Hayley, you didn't have to get right to the point.

"That famous someone doesn't even have to be particularly good looking, just powerful with maybe an aw-shucks kind of country charm."

So they *weren't* talking about Joanna who was *very* good looking and hadn't said shucks in the past 20 years, that he recalled. But he played along and said, "Okay."

Hayley continued, "I'm trying to decide whether your mother, as a young woman, could have been seduced by LBJ, and I can buy that she could have. Can you?"

"Is that your question?" Laddy asked.

"It's a preliminary one," Hayley replied.

Laddy said. "I've never thought of my mom as Monica Lewinsky, but maybe that's unfair to Monica. Not that I've ever had any great power, but, yeah, I can see a young woman being swept up by just being close to a powerful man. So, yeah, I can accept that possibility."

Hayley cleared her throat and said, "Okay, here's where things get a little trickier. What, if anything, do you remember about your mom's social life while you were growing up? Did she ever bring a boyfriend home?"

Laddy shook his head. "Not once that I can recall."

"She ever go out on dates?"

"Not when I was little. I remember, though, when I was 12, she took me out to dinner and we were joined by her attorney, Bartolo Bernstein. She introduced me to him. He ate with us and drove us home, but he didn't come in. That night, right after I got into bed, she came to me and said that every so often a woman needed to have an escort, if she was going someplace a woman shouldn't go alone. I told her I'd go with her. She kissed me and said I was very generous, but sometimes a woman needed an escort who was at least 21 years old. She said that Bartolo had been her lawyer for as long as I was her son, and she found him to be both trustworthy and a gentleman. So would I approve if he became her escort? I didn't say so, but I thought if he was a good guy and he liked my mom, maybe he'd give her a break on what he charged in legal fees."

Hayley laughed. "You came to understand later, of course, what their relationship was."

"Sure," Laddy said, "the only thing I didn't understand was why they never got married."

Hayley took Laddy's hand. "Maybe your mother would have had to give up something she felt she was owed, if she got married. Anyway, here's the really sensitive question: Do you think your mother was ever the kind of girl who'd carry on with two men in such a way that she wouldn't know who the father of her baby was?"

The question stunned Laddy. "Jesus, of course, she wasn't," he said. "I should have thought of that. Which means Win-Win's participation in the scheme was ... what?"

"Insurance," Hayley replied. "Your mother got paid never to say who your father was. But she did give you a famous surname. Maybe that made someone nervous. So my father got paid to come forward and claim paternity in the event your mother ever went public."

Laddy put his face in his hands to keep his head from spinning. Then he looked at Hayley and asked, "So we're not brother and sister?"

"Maybe we are. Maybe we aren't," she answered.

He laughed. "Glad we got that cleared up. One thing I know for sure, my mom wouldn't be keeping company, not the romantic kind, with two guys at the same time." Laddy reaffirmed this opinion and the conclusion to be drawn from it by kissing Hayley full on the mouth. Then he got up and said, "I've got to go."

And go he did. Off to Joanna Wells. But with the taste of Hayley's kiss on his lips. She thought it likely that Laddy would wind up with Joanna and probably married to her. But a Hollywood marriage was hardly a monument of durability. She could wait ... and reflect.

She'd left unspoken another possibility about the relationship between her father and Laddy's mother. One that would have been too hard for Laddy to hear even from her. What if, to further protect himself, Laddy's real father — and she didn't think it necessarily had to be LBJ; it could have been any one of the swells in that picture; in fact, Laddy's momma naming him Johnson might have been a diversion — but what if that rich, privileged Texan had insisted that Arcelia and Win-Win, in fact, had to hold their noses and actually go to bed together to get their money? Maybe even be photographed in bed together. Back in the old days, especially in Texas, that would have been enough to cast doubt on who a child's daddy was.

Such a coerced coupling would also explain the antipathy Arcelia Dominguez and Margaret Winslow held against their respective offspring ever having physical relations of their own. Well, too damn bad what the older generation wanted.

The way Hayley looked at things for the moment, if the cops caught Momma and she claimed Hayley was a spy, Hayley would simply deny it and assert her cover persona: she was a jazz singer. Famed throughout Europe and the Middle East. Momma said any different, she was imagining things. Maybe Momma could claim mental illness and serve her time in a loony bin, which beat a federal pen any day. In any case, Hayley had decided her disappearing days were over.

She was counting on any union between Laddy and Joanna being a brief one. And when he came back to her, if he wanted a DNA test just to be sure, she'd go along. Up to a point.

Because if by some mischance Edwin Winslow really had been Laddy's daddy, she would fudge the test results to show otherwise.

Having had the time to think about it, she realized she'd done things working for the G that were far worse than sleeping with her brother.

CHAPTER TEN

Still wearing her riding clothes, Ariat boots, Chic Skins suede jeans and vest by Lou Ann Kosak, Cattle Kate Tombstone Hat, and an L.L. Bean blue chambray shirt, Joanna Wells was in full cowgirl regalia. Despite her dramatic appearance, the movie star looked at her personal assistant in horror and said, "You did what?"

Erin de la Fuente calmly answered, "I arranged to have Mr. Johnson and *Señor* Thorn visit you at the same time. They should be arriving momentarily."

Her knees weakening, Joanna felt the need to sit down. She collapsed onto a leather armchair in the living room of her beautiful new ranch house. The place had been styled by a hot new interior designer out of Austin, Kyle Watanabe. He'd done the place in a tasteful combination of Western hues, animal hides, and a Japanese sense of minimalism. The latter element explaining why there was only one Winchester carbine hanging on the wall over the fireplace.

Joanna couldn't remember if the rifle was loaded.

"I'm beginning to understand why your husband beat

you," she told Erin.

Erin took a chair opposite Joanna.

"He didn't beat me, I beat him," she said, "and you know that."

"Okay," Joanna conceded, "I'm beginning to understand why he *wanted* to beat you."

Erin gave Joanna an evil look. She wanted to slap the movie star. But she couldn't. As part of Joanna's preparation to play Erin in the movie they were to make, Erin had taught Joanna everything she knew in the way of martial arts. Except Erin had been unable to explain to Joanna how it changed your soul to feel and hear yourself break the bones of a man you once loved. It had been as traumatic to Erin's psyche as it had been to German's body. Instead of being honest, she'd portrayed herself as *mas macho* than her vanquished husband. Intuitively, she felt this would be the way to sell her story. And she'd been right. Joanna had jumped on that point and told Erin she had a sale. Which might have been the expected reaction from a woman with so many failed marriages of her own. In any event, Joanna was now very nearly Erin's equal in physical combat, and not knowing any better, Joanna was likely more willing to inflict real damage.

So trying to slap her was out of the question.

Instead Erin asked, "Would you like to dissolve our partnership right now. I'll repay your investment with money I receive when I sell my story elsewhere."

Joanna was tempted to fire Erin, tell Erin her life story was now Joanna's property, and she could get herself a new immigration lawyer, too. Only doing all that would look so politically incorrect Joanna would be lucky if she ever worked again.

"Well?" Erin demanded.

Joanna was saved from the humiliation of having to back down when the doorbell rang.

"Will you please see who that is?" she asked.

Erin huffed off to answer the door.

Joanna took the Winchester off the wall, found it was loaded, removed the .32 caliber rounds and stuck them in the right front pocket of her jeans. She didn't think Lou Ann Kosak would approve of the bulge they made. But better that than a multiple homicide.

At the very moment that Lucan Thorn rang the doorbell at *La Casa de Buena Suerte*, the private jet carrying Mary Sue Parker to meet Beeb Bidwell made its final approach into Bob Hope Airport in Burbank, California. En route, Mary Sue, as the sole passenger, had had the undivided attention of both cabin attendants and for half the flight the captain as well. The chore of flying the plane was left to the co-pilot. Mary Sue took all the hospitality as her due, being polite in return but keeping enough of an air of reserve to maintain the pecking order.

Waiting for her at the airport was a limousine from TOATMA. That was what Beeb Bidwell, one month ago, had renamed his business: The Only Artists That Matter Agency. Its unofficial but relentlessly publicized motto was: *You're TOATMA or you're toast.* As Hollywood was a stainless steel cage of insecurity under the best of circumstances, every actor in town was soon begging Beeb to have one of his agents represent them.

So not only was Mary Sue arriving at a good time, but when she slid her pert bottom onto the backseat of the limo where Beeb awaited her, it was love at first sight for both of them. This came as a real surprise to Beeb who from the time he was 16 had thought that he was gay.

Maybe all that was just a fashion statement, he decided.

Too bad his father hadn't lived to see him go straight.

Well, hetero anyway.

Before Lucan could say a word to her, Joanna told him, "Please take a seat and give me a moment to think. Laddy will be here any minute."

Laddy, Lucan wondered. He had a hard time not putting a hand to his nose as he suddenly and vividly recalled the punch Laddy Johnson had visited upon it. Thorn was also more than a little curious and apprehensive about the rifle Joanna cradled in her lap. Yes, it went with her Western costume and it might be just a prop, but this was Texas, and the 19th century was never far away: fighting Indians, range wars, frontier justice.

It was only because his two divorce settlements with Joanna were more than equitable that Thorn found the composure to sit down and wait to see what happened. Being a true student of his craft, he thought he might be able to use elements of the scene that was about to unfold. Perhaps as a passage in his memoirs if nothing else. Life was grist; he was the mill.

Laddy's arrival wasn't noticed until he stepped into the room and saw Joanna to his right and Thorn to his left. This was the first time all three of them had been under the same roof since that first meeting at Beeb Bidwell's party in the Hollywood Hills 17 years ago.

Laddy, too, took note of the firearm in Joanna's hands.

He told her, "If it's just Thorn you want to shoot, I can come back later."

Joanna looked at the Winchester as if she'd forgotten she was holding it.

"What?" she asked.

Laddy said, "I can come back later. Help you dispose of the body."

Thorn hadn't cared for the first joke. Now, he didn't want to let things get out of hand where Joanna might suddenly say, "Hey, you've got an idea there, but no need to leave."

The actor had done absurdist theater that worked like that, and nothing was more absurd than life itself. As if to prove his point, Erin de la Fuente, a minor character, entered the room with a tray of drinks, iced tea, set it down on a polished plank table and said, "I've got a few things to tell all of you."

That was the problem with unscripted scenes, both of the movie stars in the room thought, you never knew when you might be upstaged.

Laddy made use of the distraction to pluck the Winchester away from Joanna.

Kirkly Osgood drove straight through the night to Boca Raton fueled by truckstop coffee and the growing conviction that she and Walker Winslow were sitting on a gold mine. She was even getting to like the little fella. He had a wonderfully funny delusional complex about who he was: Chuck Norris writ small. Only just like the mongrel puppy Kirkly had as a young girl, Walker didn't realize he was small; both of 'em would yip and yap at anything that came along. Kirkly's puppy had gotten run over by the truck that came to clean the cess pool out back of the house. Wasn't nobody's fault really that a 10-pound critter thought it could get the better of a 4,000 pound truck. But having learned that lesson, Kirkly was determined to keep a watchful eye on Walker.

More than that, if they connived themselves a good deal at the *National Enquirer* today, she might entertain Walker with her own pink flesh. Just the idea of having the little guy climb all over her gave Kirkly goosebumps.

But the first bump they encountered was one in the road. Despite the fact that Kirkly and Walker were driving a $90,000 SUV and looked like law-abiding Americans, they were denied entrance to the *Enquirer's* office complex without an appointment.

"But we've got a great story for y'all," Kirkly whined into an intercom set into a post outside the gated parking lot. "It's got a great big movie star, sex, infidelity, homewrecking, and we got some pictures that'll make your eyes bug out."

"I'm just a security officer, ma'am," a voice came back. "You have to remember, we were attacked with anthrax spores not so long ago. So we have to be careful. Call for an appointment is my advice."

"Shit," Kirkly said.

"Please leave now or I'll have to call the police," the security guy replied.

Stepping out of character, Walker tapped Kirkly on her arm and played the voice of reason. "Let's go," he said. "I saw this place coming into town that might be of use."

He directed her back to an office in a strip-mall above a Chinese noodle restaurant. The sign on the door said: *The National Despoiler, Laying Low the High and Mighty*. Below that was a picture of blonde-haired woman, you couldn't quite tell who she was, holding her hands up as a flash-camera went off in her face.

Well, the editorial approach was right, Kirkly thought, but —

"I never heard a no *National Despoiler*," she told Walker. "In fact, I can't hardly believe you even spotted that little bitty sign up there, while I was driving by at 40 or 50 or whatever."

Walker winked at Kirkly and said, "Good eyes. Always had 'em. Just one a things that's special 'bout me."

He was so damn cute, Kirkly thought. She wanted to squeeze him like a bug right there. But there was business to think about first. "All right, you did a good job keeping your eyes peeled, but what's a two-bit operation like that gonna pay us? We got a big story; it deserves big money."

"Sure does," Walker said. "But the least that talking to these folks'll do is set a floor-price for us, and who the hell knows, bein' in the same business as the big boys, maybe the ol' Despoiler up there has some connections. Maybe they can do a deal with another outfit to pay us the big money for the main story and they give us a little more to do a follow-up profile on you 'n' me, bein' the people who brought the whole thing to light."

Kirkly looked at Walker dumbfounded, like she just realized that she had Albert Einstein in the truck with her. Truth was, Walker had learned about the power of leveraging things from Norman Oklahoma, who routinely got customers of TRS to take out second mortgages on their houses to pay for their SUVs.

Kirkly showed her appreciation with a kiss that about sucked all the air out of Walker's lungs. Then she yanked him out of the truck and the two of them ran up to the

National Despoiler's offices where they presented their story and showed their pictures to a Mr. Dicky Prufrock, a dark-skinned gentleman with a bristling black mustache and a smile that would glow in the dark. Dicky admitted to them, in confidence, that he had changed his name after arriving from Pakistan.

Kirkly and Walker were more than willing to keep Dicky's secret when they learned he'd be delighted to purchase their magnificent story and titillating pictures from his own funds. True, his journal was unknown thus far, as it had yet to publish its first issue. But within a year it would appear in every supermarket and on every newsstand in the country. He guaranteed it, *inshallah.*

"God willing, and God bless you," Kirkly told Dicky.

After that, it was just a matter of haggling over the price of what would be the lead story of the first copy of a periodical with national ambitions. Dicky Prufrock's family, historically, were merchants of exotic spices. But the Winslows traded in luxury motor vehicles. This was a caste difference of no small measure. In the end, Dicky bowed to Walker's demand for $500,000 for the story of how movie star Lucan Thorn had destroyed Walker Winslow's happy relationship with Mary Sue Parker, and three photos graphically showing just how Thorn had sown the seeds of that destruction. An option for the purchase of additional photos to accompany follow-up stories was included in the purchase price. A bonus of $500,000 was to be paid if a movie was made from any of the stories the *Despoiler* published on the subject. A further bonus of $500,000 would be paid if Lucan Thorn portrayed himself in the story of his treachery.

With Dicky cutting Walker and Kirkly a check for a $50,000 advance against the balance to be paid in 90 days, business was concluded. Dicky brought out chilled bottles of kiwi-strawberry Snapple to toast their deal.

Clinking bottles with Walker, he said, "I would be most pleased if you had any further stories and pictures of this nature to bring to my attention."

Hearing that, Kirkly rubbed her hands together with glee.

"We'll see what we can do, partner," Walker drawled. Then, just like he was somebody important, his cell phone rang. He said, "'Scuse me a minute."

As Dicky politely chatted with Kirkly, Walker moved to the far corner of the room, wondering who the heck could be calling him. He was both surprised and pleased to see his mother's cell phone number on the caller ID screen. Now, wouldn't she get a draft up her skirt to hear he'd just made himself a pile of money — even if Kirkly was the one holding the check.

Walker clicked the talk button and said sweetly, "Hi, Momma."

That was the last thing he said to her. She told him she was on the run. She and Daddy had stolen 'bout a million barrels of oil from the Municipal Field. So she was gettin' out a the country while she could. But Hayley had come home. *Hayley?* Walker thought. All he could remember of his older sister was a picture that sat on the baby-grand piano nobody ever played. He didn't have any memory of actually seeing her in real life. But not only was Hayley back, Momma said, but she was seeing Laddy Johnson. Which was bad enough in any case, but was especially bad in this case because ...

It took Momma a minute to get the words out. "Walker, it's simply an abomination. Laddy Johnson just might be

Hayley's brother."

Walker Winslow laughed, until the light went on in his head and then he moaned. The only way Laddy could be Hayley's brother was if their daddy, and not Lyndon Johnson, was also Laddy's daddy. And, oh shit, if that was the case, then Laddy wasn't just Hayley's brother, he was Walker's brother, too.

Before Walker could ask Momma how the hell any of this could be true, she told him, "My plane's about to leave, Walker. But if you're a *real* man, you'll do something about all this."

"So what're you saying we should do about all this?" Laddy asked Erin de la Fuente.

"Fight for Joanna," Erin said. "She is the woman both you and *Señor* Thorn love."

Laddy said, "Unh-huh. Guess I heard you right the first time."

Thorn looked at Joanna and asked, "Are you sure this woman," he gestured to Erin, " is a Harvard MBA? Sounds more to me like she studied under Don King."

"You won't fight for me, Lucan?" Joan asked in a quiet voice.

"He's got a gun," Thorn pointed out.

Laddy, who was the only one present still standing, walked over to the fireplace and replaced the Winchester on its rack. He'd been able to tell from its relative lack of heft that the carbine was unloaded. He went and sat in the easy chair opposite Thorn. Joanna was to his right and Erin was to his left. The four of them were separated by the plank table on which Erin had placed their glasses of iced tea.

"You really think this can be settled with fists?" Laddy asked Erin.

She did, which maybe made her a hypocrite. She had no wish to inflict any great physical harm herself, after what she'd done to German. But she thought it would be just fine for these two men to fight over the beautiful woman they both desired. That was, of course, a double standard. Women, historically, had to fight against double standards. But those were the ones which placed them at a disadvantage. Any others weren't necessarily so bad.

Laddy continued, "Back when Joanna and I, and Prince Charming over there," he nodded at Thorn, "when we were a lot younger, I busted his nose for him and that didn't discourage him one little bit. He married Joanna twice and now he's back for more. I really don't know if I could hit him any harder without killing him." Laddy turned to Joanna. "And, no, I won't kill him for you."

Thorn kept a straight face, but felt greatly relieved to hear that.

"Why did you come, Laddy?" Joanna asked.

"To see if you still want to get married," he said. "To ask if it's too early for you to take one of those home pregnancy tests."

Hearing that, Thorn and Erin leaned forward, but neither said a word.

"Is that the only reason you'd marry me, to give our child a father?" Joanna asked.

Now Laddy leaned forward, too. "You are pregnant?"

Joanna told him, "I didn't say that. I asked what your reason was."

Laddy sat back and smiled. "My *reasons*, plural. Well, let's see. I started loving you when I was 18; I've loved you ever since; and I didn't stop loving you even when you were married to Luke Anne here or those other two guys. I tried real hard to stop, but I just couldn't do it."

Thorn saw how powerfully Laddy's declaration of love had affected Joanna. He hurried to say, "Me, too. I never stopped loving you, either."

Erin reached out as if she was going to pinch Thorn, but Joanna shook her head.

She said to her former husband, "You know, Lucan, I can almost believe that, but your love for me never kept you from sleeping with any woman who came within reach."

Thorn smiled ruefully. "You own the candy store and you have a sweet-tooth ..." He shrugged and added, "But you know all about that, Joanna."

"I think I've finally outgrown it," she replied, "and Laddy's never been that way." She turned and looked at him. "Or maybe the opportunity just came to him late."

Laddy considered the possibility and nodded. "Could be. But with me there's only one other woman I'd mention in the same breath with you, and she might be DQ'ed at the starting line."

Joanna asked, "And what is Hayley's disqualification?"

Laddy had thought about the matter driving to Joanna's ranch. A notion had occurred to him that was so horrible he could never mention it to anyone, not even Hayley. Especially not Hayley. What if Win-Win had been paid not only to step forward if Laddy's mother made a claim against his real father, what if Win-Win had been paid, say, to drug Arcelia, get her into bed, and actually have his way with her? On top of that, what if the whole thing had been photographed?

Short of taking a DNA test, there really was no way to

tell whose sperm had fertilized Arcelia Dominguez's ovum. Maybe his mother had never said anything to him about who his father was because even she didn't know for sure.

"Laddy?" Joanna asked once more.

"Well," he said, "there's this possibility that Hayley Winslow is my sister."

Laddy's words left Joanna and Erin dumbfounded.

But Thorn asked, "This Hayley person, she's his other woman?"

Joanna waved off his question. She asked Laddy, "If you knew this, you never ..."

Laddy shook his head. He was presuming Joanna meant to ask him if he'd ever had sex with Hayley. Which he hadn't. He'd keep the kiss and the fanny-rubbing to himself.

Thorn intruded on their moment by breaking into raucous laughter. "Oh, this is rich," he said, "one for the books. 'Honest, baby, I couldn't have anything going with that other dame. She's my sister.' Really, Joanna, does that load of bull play for you?"

Erin started to go for Thorn once more. This time Joanna didn't stop her, but Laddy did, placing a hand on her arm.

"I wouldn't expect Luke Anne to believe me," he said, "but I don't care."

"You know," Thorn told Laddy, "I'm getting really tired of that Luke Anne shit."

Erin sat back, grinning. She thought she might get to see her fight after all.

Joanna thought so, too. Her eyes shifted back and forth between the two men.

But all Laddy did was grin and say, "Sue me."

Thorn scowled and said, "That time you hit me, you prick, that was a sucker punch."

Laddy said, "Unh-huh, right after you sucker-grabbed Joanna's boobs."

Fire flashed in Erin's eyes. She asked Joanna, "He assaulted you this way?"

Joanna held up a hand. "It was a long time ago, and Laddy made him pay."

Thorn jumped to his feet and a second later he held the Winchester in his hands.

He said, "And maybe this time the stuntman will pay."

Joanna only sighed, wondering how she could have married this man two times.

"What's he really want from you?" Laddy asked her.

"A part in a movie," she answered.

"*Our* movie?" Erin demanded. She got to her feet. Seeing a new threat, Thorn pointed the carbine at Erin, who asked Joanna, "This sissy wants to be my German?"

"*Sissy?*" Thorn asked. He was getting ticked-off himself.

Erin turned a hard stare on him. "German was a swine, but he was a man."

Erin and Thorn continued looking daggers at each other.

And Laddy asked Joanna, "You do know, right?"

She nodded.

Turning to face Joanna, Thorn demanded, "Know what?"

He always hated it when people kept secrets from him. And he deeply resented the total lack of terror in the room. *He had a rifle, didn't he?* He pointed it at Laddy and brought his eye down to the notched gunsight. But that didn't scare anyone either.

"*Know what?*" he shouted once again.

Joanna took the ammunition for the Winchester out of her pocket and dropped the rounds on the table one by one. That should have defused matters right there. But as she had in Mexico, Erin showed that once provoked she was not easily stopped.

She pounced on Thorn, ripping the Winchester from his hands and flinging it away. Having disarmed her opponent, she had an eight-page menu of attacks she could launch against him. But before she could choose her appetizer, entree, or dessert, he began to cower, and she remembered the horror of what it was to brutalize another human being.

She just couldn't do it again. At least not now with this pathetic creature. But neither could she let him go unpunished. So she reached out, seized his nose, and gave it a sharp twist.

Everyone heard the cartilage snap and saw the blood spurt.

Thorn's eyes crossed and he fainted dead away.

CHAPTER ELEVEN

"I'm new to politics," Laddy Johnson told Herbert Prescott when the two of them met in Win-Win's old city hall office. A smiling portrait of the late mayor still hung on the wall, and his long-lost daughter, Hayley, sat silently in a shadowy corner of the office. Prescott had noticed her, but he made no verbal acknowledgement of her presence or if he knew who she was. He simply sat looking straight ahead with his briefcase on his lap. Laddy continued, "So you'll have to forgive me if I speak honestly."

The New York lawyer smiled, "Are we both speaking for the record here, Mr. Mayor-elect? That is, are our words and likenesses being recorded?"

Laddy shook his head. "Not by me, if that's what you mean. I'm pretty sure, though, that you, and I, and Ms. Janssen will all remember what gets said here."

Laddy and Hayley had decided to use her stage name for purposes of the meeting.

Prescott looked at her a long moment. She never blinked. Before turning back to Laddy, the lawyer glanced at the portrait of Win-Win, but made no comment on seeing any resemblance.

Prescott said to Laddy, "Very well, sir. You've heard my offer. You've convened this meeting before the deadline I set. Am I to understand you will be accepting my terms?"

Laddy shook his head. "No, your offer is rejected."

Prescott looked at Laddy as if he was trying to peer into his soul. He said, "The terms of the offer won't be increased. The sum I mentioned was top dollar."

"I'm not looking for more money, Mr. Prescott," Laddy told him. "I'm not looking for any money at all."

The lawyer went back to staring at Laddy, as if he'd stumbled on some hitherto unknown species: a politician who couldn't be bought.

Prescott said, "I've examined every last detail of your finances, Mr. Johnson. I know that you're comfortable in a *petit bourgeois* way, but you're hardly wealthy. So tell me, please, have you taken a vow never to rise above the middle class?"

Laddy grinned. "You know, I never thought about it that way, but maybe I have. I own my home; I've been driving the same car since high school; I have some good friends; and I don't aspire to more."

Prescott smiled sourly at Laddy's homespun world view.

Laddy continued, "Now, you say you've checked out all my finances. So I'm wondering if you can tell me one thing: Who paid my tuition at UT?"

A flash of displeasure crossed the lawyer's face.

Laddy said, "So you don't know that. There are some walls even you can't get past. Well, I would've been surprised if you had. Anyway, Mr. Prescott, here's the part where I really come clean with you."

The mayor-elect told Big Oil's lawyer how local brigands had robbed the Municipal Field blind, and how there wasn't nearly as much oil left in the ground as a prospective buyer might believe. Such candor was unprecedented in Prescott's experience.

He said, "You're telling me that the purchase price I offered was far too high."

"Exactly," Laddy said.

"Why would you do that?" Prescott asked.

Laddy said, "It's a little thing we middle-class folks call honesty. But if you can't buy that, well, you'd have found out the truth eventually and you lawyers love to sue people, so think of it as a way of avoiding a lot of hassle."

Prescott nodded in agreement. With Laddy's secondary explanation.

"Do you know where your current oil reserves stand?" he asked.

"Approximately," Laddy said. "We'll be getting a more precise determination soon."

Prescott told Laddy, "I could make a new prorated offer. And as it would necessarily be lower, there would be money available to add as, shall we say, an *honesty* bonus."

Laddy smiled again. The guy didn't stop pitching. It had to hurt him to think there was *anyone* in the world who didn't value money as much as he did.

"Well, here's what we're thinking, Mr. Prescott," Laddy said. "We know we've got approximately enough oil to last about three years, if we continue to consume it at the rate we've been doing at 25¢ a gallon. Now, if we raise the price of gas to two dollars a gallon, that might not extend the life of the field by a direct eight-to-one ratio, but we figure we can get at least another 10 to 15 years out of the field. Of course, we figure two bucks a gallon is going to look real cheap compared to what the market price of gas will rise to over that time, isn't that right?"

The lawyer responded only with a frosty smile of his own.

"That's what I thought," Laddy said. "The really interesting thing is we're going to take 50% of the pump price here in Gasoline as a tax that will be invested it in renewable energy technology. You know, to look ahead to the day when the wells run dry."

Prescott's smile was gone now; all that was left was a cold stare.

"We're thinking when that day comes," Laddy said, "we might rename the town Sunshine, Texas. What with all the solar panels we'll have. I hear they're even starting to make roofing shingles that produce electricity. Isn't that amazing?"

Herbert Prescott looked at his briefcase for a prolonged moment, as if he was communing with something inside the Raffaello Italian leather. Then he got to his feet and asked Laddy one last question. "Why, may I ask, did you have Ms. Janssen join us for this meeting?"

Laddy said, "She's my bodyguard."

The lawyer nodded as if that was what he'd worked out in his head. He left without another word. Hayley got to her feet and made sure he was gone.

When she returned, Laddy asked, "Prescott have a gun in his briefcase?"

"Bet on it," Hayley answered. "How'd you know?"

Laddy told her, "The last mayor of Gasoline to meet with a Big Oil lawyer was John Tyler Tunbridge, and he wound up shooting that sonofabitch. The way the world's been turned upside down since then, I thought the lawyer might be the one to do the shooting."

Shortly after sending Herbert Prescott on his way, Laddy went to the studios of KYHA, YeeHaa-TV, to address the populace of Gasoline. He'd considered wearing a suit and tie for the camera. Buck, Eveleen and his mother all favored that idea. But when Joanna and Hayley simultaneously said, "Be yourself," while never even looking at one another, he decided to go with a Western collar shirt, blue jeans, and cowboy boots.

Laddy began his speech with the immortal words of Joe Jacobs, "We wuz robbed!"

Jacobs, a fight promoter in the 1930s, had been referring to a controversial decision against his boxer, Max Schmeling, in a heavyweight championship rematch against Jack Sharkey. Laddy soon made clear how the phrase applied to everyone in town.

"The Municipal Field has been plundered by a gang of thieves who've been stealing our natural resources for the past 20 years. This has left our oil reserves far lower than anyone outside of the criminal conspiracy ever would have guessed."

Laddy's words stunned the staff at the TV station, and he could easily imagine that they had stupefied people throughout town. He knew anger would come next. And right behind that would be a gut-deep desire for revenge.

It was up to him to forestall violence. "This good news is, just about everyone involved in this crime is already in jail and will soon be facing charges. So whatever thoughts come to mind, however mad you get, don't do anything stupid."

Laddy leaned forward so his face would fill the frame and he channeled a little Tommy Lee Jones into his voice. "You behave like a criminal, we'll treat you like one."

He sat back, took a beat, and then went on. "What's done is done. Now, we have to decide what we're going to do next. As I see it, the best way to do that is to let all of you decide. In other words, we're going to have a referendum. It'll be this Sunday, two days from now.

"I'm looking for a sense of direction from the people of Gasoline. You have the most to gain or the most to lose. Sunday's voting likely won't be dressed up in enough legal niceties to make it an official election, but it'll be a fine exercise in democracy.

"I'm proposing that we make a choice between two alternatives. The first is to keep on pumping oil out of the Municipal Field just like we've always done, keep the price of a gallon of gas at 25¢, and three years or so from now run dry. The second alternative, the one I favor, is to raise the price of gas immediately to two dollars per gallon for six months and thereafter peg it at 80% of the national average price. But for every two dollars we take in at the pump, one dollar will go to developing new renewable energy technologies. There are lots of bright entrepreneurs and high-tech people just up the road in Austin. We can bring some of them down here to start new businesses and find new ways to power our homes, shops, and vehicles.

"Voting will take place in Tunbridge Square from 8 a.m. to 8 p.m. so everyone will have time to go to church or seek guidance in whatever form they choose. Voting will be public not private. You'll stand at a microphone in front of your friends and neighbors, give your name and address, and say either, 'Two bits' or 'Two dollars.' And that's all. No speeches will be permitted.

"What will not only be permitted but also encouraged is the largest possible participation of legal voters. With that in mind, we'll extend the franchise to everyone 16 and older: You're old enough to drive, you're old enough to vote.

"We'll keep a running tally of the vote, so we'll all know the results immediately. The first thing Monday morning, I'll introduce legislation in the Town Council to implement the expressed will of the people."

Laddy closed with a nod to Edward R. Murrow. "Good night and good luck."

No sooner had the red light on the camera in front of Laddy blinked out than a phone rang and a voice announced, "It's CNN. They want an upload of Mayor Johnson's speech."

Buck Musgrove told Laddy, "Boy, you done started a shitstorm."

Eveleen Nellis added, "And there's not enough Charmin to go around."

In an hour's time, word had reached the mayor's office that reporters from around the nation and several foreign countries were on their way to Gasoline to cover the story of the upcoming election. A media circus was about to arrive in town and pitch its tent.

The governor called to say, "I'm sending you a hundred Texas Rangers pronto."

Joanna had her own helpful idea, "I'm booking every hotel room within fifty miles; nobody will have a place to stay unless we say so."

Laddy liked that. He'd scheduled a snap election so people would still be mad about being ripped off — and so Herbert Prescott would be hard pressed to send an army of oil industry lobbyists storming into town with cash in hand to buy the election.

Laddy turned to Hayley. "You have any suggestions?"

She nodded and said, "Kevlar."

Joanna said, "I don't like having that woman here."

She and Laddy had returned to Joanna's ranch and currently lay side by side in Joanna's bed. Hayley had accompanied them to *La Casa de Buena Suerte,* but remained outside the bedroom. Lucan Thorn had chartered a Gulfstream to return to L.A. for cosmetic surgery; Erin de la Fuente had flown commercial to Boston to visit old B-School chums.

"She's my bodyguard," Laddy said.

"I don't like that, either," Joanna added.

By way of reply, Laddy asked, "Are you going to cast Luke Anne in your new movie?"

Despite Joanna's misgivings about her two-time and two-timing former husband, she had sympathized with Thorn after Erin had broken his nose for him. It was a movie star thing. There were only so many faces in the world that could open a movie. If you were a member in that exclusive club, you could identify with the others, even if you didn't like them.

Thing was, Laddy wasn't sure Joanna's feelings for Thorn were a thing of the past.

As if to confirm his suspicion, she snapped, "I don't know if I will or not."

Laddy nodded. "I may have loved you before he did," he said, "but old Luke Anne was the one who gave you your big break. He made you a star. In a perverse way, he's your security blanket."

Joanna glared at him. "Do you have to be so damn honest all the time?"

"It's a failing, I know," Laddy told her. "I'll go sleep on the sofa."

Which was precisely where Hayley Winslow reposed. Before he could move, Joanna grabbed Laddy Johnson's johnson.

"You'd just love that, wouldn't you?" she asked. "But if that's what you have in mind, you take it somewhere down the road."

Feeling Joanna's hand start to tighten in anger, Laddy said, "At the risk to future generations, why don't you tell me what you want to do? Be with me or Luke Anne?"

Joanna relaxed her grip on Laddy, turned him free. In a quiet voice she told him, "We didn't make a baby the other night. I don't need a test. I can tell. I'm not pregnant."

Laddy put a hand on Joanna's shoulder to comfort her, but she shrugged it off.

"I'm not pregnant, but I'm not your damn sister, either," she said, turning on her side, facing away from him.

Laddy got out of bed, bemused at how complicated life could get. He'd loved only two women in his entire life. He'd never cheated on the one who kept marrying other guys. He'd never even had sex with the one who got him to sing onstage. It seemed like something should have worked out better with one of them. He thought maybe it was time he got himself a dog.

CHAPTER TWELVE

There hadn't been so many people in Tunbridge Square since '05 when Win-Win put up a giant TV screen and passed out free hot dogs and soda to anyone who wanted to watch the Houston Astros whip the asses off the Chicago White Sox in the World Series. Only the White Sox had plans of their own and swept the series, leaving many locals to maintain that their true love was high school football, anyway. Despite the failure of the Houston team, Win-Win still made out. Between innings, he went to closed circuit commercials for Texas Rolling Stock, selling his SUVs that year under the slogan: *Proud to Be a Texan.*

Naturally, in the face of defeat, the townspeople had to assert their Texas pride and run right out and buy a new truck. In the event the Astros had won, Texas pride would have demanded that a new SUV be bought in celebration.

Laddy Johnson, much like his predecessor in office, was not above hiding a card or two up his sleeve. For instance, before the voting began, he offered five minutes to every clergyman in town to provide words of wisdom to the gathering. But this was done only after Eveleen's spies had determined that preserving God's bounty had an ecumenical appeal among Protestants, Catholics, and Jews. A public airing of such unanimity couldn't hurt, Laddy figured.

Having said his own prayers in his shower that morning, Laddy felt free to pay only passing attention to the admonitions of the clerics. He stood off to one side of the stage on which the prudent stewardship of the earth was being promoted and on which the voting would also take place. He turned to Hayley who was scanning the crowd for threats to his life.

"You mind if I ask you a question?" he said.

She answered, "If you're thinking about getting a dog, I've always liked Labs. But get a yellow one if you're going to stay down here. Texas is too hot for a black Lab."

She hadn't taken her eyes off the crowd, but he could see a smile form at the near corner of her mouth. She'd read his mind and she knew it.

"You got a name for the dog, too?" he asked.

"How about Amarillo?" she said.

Which, of course, was the Spanish word for yellow, but using the Texas pronunciation, it worked pretty well.

Laddy kept the gag going. "So, you ever do any dog training in your travels?" he asked.

"Some," she said, "but it'd be a pity to teach a sweet dog the things I know."

Which got them back to a sensitive area, but that was where Laddy wanted to go.

"What I was going to ask was this," he said. "Do you have anyone in your life who means as much to you as Lucan Thorn does to Joanna?"

Hayley took her eyes off the crowd and looked right at

him. "I did," she said, "but he's dead."

She looked back at the crowd.

"You want to know how it happened?" Hayley asked.

"Not right now," Laddy told her.

At eight o'clock straight up, Laddy stepped up onto the stage. There was one pool TV camera on him. He made a point of not looking directly at it as the crowd gave him a rousing cheer. It wasn't hard to sell people on the fact that their vote mattered — if you really meant it. It almost made him feel bad that he was doing his best to stack the deck in his own favor. Over the cries from the crowd and the rustle of a soft wind, he could hear Win-Win's ghost laughing at him.

"Boy," Win-Win said, "you ain't no better than I was."

"Maybe not," Laddy thought. "Could be I'm just a chip off the old block."

Win-Win had nothing to say about that.

Laddy held up his hands, asking for silence.

"Thank you all for coming out," Laddy said to the crowd. "Everybody hear me okay?"

More cheers and shouts came in response.

"Good," Laddy said. "We have a really nice morning for being outdoors, but as we all know it's going to get hot later in the day. So we'd like to get the voting done as smoothly and quickly as possible. To aid in that effort, since this is a new kind of election for most of us, we've picked the names of 100 people at random." Which was a lie, but Laddy pulled off with a straight face. "We'd like those people to line up, in the order that they're called, in the chute that's roped off to my left. Those people will then come onstage one at a time and say, 'Two bits' or 'Two bucks,' and leave. Then the next person will vote. After the first 100 people have voted, we'll take the next hundred. We'll ask for 50 each of the oldest and youngest voters. We'll work our way to the middle so when the temperature starts climbing the only people who'll have to sweat it out will be Texans tough enough to mount up and drive cattle to Kansas City."

That brought a cheer from the crowd. Laddy added that Town Hall and the public library would be open as cooling stations and for restroom facilities. Additional rest rooms were being provided by businesses on the square. Please keep the facilities as tidy as the ones in your own homes — or in some cases tidier.

That got a laugh.

"In just a minute now, I'll call out the first 100 names, we'll record the votes on the scoreboard behind the stage, and we'll put out some lemonade and cookies to keep you going through the day."

The news of free refreshments brought a round of applause, and just for a second Laddy thought he heard Win-Win laugh again.

Laddy called out the first two names from the list he held. "Walter Ketchum and Buster Todd Petty." Laddy looked up from his list and told the crowd. "If I call out the name of someone who's not here, somebody give them a phone call, all right? We want everyone to get a fair chance."

Right after I define the forces of good and evil, he thought.

Laddy's plan was to give the Two Bits-vote a two-to-one edge among the first 99 voters. Then would come voter number 100. In screenwriting parlance, that would be the plot point in this little drama.

With the help of Eveleen Nellis and Buck Musgrove, Laddy had selected 66 likely Two-Bits voters who represented the most self-centered, dim-witted, and off-kilter cusses in town. Walter Ketchum, 86, and Buster Todd Petty, 16, fit the bill perfectly.

Walter was a World War Two vet who called himself a war hero. He wore a Purple Heart everywhere he went to prove it. But the truth was he almost received a Section 8 discharge because he refused to stopping killing livestock. He shot 28 cows in Belgium, claiming he saw Nazis hiding behind every one of them. Then he slipped on the entrails of the last bovine he blasted and hit his head on an unexploded German artillery shell. The hiding Nazi revealed at last. But the mishap earned Walter his Purple Heart and a medical discharge.

Buster Todd was briefly a star football player for the Gasoline High Oil Barons, a two-way interior lineman. He could block and tackle like a sonofagun. The problem was, whenever there was a pile-up, Buster would tilt his facemask up and take a bite out of an opponent's leg. It was bad enough when he started out as an ankle-biter; it was intolerable by the time he worked his way up to mid-calf. He had to be cut from the team before the Oil Barons got expelled from the conference. Buster Todd's social standing at school fell from hero to pariah. Kids started calling him "Steak Tartare" Petty, but not to his face.

All of the other 64 voters deemed to be in the Two-Bits camp suffered from their own peculiar social deficits, whereas the first thirty-three Two-Dollar voters, young and old, were sober and serious people. Not the brightest kids in class or the membership committee at the country club, but people you could trust to babysit your kids or do your tax return without telling the neighbors how much money you made. Salt of the earth types.

So the first 99 voters, if all went well, would present two clear archetypes for all those who would follow. Define yourself, friend, by the company you keep. Do you stand with Walter and Buster Todd or with ...

Voter number 100. Betty Anne Bates, the closest thing Gasoline had to Mother Teresa, albeit a saint who liked to go out and honky-tonk once a month or so. An emergency room nurse at Saint Prosperina Hospital for 30 years, Betty Anne had provided medical care in emergencies ranging from the treatment of gunshot wounds of every imaginable caliber to every conceivable part of the body; to the removal of foreign objects such as pop bottles, Cuban cigars, and cucumbers which had been inserted into anatomical openings where they could serve no good or moral purpose; to the extrication of Christmas tree lights, magic markers, and lug nuts from the gullets of smallfry whose parents should have been paying closer attention. After retiring from the hospital, Betty Anne had volunteered her time as a school nurse for 10 years, visiting every school in town at least once a week. Betty Anne had organized immunization programs and blood drives. In case of any disaster, natural, man-made, or one instance attributed to a UFO, Betty Anne was always on the scene ready to help in any way she could.

And wherever she went, she always arrived in her navy blue 1969 VW Bug. She'd told Laddy she was going to vote for him for mayor because he was the only one in town who drove a car older than hers, but with a laugh she'd boasted that her car got better mileage.

Betty Anne, as hoped, voted Two Dollars. As did 98 out of the next 100 voters.

And the referendum for investing in the future was won not by four votes, as Laddy had in the mayoral election, but by four percentage points, 52% to 48%.

The town council voted to implement the will of the people the next day. Gas stations all over town immediately raised their prices to two dollars per gallon. In spite, Herbert Prescott struck back at Laddy Johnson. Not with gunfire, but with a suit to prevent the mayor-elect from being sworn in and taking office. The suit claimed that voting irregularities that occurred in the mayoral election made the alleged winner's four-vote margin of victory subject to a recount at the minimum and preferably the staging of a special election to produce a clear and unambiguous winner. A judge named Clarence Scalia issued an injunction to keep Laddy from taking office.

That gave Big Oil time to push for their do-over. With a challenger of their own choosing. One they could bankroll and control. One who wouldn't allow municipal revenues to be invested in sources of alternative energy.

Some weeks later, the governor called Laddy to say, "Much as I'd like to have a friendly judge toss this suit, I gotta stay impartial."

The state's chief executive had already proposed switching every state-owned vehicle to bio-diesel, so he had his own Big Oil fight on his hands.

"You ever think of getting back into show biz?" Laddy asked the governor.

"Sure, right after I get myself a nose job," the governor said with a laugh.

Laddy laughed, too.

He laughed even harder a month later when word came from a stuntman friend in L.A. about Lucan Thorn. It seemed that Thorn had thought he'd reached the point in his career where he could have his nose fixed not so it looked the way it had after Laddy had broken it, but the way it had looked originally. So once again it was perfect. But it was no longer the schnoz that had carried him to stardom. No longer the central feature of the face that his public had worshiped.

"Think Clark Gable without the mustache," Laddy's friend told him.

The judgment was damning, and that was before the public had even seen Thorn. His new appearance was known, so far, only to show biz insiders. But that was enough to send his career into a tailspin. Beeb Bidwell stopped representing Thorn.

Beeb's new dragon lady, Mary Sue Parker, had the pleasure of giving Thorn the ax.

Laddy's friend asked, "You ever coming back to L.A.?"

Laddy said he didn't know yet.

He got a call later that week from Joanna, who had gone back to L.A.

"Do you know what she did?" Joanna asked him.

"Who?" Laddy asked, wondering if Joanna meant Hayley.

"Erin," Joanna said. "She's suing me."

"For what?" he asked.

"Devaluing the script I had written for that treacherous little bitch," Joanna told him. "This is something she cooked up with those snooty Harvard friends of hers. I think they probably came up with the idea just for a laugh, but then they took it to court and a judge refused to throw it out. I'm surprised you haven't read about all this."

"We don't get *Variety* in Gasoline," Laddy told her, "or even the *L.A. Times*."

Joanna said, "Oh. Maybe I shouldn't say anything more."

"No, no," Laddy told her. "You don't get to just tease me. How is Erin claiming you devalued the script?"

"By casting myself as her," Joanna said. "She claims I'm too *old* to play her. Her lawyers are showing pictures of me in full makeup from *Desperate Hours*, where I was supposed to look old." Joanna's voice dropped to a whisper. "I'm not old, am I, Laddy?"

Nowhere but in Hollywood and Olympic gymnastics, he thought. But all he said was, "No, you're not."

"I miss you," she said.

"Come home," he told her.

"I don't want to be forced out of my profession," she answered. "I love acting. I don't even care about being a star anymore."

"Really?" he asked.

"Well, I do like being appreciated."

"Who doesn't? Listen, can I tell you something I've thought for a long time?" he asked.

"Okay," she said.

He heard in her voice that she was trusting him not to further attack her ego, but that wasn't what he had in mind at all.

"You may find this hard to believe," he said, "but I think Hollywood is a little too inbred. New York, too, for that matter. I think American movies would be a lot better if there were eight, nine, or even ten production centers scattered around the country. So why don't you come home, use your fame as an entree to some of the zillionaires in this state, and start your own mini-studio right here?"

There was a pause lasting long enough that Laddy knew he had her thinking about it.

"You think I could?" she asked.

"Why the hell not?" he said. "Start your production slate with a Western. I'll get you all the stuntmen you need."

She laughed and said, "I'll be home tomorrow."

Then the levity left her voice and she asked, "Is Hayley still there?"

"She's been up in Washington for a month," he said, "tending to some personal business."

What Hayley had told Laddy was she had to put the minds of some people in the G at ease so guys a lot meaner than Herbert Prescott didn't come looking for her. He hadn't heard from her since she left, but she'd told him to give it sixty days before he started to worry. If she wasn't back by then, Laddy was to e-mail a password-protected file to a lawyer in London. That and forget that he'd ever met her.

He'd said sure, no problem. But if he got even a hint that some spook shop had harmed Hayley, he was going to take a suicide run at it. He'd already imagined several scenarios, and he knew they were suicidal because they would all rely on the help of other stuntmen and screenwriters.

"Did you ever find out if you and Hayley are—" Joanna started.

"No, and my momma's not talking either," he said. "We're going to let that wait a while."

"Lucan proposed to me," she told him.

"You see his new nose yet?" Laddy asked.

"Yes, it's quite handsome."

"Unh-huh," Laddy said. "He ask you to get married after

Beeb dropped him?"

"Yes," Joanna said.

"And you said?"

"I said no."

Poor guy was really on the outs, Laddy thought.

He told Joanna, "So come on home. I'll pick you up at the airport."

"But where do we stand?" she asked.

Laddy had given that question a lot of thought. He'd missed Joanna more this time than ever before. But he was living at Hayley's place while she was away, and he'd spent a lot of time there looking for reasons why they couldn't be siblings. He wouldn't be doing that unless ...

He said to Joanna, "Hey, you know what? I got myself a dog. A yellow Lab puppy. I call him Amarillo. We never had a pet when we were together. I don't even know if you're allergic."

"To cats," she said. "I love dogs."

"Another reason to come home," he told her.

Given the way things usually worked out for him, Joanna would be landing at Austin-Bergstrom International Airport just as he saw Hayley getting off another plane. He'd have to see which one Amarillo liked better. Go with that.

Just then, he heard the puppy barking excitedly. Fearfully?

There were coyotes in the countryside around Hayley's property. The occasional feral dog and wild boar, too. Any of which would make a quick snack out of Amarillo.

"Joanna," Laddy said, "I've got to go. Sounds like the pup's in trouble. Come home and call me from the airport."

He clicked off the phone, raced outside, and brought himself up short.

Kirkly Osgood held Amarillo in her arms. She wasn't

hurting the puppy. But the little dog continued to yip and yap as it tried to squirm free. Walker Winslow stood next to Kirkly. He held a semiautomatic pistol and pointed it directly at Laddy.

"Momma told me to come take care of you," Walker said.

CHAPTER THIRTEEN

Laddy'd been in any number of spots tighter than this one, only each and every one of them was make-believe with a camera rolling and a gag choreographed down to the last detail. Despite the fact that Laddy believed that demented little twit Walker was pointing an actual gun at him with an earnest intent to use it, Laddy's stuntman mentality kicked in. As he was unquestionably the good guy in this little set piece, there would come a timely distraction that would allow him to escape unscathed or with a flesh wound at worst.

Right on cue, acting like a natural-born show-pup, Amarillo turned his snout in the direction of Kirkly Osgood's left breast and bit it for all he was worth. Kirkly shrieked loudly enough to launch a thousand birds out of an acre of pecan trees. Reflexively, she also flung Amarillo ten feet into the air. The commotion pulled Walker's eyes away from his target.

Laddy dived low at Walker's legs, intending to tackle him and drive him straight back into the ground. If the little shit got his neck broken, that was too damn bad. But Laddy's dive came up short. His injured leg just didn't have the spring he used to take for granted. Walker looked back to where Laddy had been standing. When he didn't find him there, he looked down as Laddy tried to bowl him over by rolling into him.

Walker adroitly hopped over Laddy and had his gun pointed at Laddy once more when he came to a stop flat on his back. Walker looked down and laughed.

"Big Hollywood hero," he said. "Don't seem so tough now, do you?"

But Walker had made the villain's classic mistake of turning his back on a foe who hadn't been vanquished. Amarillo showed his mettle once more by sinking his teeth into Walker's right calf. Buster Todd Petty would have been proud of the pup.

Walker leaped in the air with a yelp, giving Laddy time to get to his feet. But that was all he had time for. With one shake of his leg, Walker dislodged his six-pound attacker. Worse, he pointed his gun at the irrepressible little dog, who was gathering himself for another charge.

Laddy forgot any concern for his own safety and was about to make his own charge when a familiar voice calmly said, "Shoot that pup, little brother, and I'll shoot you."

Walker turned his head. He saw a woman walking toward him. The gun she held was pointed right at him. Reason enough for Walker to lower his own weapon. In the time Hayley Winslow had been away, she had ceased to look like Jazz Janssen. Now, she looked like a grown-up version of the beautiful girl she'd been in high school.

Even Walker recognized her from her yearbook picture, and he let his gun fall out of his hand. Amarillo took that as his cue to charge, but Laddy scooped the puppy up into his arms and began scratching him behind his ears.

"Cute dog, Laddy," Hayley said.

Walker looked at the two of them, saw the way they looked at each other.

"So, it's true," he said, "what Momma told me about you 'n' him. I couldn't believe it, but now I see she was right."

"You couldn't believe it, but you were going to shoot Laddy anyway?" Hayley asked.

"I was just going to scare him. Tell him to stop messing with you," Walker said.

Kirkly told Hayley, "This wasn't my idea. I just like to take pictures."

"Go inside and clean up," Hayley told her, "you're bleeding on yourself."

Kirkly looked at her shirt and saw that the pup had indeed drawn blood.

She frowned and said, "Damn, this was my favorite top."

Fretting, she walked to the house, unselfconsciously removing her shirt as she went. Hayley looked at her and then back to her brother. "That's a lot of woman for you, Walker."

Walker said, "Yeah? Well, I'm a lot of man for her. Just you ask her. So what're you gonna do now, Hayley. Shoot one a your brothers so you can sleep with the other?"

Hayley sighed, put her gun away. "No, Walker, I'm about to give you and your plus-sized lady friend the opportunity to have yourselves the adventure of a lifetime."

Walker regarded her with a squint of suspicion. "What do you mean?"

"I mean, you're a real Texan, aren't you, Walker? A tough hombre?"

"You bet I am," Walker said.

"And if you listen close, you just might be smart enough to work with me," Hayley said.

"Doin' what?" Walker demanded.

Hayley gave her brother a cold, thin smile. "Defending your country. Against some of the worst enemies it's ever known. As an undercover operative. You up for that?"

Walker's eyes gleamed. He straightened his spine, raising himself to new heights. Possibly five-foot-six. Then he thought to ask, "You ain't lyin' to me, are you, Hayley?"

Laddy was sure Hayley was lying. But he was wrong.

"It's the goddamn G," Hayley told Laddy. "I owe them two years separation time, but they agreed to let me go in peace if I give them one year."

Hayley had sent Walker into her ranch house to advise Kirkly that her services, too, would be required to defend the national interest. Now, she and Laddy and Amarillo were walking through Hayley's pecan orchard. The pup, as if he'd belatedly realized the danger he'd faced, walked between the two people, keeping pace, nuzzling their legs.

Laddy nodded and said, "I suppose getting some concession is better than none, but I don't understand where Walker and Kirkly fit in. I'd cast them for an Austin Powers flick, not a James Bond thriller."

Hayley grinned. "Yeah, me too. Only it wasn't my choice. It was bad luck and the perverse sense of humor of the people I work for."

She told Laddy about Walker and Kirkly selling their photos and story to a new scandal sheet in Florida.

"I never heard of the *National Despoiler*," Laddy said, "and people in show biz tend to know all of those rags."

Hayley told him, "It's brand new. Their first big story is going to be on Lucan Thorn, the big Hollywood star who got caught in the sack breaking up a poor country boy's romance. Anyway, the tabloid is all a front for Islamist terrorists. They think it's funny to make money to support their cause by trading on the decadence of the West. At the same time, they'll be circulating the same stories and photos back home, in heavily censored versions, of course, to expose the moral corruption of the infidels. It's really pretty clever, except we were onto them from the start."

Laddy said, "Glad to hear it. But you couldn't have been too happy when you learned Walker was involved."

Hayley shrugged. "It's going to keep me from sitting at a desk shuffling paper, which is what I was doing before I got the assignment. Now, I get to run the team of my bantam brother and his plump girlfriend to see if we can learn more about who the real mastermind behind the *National Despoiler* is."

Laddy looked at her. "It was a lot easier not knowing what you do, not knowing that the bad guys will be playing for keeps if they find out about you."

Hayley took Laddy's arm, forcing Amarillo to scoot on up ahead.

"Another reason I disappeared," she said.

Laddy withdrew his arm from hers and put it around her shoulders, holding her close.

"I've got something else to tell you, Laddy," Hayley said.

"What's that?" he asked.

"Before I got my assignment, while I was shuffling paper, I did some digging."

He felt her tense under his embrace. "Do I want to hear

this?" he asked.

"I think you better," Hayley said. "I found out who your daddy is."

Hayley suggested they return to the hilltop they'd visited on Laddy's first trip to Hayley's property. They sat tailor-fashion facing each other. Amarillo lay sleeping in Hayley's lap. A soft breeze took some of the weight off the midday heat.

"So who was it," Laddy asked, "LBJ or Win-Win?"

Hayley took a deep breath, let it out, and said, "Neither."

"What?" Laddy said, loudly enough to disturb the pup's sleep.

Hayley quieted Amarillo down, stroked him until his eyes closed again.

"I thought you'd be pleased that we didn't have to worry about incest," Hayley said. "And maybe a little disappointed that we'd missed an opportunity."

Laddy blinked. That was all the time he needed to think about those two topics.

He said, "You're right. I am and I am ... but come on, Hayley, if you know, tell me already."

"How about if I give you a couple clues? It's someone you know very well. Someone both you and your mother like very much. And if that's not enough, you're half-Jewish."

That took two blinks for Laddy to process.

He said, "Bartolo? Bartolo Bernstein is my father?"

Hayley nodded. "I got to thinking," she said, "maybe the situation with your father was someone using the old hiding in plain sight ploy. Which is exactly the way I worked as Jazz Janssen. I never tried to hide my movements. I had a publicist tell everyone where I would be appearing. And then I'd step out of the spotlight and do my dirty work. So I asked myself if there was a man in your mother's life who'd been with her from before the time you were born. Someone who had a plausible reason to be there in another role."

"Her lawyer," Laddy said. "And Bartolo has been there forever. But why then —"

"All the legends about LBJ and my father's possible involvement?" Hayley asked.

Laddy nodded.

Hayley said, "I called Bartolo. Told him I knew. Told him I had the DNA tests to prove it. Which I do. I had a friend come to town and surreptitiously collect a plastic water bottle you'd drunk from and tossed away and a fork Bartolo had used in a restaurant."

Laddy looked Hayley in the eye. "If you had found out I was Win-Win's son, that you and I were siblings, would you have told me?"

"I was thinking I might have to flip a coin about that," Hayley answered. "Possibly the best of seven times. But I'm telling you the truth, Laddy. Bartolo will even tell you so, if you ask him privately and promise not to tell your mother you know."

"Which gets us back to why the big secret at all," Laddy said.

Hayley's face lengthened with sadness and she said, "Laddy, something bad did happen to your mother that day the photo with LBJ was taken. Somebody started giving her drinks and she was young and afraid she'd be considered rude if she didn't take them. From what I was told it took only two or three to make her tipsy, and then ..."

"Then what?" Laddy asked. "Somebody raped her?"

Hayley nodded. "Grabbed her from behind, dragged her into a darkened room, and did it. The way Bartolo told it to me, your mother never even saw who the attacker was. When your grandfather found out, he wanted to rush out and murder a dozen or so of the most powerful men in Texas. But your mother didn't want her father to die in an attempt to avenge her. And Bartolo, who'd just passed the bar, and was your mother's secret lover, and who knew she was pregnant with his child, had another idea. After a month had passed, he went not to the men involved but to their lawyers. He told them of the rape and that the victim was pregnant. He told them they had a choice. They could provide for the victim and her child for the rest of their lives, not lavishly but reasonably, or they could face public exposure which would cause all of them embarrassment and possibly put one of them in prison for a long time."

Laddy's shoulders slumped. "So nobody 'fessed up, but collectively they paid up."

"And continue to pay until this very day. But making the bargain exacted its own price on Arcelia and Bartolo."

"Sure," Laddy said. "If they ever acknowledged me as their son, if they ever got married, all those powerful people, except the rapist, would think they'd been swindled. And I don't think they'd just shrug that off."

Hayley shook her head. "I don't either. There was one more question I had to ask Bartolo: Was my father the one who fed your mother those unwanted drinks? He said no. Which doesn't mean he wasn't the one who ... Well, your mother doesn't know who that was, but you can understand why she wouldn't want us together just on the possibility."

Hayley draped Amarillo over her shoulder gently enough that the pup only moaned but didn't wake up. She got to her feet and extended a hand to Laddy. He took it and stood next to her, looking at her, loving her, trying not to think that her father might have raped his mother.

He squeezed her hand and then let it go and looked off into the distance.

"If it matters," Hayley said, "I checked my father out, too. What I learned was he paid for sex, but there's no evidence he ever took it without asking."

Laddy nodded without looking at her.

"Bartolo told me one more thing," Hayley added. "You and Joanna were supposed to get married, but something seemed to put it off. Right about the time I showed up. I think you ought to marry her, Laddy, if she'll still have you."

Laddy turned to look at Hayley.

"That time you asked if there was ever anyone really important in my life," she said. "Well, that story's even less fun than the one I just told you. So ... so maybe you should just go and see if you can be happy with your movie star."

She took Amarillo off her shoulder and handed the pup to Laddy. He curled up in the crook of Laddy's arm, still dozing.

"And if there comes a time I want to see you again?" Laddy asked.

"Call my lawyer's office in London," Hayley told him.

Laddy stroked the sleeping pup's belly and said, "Thanks for saving my dog."

Hayley told him, "*Te adoro, Anton.*"

The next morning, Laddy was parked outside the general aviation terminal at Austin-Bergstrom International. The top was down on his Mustang and Amarillo lay asleep on the passenger seat, his leash tied around the seat-shifter bar. Parked behind the Mustang was a stretch limo four times the length of the pony car.

In the time it took for Joanna to deplane and clear the terminal, he thought about what their wedding would be like. This time he was doing the planning. Joanna could have the clergyman of her choice. They'd do it in that fellow's chapel, assuming he had one. The guest list would be small: Joanna's parents and Laddy's mother and father.

He wouldn't say a word to Momma about what he'd learned and he hoped he could inform Bartolo with nothing more than a handshake and a look in the eye. He was betting he could. He wasn't sure whether he'd stay in the race to be mayor of Gasoline; now *he* was missing the movie business, and the idea of bringing a chunk of it home to Texas was intriguing him more than ever. He supposed his decision about staying in politics hinged on how loathsome an opponent Big Oil managed to dredge up.

When he saw Joanna exit the terminal he jumped out of the car to greet her. The motion of his departure from the car awakened Amarillo. The puppy stood on his hind legs and barked as he watched Laddy and Joanna embrace and kiss.

Joanna moved over to the car and scratched Amarillo's head. The little dog's tail wagged at a hundred beats per minute and he inclined his head for more stroking.

"He's adorable," Joanna told Laddy with a smile.

"Just another sucker for a good-looking dame," Laddy said.

Which earned him another kiss. He undid the leash so Joanna could pick Amarillo up.

She turned and looked at the limo.

"What's that for?" Joanna asked.

"Well, I thought you could ride with the pup and me, but I figured we'd need something for your luggage."

Joanna laughed and just then a skycap came out of the terminal. He was carrying only two small items. Hat boxes, it looked like to Laddy.

"That's all my luggage," Joanna said.

Laddy relieved the skycap of his trifling burden and Joanna tipped the man.

He said thank you and departed.

Joanna took a box from Laddy and told him the one he held was a gift for him. He opened the box and found a white Stetson, a thing of beauty, and just the right size. Joanna had one for herself and put it on, grinning like a kid.

"When in Texas," she said.

"Welcome home, sweetheart," Laddy told her.

They got in the Mustang and with Amarillo on Joanna's lap, Laddy drove down the highway to the House of Good Luck.

About the Author

JOSEPH FLYNN is a Chicagoan, born and raised, currently living in central Illinois with his wife and daughter. Mr. Flynn is the author of *The Concrete Inquisition, Digger, The Next President, Hot Type,* and *Farewell Performance.*

www.ingramcontent.com/pod-product-compliance
Lightning Source LLC
Chambersburg PA
CBHW050020180626
46810CB00002B/498